P9-BJX-916

HERE, THERE & EVERYWHERE

CHRIS ROBERSON

HERE, THERE & EVERYWHERE

an imprint of Prometheus Books
Amherst, NY

Published 2005 by PYR™, an imprint of Prometheus Books

Here, There & Everywhere. Copyright © 2005 by MonkeyBrain, Inc. All rights reserved. No part of this publication may be reproduced, stored in a retrieval system, or transmitted in any form or by any means, digital, electronic, mechanical, photocopying, recording, or otherwise, or conveyed via the Internet or a Web site without prior written permission of the publisher, except in the case of brief quotations embodied in critical articles and reviews.

Inquiries should be addressed to
PYR
Editorial Department
Prometheus Books
59 John Glenn Drive
Amherst, New York 14228–2197
VOICE: 716–691–0133, ext. 207
FAX: 716–564–2711
WWW.PROMETHEUSBOOKS.COM

09 08 07 06 05   5 4 3 2 1

Library of Congress Cataloging-in-Publication Data

Roberson, Chris.
 Here, there & everywhere / by Chris Roberson.
  p. cm.
 ISBN 1–59102–310–6 (hardcover : alk. paper)
 ISBN 1–59102–331–9 (paperback : alk. paper)
 1. Women travelers—Fiction. 2. Time travel—Fiction. I. Title.

PS3618.O3165H47 2005
813'.6—dc22

2004030014

Printed in Canada on acid-free paper

For my daughter,
Georgia Rose Roberson.
May you grow up in the best of all possible worlds.

ACKNOWLEDGMENTS

I would like to thank my parents, Mike and Becky, for allowing me a childhood filled with books, comics, movies, and endless hours of television (in a very real sense, this is all their fault); John Picacio, for gracing my humble prose with his extraordinary talents; Lou Anders, for championing my work for years; and Allison Baker, wife, partner, and mother of my child, for everything else.

PRELUDE

DAY TRIPPER

LONDON, 1995

he woman was there again, haunting him, when the phone rang.

"Avram here."

"David?" came the voice at the other end of the line, peppered with transatlantic static. "It's Ron."

An executive producer of the project so far as the end crawl was concerned, Ron Stein was really just a watchdog ABC had tapped to watch over expenditures, in particular those racked up by David Avram over in England. David had come to dread the twice-weekly conversation, wherein he was called upon to account for every cent and pence.

"Yes, Ron, what is it?" David answered wearily. His gaze drifted across the room, as it always did, pulled by the gravitational force of the blown-up black-and-white photo tacked on the far wall. In the half-moon of white at the photo's center were positioned four young men in white shirts, black vests and ties, two guitars, a bass, and a drum kit, framed by the dark crescent of the ceiling above and the range of heads below. In the foreground, with bobbed blonde hair, leather jacket, and knapsack, stood the woman, caught in profile, blurred in the instant of turning back towards the camera, or else turning back from the camera towards the stage. She wore a strange Mona Lisa half-smile, and seemed to mock David with her mystery.

"Don't worry, David, I'm not calling to bust your balls. Not today, anyway. I just got some news off the wire that I thought you'd be interested to hear."

"Okay," David replied, his tone noncommittal. He didn't consider Stein the best judge of what he might or might not find interesting, but as Stein held the purse strings, there wasn't much he could do about it. "Shoot."

"Get this," Ron continued through static. "Your boys are putting on a little show."

"Boys? What boys?"

"The Fab Four," Ron answered. "Or what's left of them, anyway. The surviving three have scheduled a press conference at the London Hilton, for tomorrow."

David found he had trouble swallowing, as though he'd forgotten the trick sometime in the last few seconds.

"Press conference?" he repeated. "But . . . they've said they wouldn't promote the project. Only the private interviews, and no public appearances."

"Hey, pally, I can read the contracts as well as you can, but I'm telling you that they're going to be at the London Hilton tomorrow. We've confirmed with their people, and it's a go."

"What . . ." David began, finally remembering the trick to swallowing. "What, what are they talking about?" He paused, and then added, "At the press conference, what are they talking about?"

"That's just the thing," Ron answered. "Nobody's got any idea. How's that for a kick in the drawers. Now, I think you see where I'm going with this, right? Have you still got that film crew on the leash —the one that you used for those pickup shots over on Apple Road?"

"Abbey Road," David corrected automatically, then nodded. It took a moment to remember that his nod wasn't likely to translate down the transatlantic line, and he added, "Yeah, yes, they're here in town. I should be able to get them together."

"Great," Ron said. "So here's the plan. We've wrangled a press pass for you and the crew—should be waiting for you at the gig. You get your ass over there tomorrow at noon, get the whole shindig on film, and maybe we've got a new ending to this story, right? You with me?"

David nodded again.

"Yes," he said finally out loud. "I'm with you."

"Great," Ron said. "Okay, go get 'em, man. Let me know as soon as you've got something golden, you got it?"

"Got it."

David set the handset back down on the cradle, and rubbed the heels of his palms into his squeezed-shut eyes. When he opened them again, he looked up to see the woman, standing there beneath the half-moon of light, laughing at him in grainy black and white.

David Avram had been working on the Anthology project for ABC for about a month when he'd first noticed the woman. Brought in on the project first as a second unit director, on the basis of a little documentary he'd done about the last days of Elvis while still in film school, David quickly began to feel that he was out of his depth. His senior thesis project, *The Face of Elvis*, had been shot on video, on a shoestring budget, and really only worked as a result of some of the extraordinary interviews that David had lucked into in the course of shooting in Memphis. He'd had no idea when he sat down to interview the barber that the man had briefly been a member of the "Memphis Mafia," or that the man would be so forthcoming with theretofore undisclosed scandals.

Now, traveling all over the United States, England, and the rest of Europe, David was sure they'd picked the wrong man for the job. The woman, and her mystery, were really only symptoms of a larger disease.

The Anthology project was originally intended to be a bit of fluff, coproduced by ABC in the States and ITV in the UK, timed to coincide with the release of a new series of compilation CDs. Months and hundred of hours of footage later, it was decided that the Anthology would be released as a six-hour miniseries in the fall of '95, the week of the CDs' release. To make matters worse, they'd so far overshot the mark of six hours that the Anthology was scheduled to be released in an expanded format on video the following year, ten hours in all.

Ten hours. Threading his way through the mountains of stacked beta cassettes and film canisters in his temporary London offices, David was sure he could cut together ten hours from the detritus he'd dropped on the floor in the last week alone. Ten hours. They could do a hundred and not blink.

The problem was, so far as David was concerned, that the piece lacked a center, a focus around which the rest of the project could orbit. Due to contracts and agreements signed with the surviving band members and various estates and family members, the Anthology was hardly the insightful and hard-hitting exposé David had imagined when he'd first interviewed for the position. Instead, the rough cut of the footage so far soft-pedaled its way through the decade or so of the band's career, showcasing the albums and concerts while glossing over anything meaty.

Just one nugget would do, David was convinced, just one gristly morsel. The woman, he was now convinced, could well be it.

He'd first caught sight of her in a photo of the band's early days in Hamburg in 1961: the four Liverpudlians, just steps away from their teddy boy roots, in leather jackets and pants, their hair only now shading down from greased-up pompadours to the bangs-forward style they'd make famous. She'd been partially visible at the edge of the stage:

blonde bobbed hairdo, leather jacket, and backpack. In her knee-high boots and black miniskirt, she'd looked like something out of a dark mirror *Star Trek* episode, which put her, David had to admit, somewhat ahead of the curve so far as fashion was concerned. He'd not thought much of her, assuming she was just another of their hundreds of adoring German fans who'd come to know and love them in the Reeperbahn.

A few weeks later, while editing together some still shots and film clips of the Cavern Club from 1962, he'd noticed her again. At first he thought it a coincidence, just another similar-looking woman in the same sort of outfit, but after blowing up the two images and comparing them side by side, he was sure the two were of the same woman. Was she a German who'd followed the boys back to England, or an Englishwoman who'd followed them to Germany in the first place? He had photos of all the boys' girlfriends at that time, and none of them looked a bit like her. It was a mystery, but a minor one at best.

A month went by, and David was sent to England to film some framing sequences at the site of the old Apple offices on Savile Row. To familiarize himself with the location, in an attempt to show the passage of years from then to now, he'd watched the footage of the rooftop concert over and over again before heading out for the shoot. It was on the fourth viewing that he caught sight of a woman with short blonde hair in a leather jacket, knee-high boots, and miniskirt standing on the roof of the building adjacent Number 3 Savile Row, watching the performance with an amused half-smile on her face. The same woman, looking as though she hadn't aged a day, in precisely the same clothes and hair.

David felt himself becoming obsessed, but there was nothing else for it. Returning to the offices after wrapping up the location shoot, he dug out every bit of archives film, video, kinescope, and still photography he'd amassed over the previous year, hunting down the mystery woman. He found her again sitting a few feet from the drum kit in the color footage of the "Our World" satellite broadcast of June 25, 1967, incongruous amongst the baroque flower power of beads and spangles in her black leather and miniskirt. There she was again in black and white in photos of the tour performance in Hong Kong, where the band's manager had hired a session musician to sit in for their ailing drummer, left home with tonsillitis back in England. And again in the stands at Candlestick Park in 1966, at the last performance of the last tour the band would take.

Time and again he found the woman at the sidelines of key points of the band's history, always looking precisely the same, as though it was the world around her that changed while she remained immutable and static. Same half-smile, same bobbed hair, same clothes, boots, and backpack. David took to carrying a photo of her, a blown-up screen capture from the "Our World" broadcast, the best likeness he'd found, whenever he went out to pick up an interview. He fidgeted his way through each interview, every old girlfriend, classmate, and cousin, waiting until that moment when the camera would be shut off and he could produce the photo, but none of them would admit ever having seen her before, or to knowing why she haunted the periphery of the band's career for so long.

Now, months later, work on the project drawing to a close, David had begun to feel that the mystery woman in the photo was the linchpin to the project, the one question around which the Anthology would crystallize. But no answer had surfaced, and he began to suspect that one never would.

The next day, film crew in tow and press passes in hand, David arrived early at the large hall of the London Hilton, a strange mix of giddy anticipation and dread gripping his chest. He found a seat near the back, after instructing the crew where to position the two cameras, and waited for the hall to fill.

A few minutes before noon, nearly every seat taken and the back and sides of the hall crowded with cameras and sound equipment, a gentleman in a finely tailored business suit entered through a door at the front of the hall and stepped up to the podium. To one side of the podium was a table and four chairs, behind a banister set up as a barricade separating the table from the audience. Four chairs? David could hardly guess.

The business suit began with some preparatory remarks, introducing himself as a press agent whose name David recognized and indicating that he'd been hired by the former bandmates to arrange the press conference. After fielding a few questions from the assembled reporters, none of which he was at liberty to answer, the suit indicated the door behind him with a wave of his hand.

"Ladies and gentlemen of the press," he announced, his tone becoming that of a circus ringleader. "May I present, in no particular order—" Ripples of laughter ran through the crowd. "—Paul McCartney . . ."

The man himself came through the door, looking just as he had in the interview footage the Anthology's first unit director had shot the fall before, appearing young for his age, smiling, still handsome, still a presence.

Flashes snapped, questions were shouted out, all but drowned out by the applause from the audience. Applause, from reporters no less. This was something David hadn't seen before. He glanced around him at the sparsely populated seats at the rear of the hall, the bulk of the reporters having squeezed as far forward as possible, all of them eager for a closer look, some seeming as though they'd go into hysterics if they could only touch the hem of his garment. The boys, after all of these years, still held some sway over people.

"George Harrison . . ." the press agent finally continued, having to shout over the applause and shouted questions, the room refusing to calm.

The second of the survivors entered the hall, dressed casually in denim jacket and jeans, gray-streaked hair brushed back and his face clean shaven under wide sunglasses, grinning like a Buddha at the tumult of the room. David glanced to his side, a movement catching his eye. He was about to turn back to the stage and await along with the rest of the throng the appearance of the third, the last survivor of the original three, when he was frozen in place, his gaze riveted.

One row up from him, a few seats down, sat the woman. Blonde bob, leather jacket, knee-high boots, and all. The mystery woman, not having aged a day, looking as though she'd stepped out from the photo in his pocket, crossing the distance between the lacy swirls of 1967 and the present day without missing a beat.

The press agent was introducing the third survivor, but David couldn't bring himself to notice. He was entranced, transfixed. Pushing off his chair onto shaky legs, he worked his way down the row towards the woman without collapsing, and took the seat at her side.

The woman, half-smile on her face, glanced over at him, nodded, and turned back to watch the show.

David, struck dumb, could only pull the folded and water-stained photo from his pocket, unfold and smooth it as best he could, and then present it to the woman as his silent question.

She looked down at the photo for a long moment, her smile widening to three-quarters for an instant, and then looked up at David.

"Do my eyes really look that puffy?" she said casually, reaching up to brush her eyelid with an outstretched finger.

David meant to say "No," or to shake his head, or to ask her any one of a hundred questions, but he only managed to swallow. At least he hadn't forgotten how again.

"This is really going to be something," the woman went on, turning her attention back to the stage. "You're going to want to see this."

David gaped, trying to work out any kind of rational explanation for the woman's appearance. It had been more than thirty years since that first photo of her was taken, and she hadn't aged a day.

"Are you . . . ?" he began, fishing desperately for something coherent to say. "Are you from around here?" he finished, not even sure why he'd asked.

"No," the woman answered, shaking her head just enough for her short blonde hair to shift, still smiling. "I'm just visiting a few days."

There was a trace of America in her accent, overlaid with refined British and something else besides.

"Look at them, will you?" she continued, pointing to the three men on the stage with her chin. "You wouldn't think it'd been so long since they'd been together. They belong together, don't you think? The whole greater than the sum of its parts?"

David nodded.

"Can you imagine what things would have been like if they'd never gotten together?" the woman went on before David could compose an intelligent response. "If Paul had refused John's invitation to join the Quarrymen? John on his own would never have made it, just like Paul by himself couldn't have. It was the alchemical fusion of the two that made them great. Or imagine if Williams hadn't booked them for Hamburg? It was Hamburg that did it, you know. The crucible that turned their raw talents into skill, and then skill into genius. If they'd stayed in Liverpool the whole time, they'd just have been another skiffle band turned rocker, another lesser light in the brief constellation of the Mersey Beat. And don't get me started on what would have happened if George Martin hadn't produced them."

"Um, yes," David managed. "Okay."

"I've seen it, you know," the woman said, eyes fixed on the stage, and the three men smiling for the cameras. "Ten years of genius, changing the musical landscape forever, and then they walked back into the pages of history, their job through. Oh, there's some variance in the Myriad, here and there, the breakups coming later or earlier, but in most cases the band doesn't make it much into the seventies before they call it quits. Some lines didn't even get to hear 'Abbey Road,' while in others 'Mandala' was never even recorded."

"Mandala?" David parroted back. He was confused. The woman he'd seen as the answer to the question his film was asking looked to be only another question herself.

"I'm sorry," the woman answered, glancing over at David and shrugging apologetically. "I'm rambling, I know. I've just been such a big Beatles fan my whole life, and this is such a big day for me."

David's face screwed up in confusion.

"A big day? Today? Why?"

The woman held a slender finger up to her lips, and David caught sight of light glinting off a wide silver bracelet on her left wrist, the suggestion of a faceted jewel around its curve.

"Shh," she breathed, nodding her head towards the stage. "Watch and you'll see."

The fervor from the audience had mostly died down, and the press agent was handing things over to the three men. McCartney, sitting to the far left of the table, began things, still the consummate showman.

Promising to field questions after their prepared speeches, McCartney spoke briefly about the long history and friendship the three men shared, and of the hard times following the tragic death of their fourth, missing friend in 1980. He spoke about the continued impact of their music on generation after generation of fans, and about the ongoing musical projects the three men pursued individually. He spoke, finally, about the persistent questions about and calls for some kind of reunion of the three, and of their long and stalwart reluctance to pursue the idea.

"It always seemed to us, you know," McCartney concluded, "that with just the three of us, it wouldn't be the Beatles; it would just be the three of us making music. There was no way we could ask someone to fill in those shoes, because frankly, who would want to? They were just too big."

"So we've found someone with big feet," interrupted the next man down.

"Okay, okay, you'll get your turn," McCartney answered, miming offense. "Here you go, you bastard, take it." He pushed his mic away in a mock show of disgust and leaned back, arms across his chest. "Take it away, John, it's all yours," he finished with a smile.

"Thank you kindly, Paul," Lennon answered. "Now, like I was so rudely interrupting, when Pete was killed back in 1980, I figured, well, that's the end of the Beatles for sure, isn't it? You can dissolve business partnerships, break up contracts, and piss on each other's shoes, but so long as everyone's still around and breathing there's still a chance, right? But with Pete gone, well, that's it. Who's going to want to step into Pete Best's shoes, right, even if we asked them to? Nobody. And then, last year, we found somebody that was more than willing to, 'cause he already had."

"Back in the Beatles days," George Harrison interrupted, leaning into his mic, "Pete came down with tonsillitis or some such right before we had to go on a tour of Holland and Hong Kong. Sick as a dog, really. We wanted to cancel the tour, but Brian Epstein, our manager, wouldn't have it. He wanted to hire up a session musician and finish out the tour without Pete."

"We didn't care much for the idea," McCartney chimed in, "but in the end we figured we'd pick somebody we knew to sit in, and then maybe it wouldn't be so bad. So we found this guy, still playing in Liverpool, who we'd known back in Hamburg, when he played with a band called Rory Storm and the Hurricanes. A hell of a nice guy, and probably a better drummer than Pete at that point, if we were honest."

"Pete didn't really get grooving as a drummer, I don't think," Lennon cut in, "until around the second American tour."

"Anyway," Harrison went on, raising an eyebrow at his two former bandmates, tapping his watch and indicating they should move on, "last year I was up in Liverpool visiting relatives when I ran into this guy again. He's still playing, in a church band or something, but works days as a foreman at the docks. We got to talking, and he invited me around to hear him rehearse, and I just couldn't believe it. Here was this guy, a dockworker who hadn't played professionally in what, twenty years, thirty, who can play like no one I've heard in years. Later I was talking to Paul about him, and then to John, and one thing led to another . . ."

"And to another . . ." Lennon added.

"And here we are," McCartney said. "And here he is. Ladies and gentleman, may I introduce to you, once again after all of these years, Ritchie Starkey."

David recognized the man who appeared at the door from archival footage from the 1964 Holland performance. A little more haggard, balding with a beard, he grinned beneath his prominent nose and joined the three Beatles at the table, taking the fourth seat at the end. The four Beatles, David corrected himself. He turned back to the woman at his side to find her climbing to her feet.

She was smiling broader than before, three-quarters shading to full, and heading towards the door.

"Wait!" David shouted, jumping up and rushing after her. "Where are you going?"

"They're performing together in a month, the four of them, in New York at the Ed Sullivan Theater, and I don't want to miss it." Turning away, she hiked up the left sleeve of her jacket, then laid her right hand on the silver bracelet on her arm.

"But . . ." David answered weakly, and followed after, towards the rear of the hall and the door. "Who are you? What's your name?"

The woman, moving faster than he, was already at the door. She turned around, and gave him a little wink.

"Roxanne," she answered, shouldering open the door, letting a bright white light spill into the hall from beyond. "Roxanne Bonaventure."

She slipped through, the door closing shut behind her. David made it to the door, out of breath, and shoved it open. The brilliant white light beyond was gone, replaced by the pale incandescence of the chandeliers overhead. The woman was also gone.

Later, after a fruitless search of the lobby and grounds for the woman, he returned to the hall, partially to rejoin the film crew, but primarily to retrieve the photo he'd let flutter to the ground beneath the woman's seat. He picked it up, smoothing out the wrinkles and dusting it off. The woman, half-smile in place and head cocked to one side, listening intently as John, Paul, George, and Pete informed the world that all it really needed was love.

SECTION I

CHAPTER 1

YESTERDAY

OXFORDSHIRE, 1980
AGE: 10 YEARS OLD

Roxanne Bonaventure sat on the hard, unforgiving seat of the straight-backed wooden chair, the work of weeks lying in ruins on the headmaster's desk before her.

The headmaster, Mr. Campbell, all puffed cheeks, sweat-dappled forehead, and fringe of ratty white hair, glowered at her from behind his desk, joining with her teacher Mrs. Roth in a silent chorus of condemnation. That her father had still not arrived, she was sure, only proved that she was beyond all hope. Nature and nurture, dually embodied in the form of her absent parent, conspired against her.

Scattered on the desk lay the battered and brutalized remains of Roxanne's Junior Four Science Fair project. Pristine and new only a few short hours before, sparkling with possibility and the hint of mysteries revealed, it was now only a disheveled mass of developed photographic plates, a shoebox affair, and a mangled electrical apparatus and low-wattage lightbulb. At the tender age of ten years old, still a week away from her eleventh birthday, Roxanne understood how Galileo had felt, pilloried for his insistence on speaking the truth. That Roxanne only barely understood the truth upon which she insisted hardly entered into the equation.

After a long quarter hour more, marked at regular intervals by Mr. Campbell consulting his wristwatch and Mrs. Roth clearing her throat dramatically every sixty seconds on the dot, there was a clamor from the hallway. The door swung open, clanging noisily against the wall, and a scarecrow masquerading as a man appeared in the doorframe: tall, thin, and lank, with a mess of brown hair and circus fun-house glasses.

Professor Stephen Orien Bonaventure, Roxanne's widower father, rushed into the room, muttering sincere apologies and hurrying to the seat at his daughter's side.

"Terribly sorry," Professor Bonaventure said, sliding the chair across the hardwood floors with a deafening squeak. "Lecture ran long, you know."

"I'm sure I don't, Mr. Bonaventure," Headmaster Campbell replied, pointedly omitting the appropriate honorific. "Mrs. Roth," he continued, his voice growing icier with every passing syllable, sending shivers down Roxanne's spine, "do you 'know'?"

"No, sir, Mr. Campbell," Mrs. Roth answered. "I'm very much certain that I don't either."

Roxanne fidgeted on her chair, wishing that she could shrink to tiny size like some American comic superhero.

"Well, Mr. Bonaventure," Campbell continued, turning back to Roxanne's father and steepling his fingers. "It appears that neither I nor Mrs. Roth in fact 'know' about lectures running long. You'll have to forgive us, of course, as we are merely humble laborers in the field of primary education, and not honored academicians of your caliber."

Bonaventure shifted in his seat, suggesting some genetic predisposition to unease that had passed from father to daughter.

"Erm," he began uneasily, "quite all right, Mr. . . . Campbell?" That he'd obviously picked the name from the brass stamped plate on the headmaster's desk, any previous memory of the man's name lost to him, did not seem to fool anyone. "I understand," he went on to deafening silence and pointed stares, "that there was some trouble with Roxanne today?"

Headmaster Campbell sighed dramatically, and Mrs. Roth echoed by clearing her throat yet again.

"You might say that, Mr. Bonaventure," Campbell answered, "if you consider physically assaulting another student and verbally abusing a teacher as 'some trouble.'"

"She's a menace," Mrs. Roth added, her voice shrill. "It shouldn't be allowed."

"And it won't, Mrs. Roth," Campbell said.

Through it all, Roxanne kept quiet, eyes fixed on the ground, wishing she could disappear.

"I'm not sure I follow," Bonaventure said. He leaned forward in his chair, apparently trying to regain lost psychological ground by taking a more aggressive posture. "What, precisely, is Roxanne supposed to have done?"

"Do you recognize these items, Mr. Bonaventure?" Campbell asked, indicating the ruins of the science project scattered on his desk.

Bonaventure peered over the plastic rims of his glasses at the photographic plates, box, and electrical equipment. He nodded slowly.

"Yes," he answered. "It's a variation on Feynman's double-slit experiment, with a forty-watt bulb modified to release only one photon per half-second, set into a sealed box with a photographic plate positioned at the far side of the barrier. The barrier has a variable number of apertures, or 'slits,' and with the box sealed shut the only light in the system is that emitted by the light. After a set amount of time, the apparatus is dismantled, the photographic plates developed, and the results compared to previous trials with different slit configurations." He paused, and then looked up at Campbell, and over at Mrs. Roth, and back. Neither seemed terribly interested in his explanation.

"Well, if you're worried," Bonaventure continued, straightening, "I can assure you that Roxanne did all the work on her own. I gave her a bit of guidance now and again, but at no point did I contribute materially to the project's construction or design."

Campbell began to shake his head slowly from side to side, and drummed his fingers on the desk's surface.

"No, Mr. Bonaventure," the headmaster answered, "that is not our concern here."

"Then what is?" Bonaventure asked, growing exasperated. He turned to his daughter, who sat as still as a mannequin by his side. "Roxanne, what's going on here?"

"She's filling the other students' heads with stuff and nonsense is what," Mrs. Roth fairly shouted, rising up. Campbell waved her to remain seated, so she crossed her arms over her generous chest and huffed. "Stuff and nonsense."

"Mr. Bonaventure," Campbell continued, "our concern with Roxanne today is not so much different from our concerns on days previous, spanning back over several years, to the point when she first arrived at our school. That Roxanne is inspired by your profession to produce"—he paused, indicating the experiment components—"objects . . . such as these, is hardly grounds for chastisement. It should be encouraged, in fact, and to my certain knowledge has been at many different points. No, our concern is more with your daughter's general attitude and conduct."

Campbell swung his chair to one side, and pushed his not-inconsiderable bulk off the seat. Hands clasped behind his back like a movie detective putting together the final clues to solve the case, he walked around the edge of the desk, and paced back and forth in front of the beleaguered Roxanne and her father.

"It appears, Mr. Bonaventure," he continued, beginning to use the man's name more as punctuation than a form of address, "that in presenting this 'slit experiment' to her classmates and to the judges of the Junior Four Science Fair, Roxanne made some rather outlandish claims which disrupted the remainder of the proceedings."

"What claims?" Bonaventure asked. He turned to his daughter. "Roxanne, what did you say?"

"She said that that little box of hers proved there were aliens and such," Mrs. Roth answered for her, tone climbing shrilly to a near scream.

"Did not," Roxanne said in a small voice, not looking up, not moving.

"What was that?" Campbell snapped. "What did you say?"

"I did not," Roxanne said in a slightly louder voice, her eyes still on the grain of the floor. "I said 'other worlds'; I never said 'aliens.'"

Roxanne's father sighed, and began to nod. "I think I see," Bonaventure said, his expression softening. "It's okay, dear," he added quietly, placing a gentle hand on his daughter's shoulder. He turned back to the pacing Campbell and fuming Roth, his look hardening.

"And when my daughter," he went on, looking from one to the other, "explained that the unexpected results of the double-slit experiment provided compelling evidence of the existence of other worlds, what exactly did you say to that, hmm?"

"Well, I . . ." Mrs. Roth began, sputtering. She'd obviously hardly expected the father to share the daughter's madness. "I told her it was nonsense, of course. The other children had started asking me if it could possibly be true, and I naturally told them that it couldn't. What would you have said?"

"For starters?" Bonaventure answered, climbing to his feet. "I'd have said you were an ignorant cow."

"That's what I said," Roxanne said in a low voice, a slow smile creeping across her face.

"Mr. Campbell?" Mrs. Roth's expression was one of pure shock.

"Now look here, Bonaventure," Campbell said, stepping nearer Roxanne's father.

"No, Mr. Campbell. You look here! I'm sure that my Roxanne might not always be the best-behaved student in your blasted school, but I'm just as damned sure that she's not the worst. And so far as her mind goes, she's worth the rest of your school rolled together, and that's including the damned teachers. Now, she's not had it easy these last years, with her mother gone and only me to look after her, but it can't be helping matters at all that she comes here to be bullied by you lot every day. She exceeds the limited grasp of your students with every step, and when they attack her for it your staff doesn't help her; they jump right in with the attackers. It's shameful, and I won't have it."

Campbell bristled.

"Say what you like, Bonaventure, but we'll have order and discipline in this school."

"You can have what you damned well please, you ignorant bastard, but you won't be having my daughter." He turned his back on the headmaster and stalked over to his daughter. "Come on, Roxanne, we're getting out of here."

Roxanne, her heart stopped in her chest, climbed unsteadily to her feet on liquid knees. Her father stormed to the door, slammed it open, and then stood waiting to usher her through. Roxanne followed in a daze, but paused at the threshold to look back at the flabbergasted headmaster and teacher.

"You can keep my experiment," Roxanne said, in as even a tone as she could muster. "I've got a better one at home."

With that, Roxanne turned away and—her father at her side, his arm around her shoulder—walked out of the school forever.

That evening, in their little flat in the faculty housing just off the Oxford campus, Roxanne waited in her darkened bedroom while her father talked in hushed tones on the hallway phone. Roxanne felt as though she'd just immigrated to a new world of questions, leaving her old world of answers behind. What the future held was a baffling, frightening mystery.

She'd never liked the school; she had to admit that. But it was the only school she'd known. What else was there? Where else would she go?

Roxanne sat on her bed, knees up to her chest, eyes wide, waiting for her father to come and provide some answers.

She didn't have long to wait. The click of plastic on plastic as the handset fell back on its cradle, footsteps sounding on the thin and threadbare carpeted hall, and the rustle of her doorknob turning and her father was there, framed against the bare bulb light beyond.

"Roxie?" her father said to the darkness. "Are you awake?"

"Yes," Roxanne replied in a little voice.

Roxanne's father flicked on the overhead light, and sat down on the edge of her bed.

"I've just been talking with your Aunt Diana in America," he said, painting on a smile. "You remember how much fun you had when she and little Jon visited last Christmas."

"Uh-huh." Roxanne gave a reluctant nod.

"Well, she and I were talking about you, and how much fun you could have in America. There's this ace school that your cousin Jon attends in California that Diana thinks you'd just love."

"Uh-huh." Again, the reluctant nod.

"You see, that is . . ." Roxanne's father left off, breaking eye contact. "Roxie, it wouldn't be easy to send you away, and you know that, but I just think that—"

"You're making me go away?" Roxanne's vision began to blur, her eyes pooling. Her voice quivered, no matter how much she tried to sound like a real grown-up.

"No, no, Roxie, it's not like that—"

"I'm sorry, I'm sorry." Roxanne leapt up and wrapped her arms around her father's neck. "I won't do it again, I promise, I'll be good."

Roxanne's father took her up in a strong embrace, unbreakable despite his spare form.

"Of course you'll be good, dear, you couldn't be anything else," he answered softly, stroking her blonde hair. "But this isn't about you. It's never been about you. This is about me, and what I can't give you."

"I don't . . . I don't understand. . . ."

"Roxie, I know it hasn't been easy for you, with only me here to raise you; and I've tried my best for you, but I just don't think that I'm doing right by you. Between my hours at the university, and my hours here working, I've not been giving you the attention you need, the attention you deserve. I'll always love you, poppet, and I'll always be here when you need me, but I think you need more than me now, if you're to be the woman I know you'll be."

"But . . ." The tears fell now in earnest. "But I don't want to go. I want to stay."

"I know you do, I know." Roxanne's father hugged her closer. "And you can come and visit me whenever you like, and I'll come visit you whenever I can. But in America you'll have your Auntie Diana there to help you grow up into a woman, and a school where they'll nurture your talents and not just shove you down into a box, and you'll have children of your own caliber as friends. You like your cousin Jon, don't you?"

Roxanne nodded weakly, her tears dampening her father's shoulder.

"Listen, Roxie, it's all worked out. You're booked on a transatlantic flight to America next week, first to New York and then all the way to San Francisco, where your Aunt Diana and Uncle Jake will meet you at the airport. You'll stay with them for a few weeks until they work out your enrollment at Jon's school, and then you'll be living the life of Riley."

"Riley can have his life," Roxanne muttered, choking back tears. "I want mine."

"There, there, Roxie. You'll see. You'll love it."

Roxanne's father tucked her into bed with practiced hands. After he'd shut off the light, and just before closing shut the door, Roxanne stopped him with a still-cracking voice.

"Daddy?" she said. "Is it true?"

"Is what true, poppet?"

"About the other worlds—the experiment, I mean. That every time a little something—"

"A subatomic particle," her father corrected.

"That every time a particle is faced with a choice of two or more options, that it chooses them all, branching the world out into different worlds every time, one for each of the paths it could have taken?"

"Well, it's a theory that fits the known facts. And the most plausible explanation for the double-slit experiment, if you ask me." He began to shift subtly into a lecturing mode, as he frequently did. "Collapsing probability states is just madness, so far as I'm concerned, as is just blithely swallowing the wave-particle duality of subatomic particles. Only by accepting that the photons are interacting with their equivalents in branching and bifurcating worldlines can one really explain the interference patterns the experiment produces."

In the dim light, Roxanne nodded, her habitual response to her father's impromptu lectures, even in circumstances such as these.

"So," she went on, her tone grave, "with a really big number of worlds—"

"Approaching infinity," her father added, "and it's 'worldlines.'"

"—worldlines, then there is just a big number of *different* worlds, right? Where everything that could have happened at any time happened in one of them?"

"Yes, I suppose so." Her father nodded. "That's a valid reading."

"So, I guess," Roxanne went on, her voice growing quieter and more deliberate with every syllable, "that means there must be a world somewhere where my mother is still alive, and where we all three live together, happy families?"

Her father took a deep breath, and held it for a long time.

"Yes, Roxanne," he answered slowly. "I suppose there must be."

After standing in the doorway, looking in at her for a long moment, Roxanne's father closed the door, leaving her alone.

A week later, the day before her birthday, Roxanne boarded a flight at Heathrow, still crying, her father in silent tears standing at the terminal. She cried through the preflight check, and takeoff, and the first round of complimentary drinks. By the time the in-flight movie started up, about a group of girls just a little older than Roxanne at a American summer camp, called *Little Darlings*, she was all but out of tears. Trapped in her cramped seat, unable to budge an inch, the little screen became her entire world, the focus of her every attention. By the time the movie was over, she wanted it run again from the beginning. She felt this was her introduction to American life, and was worried she might have missed something. For one thing, she was going to have to get a new haircut, and figure out how to get those wings to appear on the sides of her head. For another, apparently, she'd have to start smoking Marlboros.

The plane touched down, hours later, in New York, though Roxanne never saw beyond the terminal doors. After an interminable layover, and delays on the runway, she was finally in the air. Somewhere over the middle of America, down there where cowboys and Indians still roamed, where cops chased robbers day and night and girls with feathered hair had sex with boys and smoked Marlboro Reds nonstop, the clock rolled over and it was Roxanne's birthday.

She was eleven years old, and immigrating to a whole new world of questions.

Two months later, winter break still weeks away, Roxanne had become firmly convinced that she was nothing special. After a few weeks staying with her aunt and uncle in San Francisco, going to all the restaurants and shops and cinemas, she'd begun to feel that maybe her father had been right after all. She still missed him, and home, and even her bloody old school, but was slowly coming to see that America could be something else entirely.

Her Aunt Diana had lavished affection on her from the start, seeing in Roxanne the daughter that she'd never had. While having nothing but praise for her own son Jon, or "Jaby" as he preferred to be called these days, Diana missed the chance to have a daughter of her own eager to go shopping with her, or to have afternoon tea at fancy restaurants, or to go with her to pampering day spas in the East Bay. In those few short weeks, Diana had gotten a glimpse of a world where she'd had a daughter, and Roxanne a glimpse of a world where she had a mother. It was a brilliant fantasy for them both, and each of them was reluctant to leave it behind.

In the end, though, the day came when Roxanne had to start school at the Saint Anthony Academy. The school was north of San Francisco, up in Marin County. During the drive up from the city, Diana put on a chipper disposition and told Roxanne everything she could ever want to know about the place. The Academy was a coeducational boarding school, at which Cousin Jon had been a student for the last few years. The school's focus was on academics, but included a strong program in real-life experience. Between school-sponsored travel; student exchange programs; and semesters at sea, in deserts, and on tundra, there were any number of opportunities for adventure, should a student desire it. That the school was named in honor of Saint Anthony of Padua, the patron saint of "seekers after lost objects," had done a great deal to attract the primarily agnostic Diana and her husband to the institution in the first place.

All this adventuring, though, was the source of much of her trouble. Her cousin "Jaby" and his friends were nice enough—when they were around, that is. They seemed to be gone so much of the time, leaving her behind with all the little kids. Jaby and his friends were older than Roxanne by years, and despite its progressive attitudes and acceptance of independent spirits, the school didn't allow younger students off campus during session without supervision, and even then only on rare occasions.

To make matters worse, Roxanne hardly felt the standout at Saint Anthony that she'd been back at her old school. Back there, Roxanne had always thought herself the brightest star in a sky of dim lights, but here she was just a minor twinkle in a constellation of brilliance. Jaby and his friends—Galen, Sindy, Rene, the whole lot of them—all worldly, brilliant, and dead clever, and her just the same old Roxanne she'd always been. Even the little kids, as she thought of them, the classmates in her own grade, were every bit as bright and clever as she'd ever been on her best day. She was nothing special, she was sure. Just another twinkle.

That weekend, just before winter break, Jaby and his friends had gone off to visit someone's parents, somewhere fabulous and cool, leaving Roxanne behind on her own. The other kids were putting the finishing touches on their semester projects, from which Roxanne had been excused due to her late admission, or else were practicing fencing or lacrosse or loitering down at the stables. Roxanne felt like an interloper everywhere she turned, without the protective shadow of her older and well-liked cousin to hide under, so she opted instead to roam around the grounds on her own.

The Academy was positioned in the heart of the wine country, at the foot of a line of hills that marched steadily south to north a few dozen miles from the coast. All around was virgin forest, with only the main road and a few trails marring the growth of centuries. With a canteen in hand, and a jacket against the threat of chill, Roxanne set off to wander the woods, whiling away a long Saturday afternoon with only the evergreens and her own thoughts for company.

Near dusk, the sun having slipped down past the tops of the tallest trees, Roxanne heard the distant tolling of the school's bell, signaling the students to convene for dinner. Taking a last swallow of her canteen's water, she turned back, shouldering into her jacket as the temperature slowly crept downward.

Without warning, there came a brilliant flash of white light at the corner of her vision, somewhere off behind a stand of trees. Roxanne was so startled she cried out, and immediately scolded herself for her childishness. If this was adventure, then she'd have to do a better job in future to keep up. Steeling herself, she tightened her jacket around her, and hurried towards the source of the flash, her mind racing for some explanation.

Her father had so often told her that the world was fantastic and miraculous enough without having to resort to fairy tales and mythology. The behavior of a single electron in the laboratory was more wondrous and strange than any unicorn could ever be, he would tell her, but more wondrous than the electron itself were the mysteries of the laws that governed it. Everything in the world, he assured her, could be explained. It was simply a matter of finding the theory that best fit the facts.

What, then, could explain the brief flash of light, and the elderly woman lying on the underbrush, her life's blood spilling out through the massive wound in her side?

Roxanne rushed to the old woman's side, and reached out a tentative hand to brush against the chalk-white hair that framed the lined and wrinkled face.

"Are you okay?" Roxanne asked ridiculously. She scolded herself again, silently, for asking such a foolish question. No wonder Jaby always left her behind. "I mean, what can I do to help?" she added, trying for a more responsible tone.

The sight of the blood, and the quavering of the deathly pale woman's lips, unsettled Roxanne, reminding her of another woman she'd seen die, years and years before.

"What is your name, child?" the old woman asked, her voice already sounding like a death rattle.

"Rox-Roxanne," she answered in a breaking voice. "Roxanne Bonaventure."

The old woman nodded, and brushed the girl's cheek with a bony hand covered in skin the thickness of brittle paper.

"Roxanne," the old woman repeated. "I have a question for you."

Roxanne could only nod dumbly.

"I have something to give you, but it will carry a terrible price," the old woman went on, the pauses between words lengthening as her breath came shorter and more shallow. "It will bring you everything you could ever want, in time, but you will forever be unique, alone among the myriad. A singular creature, with no analogue or equivalent."

Roxanne could scarcely hear everything the old woman was saying, much less completely follow her meaning. What she did hear involved a gift, everything she could ever want, and being unique.

"Um, okay." The woman must be delirious. That was the only answer. "Okay," she added, a bit more forcefully, hoping to calm the woman.

"Stretch out your arm." When Roxanne failed to respond, the old woman reached out and grabbed hold of Roxanne's left hand. "Your arm, child."

Bewildered, Roxanne held her left hand palm up, as though the woman might produce some little trinket from a pocket and drop it into her hand.

The woman wheezed herself into a sitting position, blood pooling on the leaves and needles beneath her, and pulled up the baggy black sleeve that covered her own left arm. There, on her wrist, was a bracelet of brilliant silver, broad and unmarked, with a faceted jewel the size of a watch face inset on it, dazzling in the fading light. The bracelet was smooth and unbroken, and seemed to have been forged directly on the old woman's arm, so tightly did it fit.

The ancient woman reached out a bony finger and tapped the faceted, lenticular jewel. The bracelet suddenly fell into two pieces, hinged invisibly on one side. She then took hold of Roxanne's left arm, and without another word snapped the bracelet closed over the girl's left wrist. It sealed tight, any seam hidden, an unbroken piece of metal again.

"The Sofia will have the answers you need, when you know the questions to ask," the old woman said, her voice now just barely above a whisper. "It will be years yet to come, but it will all make sense in time."

"But . . ." Roxanne began, looking from the bracelet on her wrist to the old woman and back. "I don't—"

"Shh." The old woman reached out to touch the jewel on the bracelet one last time. "There's no time now." She paused, and then laughed, a sick rattling noise deep in her lungs. "No time," she repeated, and then coughing again spat up blood.

Her touch lingered on the jewel for a long moment, and then the old woman cocked her head to one side as though listening to a voice Roxanne couldn't hear.

"All right," the old woman said, looking at the bracelet. "It's time."

Suddenly, a blinding white light shone in Roxanne's eyes, and a strange prickling sensation ran up her arm, like the pins and needles she felt when a limb fell asleep. She blinked, and when she opened her eyes again, the blinding white was gone. The old woman was gone, too, leaving only the bloodstained leaves on the ground before Roxanne.

In the distance, the dinner bell tolled again.

Roxanne was stunned into silence, unable to move, unable even to think. After long minutes, she numbly climbed to her feet, and slowly began to walk back to the school.

The other students didn't believe her, insisting that Roxanne had only found the bracelet in the woods. The teachers and staff evinced concern, and followed the frantic Roxanne back into the woods, but in the full light of day Roxanne could not seem to find the spot where she'd spoken to the woman, nor the bloodstained leaves, nor any strange flashes of light. The next day, torrential rains washed clean the Academy grounds and the woods surrounding, and that was that. After a few weeks with the school counselor, long sessions about what the image of the old woman might have meant to her, Roxanne half believed she'd imagined the whole thing herself.

There was still the bracelet to consider, which she couldn't seem to remove, no matter how hard she tried. But she'd grown to quite like it over the weeks since, and when the counselor offered to have the Academy's building staff try to remove it with a hacksaw, she politely declined. She parroted back the accepted story that she'd found the thing in the woods, so many times that she almost believed it herself, and got on with the task of making a place for herself in the school. She wanted to be unique, wanted to stand out from the crowd, and Roxanne felt that somehow the bracelet would help her do that.

Extract from Roxanne's Diary

Monday, 10 June 1982

So my English teacher Mr. Farmer has insisted that we keep a diary over the summer term, when the older kids are away studying abroad or doing their semesters at sea or whatever, so this is my diary. It'll be graded at the beginning of the fall term, but it's a pass or fail kind of thing, either you do it or you don't. Mr. Farmer says that he won't even read them, just grade them on weight, so that we can feel free to say anything we like without worrying about what he or anyone else might think.

Mr. Farmer said to think of the diary as a letter to our future selves. When people grow up, he says, they can forget what it was like to be a kid, and if we do the assignment right, then one day we'll thank him for making us do it, because then we'll be able to see what we wrote when we were twelve, and then remember all the great stuff we might otherwise have forgotten about.

I'm not sure just what kind of future-self Mr. Farmer thinks I'm going to grow up into, or what kind of present-self I am, for that matter. Heck, I'm twelve right now, and can't think of any great stuff to forget.

But I won't be writing "Dear Diary" at the beginning of every day, like some sort of corny movie from the Fifties. That I just couldn't stand. Bad enough I have to spend part of every day inside, without having to turn into a Doris Day movie.

So, here's my diary.

Hello, Future-Self Roxanne. I hope I've done all sorts of great stuff to forget between now and whenever you're reading this, because at the moment, I've got nothing going on.

My second year at the Saint Anthony Academy is about over, and things are going pretty good, I guess. I've made a few good friends, and have been hanging out more with kids my own age. The first year I mainly tagged around behind my cousin Jaby and his friends, which was okay, I guess, but they always treated me like the runt of the litter.

EXTRACT FROM ROXANNE'S DIARY | 41

Some of Jaby's friends started calling me a Reverse-Jinx last year, and then everyone called me "R. J." for almost a whole year. I guess it all started during that school field trip to those caves, when I fell off this ledge and landed like thirty feet below. Without a scratch on me, if you can believe it. Thirty feet, and I managed to land in the one patch of sandy ground in the whole cave. If it had been a few inches to either side, I would have landed on these nasty, pointed rocks, and that would have been it for me. No more future-self, I guess, just mangled present-self Roxanne in a box.

I'm just lucky, I guess. The whole time I've been at the Academy, I've never gotten sick, never gotten really hurt, never broke a bone or anything. Jaby and his friends are always getting into trouble, and ending up in casts, or splints, or Band-Aids, but I always just skate by.

Maybe this bracelet of mine is some sort of good luck charm. I've never taken it off, since I found it in the woods, and ever since I've just been lucky.

{If what Mr. Farmer says is true, and he won't be reading these, then this is a good place to test him. Even though the teachers and everyone else insist that I just found the bracelet in the woods, I can still vividly remember the old lady who gave it to me, and then disappeared. I don't care what anyone says, it HAPPENED. Now, if this fall term I get dragged in to see the counselor for some sort of therapy again, asking me about my "delusions," then I'll know Mr. Farmer is a big fibber and went ahead and read my diary anyway. If that's true, shame on you, Mr. Farmer. Fibber.}

Oh, one more thing. I keep thinking of this name, or this word, and I can't remember where I heard it before. Sofia. Future-self, does that make any sense to you?

Okay, that's all for now. Tune in tomorrow, future-self, for more exciting stuff.

CHAPTER 2

GET BACK

SAINT ANTHONY ACADEMY, 1986
AGE: 16 YEARS OLD

Roxanne was sixteen, and just like the song said, she did look pretty in pink. The black Doc Martens boots, Roxanne was convinced, were the perfect complement to the outfit, and set her eyes off nicely.

In the last few years, Roxanne had learned that many of the things she'd liked as a child (the Bay City Rollers, the soundtrack to *Xanadu*, and *H. R. Pufnstuf*, to name just three) were not, in fact, good, and were, in fact, crap. Turning sixteen this last year had been Roxanne's final step on the road to maturity, and her tastes, and her personality, were now fully formed.

Her favorite band was the Cure, her favorite album was *The Head on the Door*, and her favorite movie was *Pretty in Pink*. Roxanne knew, with the white-hot certainty that only sixteen-year-olds can know, that these would be her choices for the rest of her natural life.

It was the day of the junior prom, and Roxanne didn't have a date. Not that she minded at all. The boy she really wanted to go with, the exchange student Julien, was just too shy to ask her. Roxanne was convinced of it. So Roxanne had taken matters into her own hands.

She'd picked out a dress, purchased her own corsage, and prepared to go to the dance alone.

Just like Andie in *Pretty in Pink*.

And just like Andie in *Pretty in Pink*, Roxanne would find her true love waiting at the prom for her, but unlike Andie in *Pretty in Pink* Roxanne wouldn't be going home with some gormless twit like Andrew McCarthy. Hardly. Roxanne always thought that Andie should have gone home with Duckie. She knew *she* would have, anyway.

Roxanne arrived at the prom fashionably late, just like all the magazines suggested, with her frilly pink prom dress arranged just so. Much better than the disastrous number that Andie had turned up in at the end of the movie. Roxanne wouldn't have been caught dead.

Still, despite the dress, Roxanne had maintained certain concessions to her normal attire. The twenty-hole Doc Martens work boots for one, black leather buffed to a high mirrored sheen, hair and makeup for another. Her normally limp, uninspired hair was spiked up to a dangerous, vertiginous height, and she was wearing more eye makeup than a Navy SEAL on maneuvers. But she was confident, collected, and cool.

She was ready for the prom, and hoped the prom was ready for her.

Roxanne pushed through the doors to the gymnasium like an arriving dignitary, like a queen, picturing the next few seconds in her mind with crystal clarity.

She'd pictured it all wrong. In the movies, places like high school auditoriums and gyms were magically transformed for school dances by lights, thousands of balloons, and tasteful decorations. Here, at the Saint Anthony Academy, there was just one ragged banner that said WELCOME

SENIORS, hung up over the basketball hoop, a few tangled streamers, and a cafeteria table with a jumble of plastic cups and a big punch bowl.

She'd also not considered that Julien would be standing in the middle of the "dance floor," just outside the free throw line, dancing close with some big-haired girl in a short skirt, their lips smooshed together, slobbering all over each other. Some townie she'd never even seen before.

Julien. With some other girl. That Roxanne had never seen before.

Roxanne could hardly breathe.

She couldn't look, but couldn't tear her eyes away. Her heart felt as though it were going to pound right through her rib cage, and she'd suddenly forgotten completely how to swallow.

Just get away. That was her only thought. *Get away. Fast.*

Her eyes on the floor, her every attention concentrated on the shiny tips of her Doc Martens, Roxanne started across the floor towards the girls' locker room. Shoulders hunched, arms crossed tightly over her chest, she was convinced that if she could make it to the locker room without being seen, she'd be as good as invisible.

Julien. With some townie girl.

Roxanne was holding her breath, racing as fast as she could without either seeing where she was going or appearing like she was in a hurry, when she ran into something with her head. She hit hard, with a solid thunk, and reeled back, dazed.

It was Julien, and some townie girl. They'd continued dancing, their orbit carrying them directly to Roxanne's path, and she'd managed to plow right into them.

The townie girl had spun around, one hand held out defensively while the other still possessively clutched Julien's own hand.

Julien looked over at Roxanne, a distracted and disinterested smile painted on his perfect mouth.

Roxanne backed away, stammering her apologies. She just wanted to be away, somewhere far away. She rushed across the gym floor, all pretense aside, slammed open the door of the girls' locker room, and darted for the safety of the stall farthest from the door.

Perched on the closed toilet seat, her knees pulled up to her chin, Roxanne could hear the sound of laughter from the crowded gym outside.

A small part of Roxanne's mind knew that the sound was just that of other students laughing, having fun, nothing to do with her; but a larger part of her, the part that had pushed to the front of her brain and taken control, was convinced they were all laughing at her. It was like that movie with the psychic girl and all the pig blood at the prom, but here was Roxanne without the ability to telekinetically explode the school and her classmates, and what fun was that?

She heard footsteps approaching: high heels. Someone else in the locker room.

"Rox? Roxie?"

It was Nancy, her roommate and (current) best friend. She sounded concerned, but then Nancy *always* sounded concerned. It was her thing. Some kids played musical instruments, or went out for the track team, or were really good at math. Nancy was just concerned.

"Roxanne?" The voice was coming closer, towards Roxanne's hiding place.

Roxanne had been telling Nancy for weeks about her big plans for prom night, all about how she'd picked out a dress, and shined up her Doc Martens, and would go to the prom alone and find Julien there waiting for her. All about how she and Julien were destined to be together, but he was too shy, and how the dance would be Roxanne's chance to bring him out of his shell.

Roxanne couldn't face Nancy, not now, not any more than she could face Julien.

Roxanne still wanted to get away, far away. Nancy was coming closer. She'd find her; she'd make her talk. Worse, she'd be *concerned.* Roxanne didn't want to talk, didn't want anyone to concern themselves with her. She just wanted to get away.

Roxanne squeezed her hands into fists so tight that her tastefully painted fingernails cut half-moon red welts into her palms.

From the gym outside, she could still hear the other kids laughing.

Get away, Roxanne thought.

There was a tiny, almost imperceptible *pop* noise from behind her, and a bright light played suddenly over the metal walls of the stall.

Roxanne turned, and floating in the air only inches from her face was a small, silvery ball, mirrored like a Christmas tree ornament. Rather than seeing herself reflected in it, though, fun-house mirror style, inside she saw traces of bright greens, and browns, and brilliant spring-sky blues.

"Roxanne, I know you're in there," Nancy called, from just beyond the stall door. Coming closer, closer.

Roxanne couldn't help herself. She was torn between curiosity over the strange thing, and utter horror at everything else. She reached out, trying to take the hovering sphere into her hands. Her fingers brushed against it. It was smooth, and warm, like a living thing. That was the impression Roxanne got for the briefest of instants. Then it was over, and she was . . .

Elsewhere.

Roxanne blinked her eyes. The metal walls, and the toilet, and the locker room and Nancy, the gymnasium and Julien and his townie girlfriend and a hundred laughing kids had all disappeared.

She stood on top of a high, rocky outcropping, a jungle of massed greens and browns spread out before her, a brilliant blue sky stretching overhead.

Roxanne looked up, and a pterodactyl wheeled overhead on leather wings, calling out its alien song.

Suddenly, the prom didn't seem so bad.

It was prom night.

Or, at least, it had *been* prom night, somewhere, somewhen, but here was Roxanne in her Doc Martens and frilly prom dress, standing in the middle of a prehistoric rain forest, surrounded by dinosaurs.

This is . . .

This is what happens to girls who take relationship advice from John Hughes movies, Roxanne thought. Things go horribly wrong. At this rate, she'd even have preferred Andrew McCarthy.

It took her brain a few seconds to catch up with the rest of her body, which had already begun sweating, breathing faster, and speeding up the heartbeat. Her thought processes were surprisingly lucid at first, and only began to swell toward panic as things went along.

Oh, there's a dinosaur, Roxanne thought. *And there's another one. What's that one called, again? Triceratops, something like that. Well, never figured them on being quite that shade of purple. Oh, and there's that flying dragon thingee again. Hey, it's looking this way. Hmm. Holy crap, I'm in* Land of the Lost, *and I'm about to become something's dinner.*

That's when panic set in. Full, honest, unclouded panic. Roxanne started to run.

She wasn't really running *to* anything or anywhere in particular—more a general running *away*. As in running away from everything, and everywhere, around. She had no idea how she'd ended up in this prehistoric nightmare, but was clinging with desperate tenacity to the idea that anywhere, even the loathsome prom, would have to be an improvement. She'd even take Concerned Nancy in the girls' locker room over dinosaurs.

And then it struck her. This was precisely what she'd wished for, back in the bathroom stall. She'd wanted to go somewhere, far away, where there weren't any people to point at her, or laugh at her, or feel sorry for her, or anything else. Just somewhere away.

Well, you couldn't get much farther away than dinosaur park, and unless the Flintstones had set up camp somewhere just up ahead, Roxanne wasn't liable to run into people of any stripe or variety, whether pointing, sympathetic, or anything.

She'd made a wish, and it had come true. Just like the girl in the movie with the pig blood and the exploding prom.

Had she somehow procured a genie, and just not ever realized it? Or did she have a fairy godmother she'd never known about? Either seemed as likely as any other absurd option.

Running through the underbrush, branches snatching at her clothes, mud sucking at the heavy soles of her work boots with every squelching step, Roxanne took a deep breath, and then shouted as loud as she could.

"I wish I had a helicopter!"

She kept running, panting and out of breath, past the place where she'd wished her helicopter would land.

"How about a Jeep? No? A Vespa?"

She kept running, her breath ragged, her dress muddy and torn, until she came upon the *Tyrannosaurus rex*.

Roxanne had never learned much about dinosaurs, but she did know a little about the *Tyrannosaurus rex*, if only from watching cartoons and King Kong movies. And what little she knew about the *Tyrannosaurus rex* suggested that, if she were to run into *any* type of dinosaur after inadvertently wishing herself back into the Jurassic, the *last* type of dinosaur she'd want to run into would be a *Tyrannosaurus rex*. And yet, here she was.

If Roxanne had a genie, it sucked at granting wishes. If it was a fairy godmother, Roxanne wanted to put herself up for adoption.

Roxanne paused just long enough to sigh—a long-suffering, undeserved kind of sigh—spin on her heels, and then run back helter-skelter the way she'd come, screaming at the top of her lungs.

She didn't look back, couldn't look back. Just hearing the thing's pursuit was bad enough. It roared, loud enough that the bones in Roxanne's chest vibrated in harmony and her teeth ached, and the noises of the trees falling and branches breaking as it charged through the forest sounded like the worst thunderstorm Roxanne had ever heard.

"I want to go home, I want to leave, I don't want to be eaten by a dinosaur," Roxanne shouted, hoarse and breathless. "I don't care about Julien, and his townie girlfriend, and Nancy and the toilet and all of that. I just want to go home. That's all I care about."

But in a secret place, deep inside, a small part of Roxanne added a footnote: But it would be nice if Julien would just notice me. Even in imminent danger of becoming something the *T. rex* would have to pick out of its teeth, Roxanne was still thinking about Julien, and his dreamy brown eyes, and that hair, and the records he listened to, and the cool European fashions he wore.

Don't let the dinosaurs eat me, Roxanne wished with all her might, *but please let Julien notice me.*

The *Tyrannosaurus rex* was almost upon her.

From just in front of Roxanne came a brilliant flash of light, and hanging in midair, just a few feet in front of her, was a silvery ball, just like the one Roxanne had seen in the bathroom stall.

It was too late to slow down, too close to do anything but plow right into it. Just as the thing was about to hit her in the chest, Roxanne closed her eyes, wincing, and the noise of the *Tyrannosaurus rex* was upon her.

"Roxanne, are you okay?" came the voice of Nancy from the other side of the stall door.

Roxanne collapsed to the floor, out of breath, her head swimming.

Nancy knelt down, and stuck her head awkwardly, sideways, under the stall door.

"Hey, what's wrong with you, anyway?" Nancy said, her eyebrows knit over deep blue eye shadow and overly generous mascara.

"Wha—?" Roxanne managed, before almost throwing up.

"Come on out of there, Rox," Nancy said. "You look like crap, and Julien was worried about you."

"Julien? Worried. About me?"

Roxanne climbed uneasily to her feet, her Doc Martens still caked in mud, her dress torn, sweaty, and covered in leaves, broken twigs, and even more mud. Her hair, if anything, was even worse than the dress.

Roxanne thumbed open the stall door. Nancy looked at her, horrified.

"What did you *do* in there, Rox?" Nancy looked from Roxanne to the toilet and back.

"Um, I'm not sure?"

If not for Nancy's reaction to the state of Roxanne's appearance, Roxanne would have been tempted to think of it as some sort of *Wizard of Oz* kind of affair, except horribly in reverse. She'd slipped and fallen and hit her head on the toilet bowl, or something, except there was no "And you were there, and you were there, and you were there." It was more like "And *no one* was there, and *no one* was there, and so on." Except for that to be the explanation, Nancy wouldn't be able to see the yellow brick road dust of Oz, or in her case the dinosaur crap and mud of the Jurassic, all over Roxanne's hair and clothes, which she most obviously could.

"Hey, is everything okay?" came a sultry, European-accented voice from the doorway.

It was Julien, with his townie date following close behind, her arm through his.

Oh God, Roxanne thought, grabbing her stomach. *I think I'm going to be sick.*

"Roxanne!" Julien said, with genuine concern. He shoved his townie girlfriend out of the way, and rushed to Roxanne's side. "Are you all right, my sweet?"

"My sweet?" both Roxanne and Julien's townie girlfriend said, practically in unison.

"You know," Julien went on, brushing Roxanne's cheek with his fingers. "I'd never noticed just how beautiful you are until just this moment."

"Um, what?" Roxanne asked, pulling a bit of leafy twig from her mouth.

"Jules?" the townie girlfriend said. She started out confused, worked her way through annoyed, and was at full blown mad by the time she'd said his name four times without him answering. "*Jules!*"

"What, oh, I'm sorry, um . . ." Julien looked at the townie distractedly, his arm around Roxanne.

"Courtney. Gah," the townie girl said.

"Right, of course, Courtney," Julien said, smiling sheepishly. "I'm sorry to do this to you, but I've just now realized that I really should have asked Roxanne to the dance, and I'm afraid I won't be able to escort you home."

"Her? But she's all covered in shit, and she smells funny."

Julien looked from the townie to Roxanne with crazy devotion in his eyes.

"I think she's never looked better."

"Whatever," the townie said. "I think you're both freaking nuts, and you deserve each other."

The townie turned, and stormed from the room.

Nancy looked at the retreating Courtney, and then back to Roxanne, who stood awkward and stiff, and Julien, who wrapped both arms around her in a crushing bear hug.

Nancy shrugged, and walked after Courtney back to the dance.

Roxanne, then, was left alone with Julien.

"Oh, my sweet," Julien whispered into Roxanne's ears, past the twigs and leaves and prehistoric bugs caught in her hair. "At last we are together."

Roxanne smiled awkwardly, and looked over Julien's shoulder at the open stall. It looked unremarkable now, drab green-painted metal walls and a white porcelain toilet. Hardly the thing you'd expect from some sort of door in time. At least proper English children in books got to travel through wardrobes and garden holes, not through un-hygienic high school bathrooms.

"Together," Julien repeated, sincere in his ardor.

"Um, right," Roxanne said, unsure.

As her newfound love led her from the locker room, Roxanne found it difficult to decide which was stranger: the sudden change in Julien's personality and behavior, or the attack of the killer dinosaurs.

She wasn't sure, but for the moment, amorous Julien was definitely in the lead.

Extract from Roxanne's Diary

Sunday, 15 Feb 1987

Dear Future-Self,

Well, it's Valentine's Day again, and your poor past-self is left without a Valentine again. I broke things off with Julien last month, and somehow deluded myself into thinking I'd meet someone else, but that doesn't look like it's going to happen any time soon.

Things with Julien were always kind of weird, and I guess if I'd had a little less inertia I would have broken up with him a long time ago. He was more like a pet than a boyfriend, really, always following around behind me, hanging on my every word. It got to be really boring, but it was nice to have the attention, so I guess I let things drag on longer than I should have.

Still, with Julien out of the picture, it's not like there's a lot of other fish in the sea. Not here at the Academy. God, it'll be so nice to graduate, and go off to college, with a whole new population of guys to meet. Every boy at the Academy I've known for years, for way too long. They're like brothers to me, or distant cousins at least, and it just wouldn't seem right to kiss on any of them.

Anyway, without Julien nipping at my heels, I've had a lot more time to test out the Sofia.

Oh, I guess I forgot to mention that the other day. It got to be too big of a pain to keep writing "the weird bracelet I wear that lets me travel in time" every time I mentioned the thing, so I decided to give it a name. I picked Sofia, which is a Greek word that means "wisdom." These early Christian guys called the Gnostics worshipped Sofia almost like a goddess, as the spirit of holy wisdom. The Gnostics had something to do with the Manicheans that Saint Augustine was so worked up about, and were called heretics by the later church leaders, but my Religious Studies teacher Ms. Ecole says that history is written by the victors, and that the loser's religions always become either heresies, or mythologies, or both, so I wouldn't worry too much about that.

Anyway, with the newly dubbed Sofia I've been testing the limits of this whole time-travel deal. I've been watching a lot of science fiction movies, and reading a lot of science fiction books, trying to find out as much about time travel as I can, but the problem is that no two people seem to agree on what it's all about. I mean, there's this whole Grandfather Paradox thing that everyone is so worked up about, where someone could travel back in time, kill their own grandfather, and then they wouldn't ever get born, so they wouldn't be around to travel back in time, and then their grandfather wouldn't get killed, so they WOULD get born, and could travel back in time to kill him, and so on.

What I don't really understand is why all of these guys want to kill their grandfathers so badly. Is it some sort of displaced Oedipus thing?

Anyhow, there's also this Butterfly Effect, or something like that. This one story I read was about a guy who traveled back to the time of the dinosaurs, stepped on a butterfly by accident, and when he returned to his own time everything had changed. Because making such a minor alteration to the past made HUGE changes in the future.

Well, the first place I went (don't remind me!) was the age of the dinosaurs, and I'm sure I stepped on my fair share of butterflies and bugs, but things weren't so changed when I got back. Except for Julien suddenly turning into Julien the Wonder Puppy, of course, but that was about it.

So what's the real answer? Does changing the past change the future, or is there some way that changing history doesn't really affect the present at all? And how can that be?

I don't know. I really should ask my dad about this kind of thing. He's the scientist, after all. But it's not the kind of thing I want to tell him about on the phone or in a letter, you know? I've kept it secret from everybody at the school, so far, because if they thought I was crazy for saying I'd met an old lady in the woods, what the heck would they say if I told them I could travel in time? They'd lock me up for life, until I was grown up into you, Future-Self, and what fun would that be?

Anyway, I've got to run. I've got Latin homework tonight, but I want to test out my verbal skills in Ancient Rome before I go in for the exam. Luckily,

I've got this nightgown that Nancy loaned me that can pass for a killer Roman toga, and with my lace-up sandals I totally look the part. More tomorrow.

CHAPTER 3

GETTING BETTER

OXFORDSHIRE, 1987
AGE: 17 YEARS OLD

Roxanne stood in the hallway of her father's home in Oxfordshire. She hadn't been back in years, and even then just for a brief visit over the Christmas holidays, with her cousin and his friends in tow. But now she was back, for as long as she liked. And she was terrified.

It was a week after graduation, a week after she'd packed up her things and left the Saint Anthony Academy, and the only life she'd known, behind. Her father had been too ill to make the trip to California for the ceremony, but had sent her a card from the hospital, with a little note on the inside written in a crabbed, small hand it pained her just to look at.

Her father had been released from the hospital in the time it took for Roxanne to travel from northern California to England, sent home to convalesce.

He was in the living room, in the chair by the fireplace, waiting for her. She could hear him breathing from where she stood, rooted to the spot.

"Roxie?" came his voice again, weak and distant, from around the corner. "Is that you?"

If Roxanne hadn't known it was him, she might not have recognized the voice. Who was this person in her father's house, she wanted to ask. Who was this old, sick man who'd moved into their lives?

Roxanne set her bags down, and took a deep breath.

She'd have to face him, and her fears, sooner or later.

But why, oh why, couldn't it be later?

"Roxie?" he said again.

Roxanne gripped her hands into tight fists, and took slow, deliberate steps down the hallway.

She rounded the corner, entering the living room.

There was a stranger sitting in her father's chair. A stranger with her father's eyes.

"Come give us a hug," her father said, holding out matchstick-thin arms to either side.

She'd never seen her father look so sick, so pale, so old. The doctors had said on the phone said that he was responding well to the chemotherapy, that there was no reason to believe that he didn't have years left to him even if the cancer wasn't yet in full remission. But Roxanne couldn't bring herself to believe any of that. The last time she'd seen her father he'd been well—had looked well, at least, like the man who'd raised her. Now he was only a sort of echo, as though her father had just walked out of the room and left his shadow behind.

"Dad," Roxanne said, and fell into his arms. "I'm home."

A few hours later, and Roxanne sat across from her father at the kitchen table, the bones of a takeout meal littering the table between them. The food hadn't been very good, but it didn't really matter all that much. Neither of them had much of an appetite, but each for different reasons.

The awkward silence of a few minutes had stretched out interminably, into what felt like an eternity. She tried to think of something to say that didn't involve her dad's illness, or loss, or the possibility of one of them going away forever.

"I've discovered time travel," Roxanne blurted out. "Or it's discovered me. Either way, I can travel backwards and forwards in time, but I don't know how it works, or how to control it, really."

Roxanne had planned to wait to tell her dad about the Sofia, the strange thing stuck on her wrist that opened doors in time and whispered to her in her sleep. She'd wanted his help for over a year now, but hadn't been able to think of the right way to tell him. He'd been so sick, she hadn't wanted to burden him. But she couldn't help herself.

Roxanne's father looked at her with his mouth hanging slightly open for a good, long while.

"Erm, what?" he finally asked.

"Here, look," Roxanne said. "But don't touch." She closed her eyes, and concentrated.

In the space between her and her father, a silvery sphere popped into being.

"If you touched that, you'd end up somewhere in the Middle Ages," Roxanne said. "I think. Or maybe the industrial revolution. My aim is still pretty spotty."

Roxanne closed her eyes again, and the sphere winked out of existence.

"Remarkable," Roxanne's father said, breathless. "It's . . . it's . . ."

"It's time travel, Dad. This old lady gave me this bracelet"—she pointed at the Sofia on her wrist—"and then promptly died without explaining how it works. I know that it can open up doors in space-time, but I don't completely know how to control it."

Her father leaned forward, and touched the surface of the bracelet with his fingertips.

"It's like *The Greatest American Hero*," Roxanne explained. Her dad looked at her with a blank expression. "The poof with the blonde perm? Anyway, it's this crap American TV show, where a schoolteacher find this alien suit that gives him superpowers, just like Superman. The only problem is, he loses the instruction book right off the bat, so he doesn't understand *how* anything works, just that it does. That's exactly how I feel. I've been given this thing, and it lets me travel in time, but I don't really understand how it works, or how to control it with any kind of real accuracy."

Roxanne's father looked at her, eyes narrowed.

"So this old woman who gave it to you," he said, his tone leading. "Did she seem . . . familiar?"

"Not really," Roxanne answered, "but I figure that she had to be me. I mean, me when I'm an old woman, come back to the past to give this thing to my younger self. It's the only thing that makes any sense."

Her father looked at her for a long moment, blinking slowly and trying to digest what he'd just heard.

"Yes, well . . ." he said. "I thought it might be . . ." He broke off, shaking his head. "Sounds like something out of *Doctor Who*."

"More like *The Man Who Folded Himself*, really," Roxanne answered. "Or Heinlein's 'All You Zombies' or something like that."

Roxanne had been reading a lot of science fiction, watching a lot of movies and TV shows, all in an attempt to find out anything about time travel that she could. But no one seemed to agree on what time travel was, or how it worked.

Her dad laughed as she explained her references, and then coughed blood into a Kleenex.

"You should have studied more science and less fiction," he said. "Time travel is certainly a theoretic possibility, even if no one has yet been able to provide empirical evidence, and there is a sizable body of research that describes possible models for how such a thing might work."

"There's more," Roxanne said, after a long pause.

"More?"

"Yeah. Sometimes it seems like I don't just travel in time, or space," she said. "Sometimes it seems like I'm going . . . somewhere else."

Roxanne's father, who just moments before had looked as though he might keel over dead any second, perked up, his eyes brightening.

"The Many Worlds Theorem," he said, climbing up out of his chair. "Do you sometimes seem to find yourself in places where things have gone slightly different than those to which you're accustomed?"

Roxanne was puzzled, and shrugged and nodded simultaneously.

"Divergent timelines, Roxie."

Her father paused, a hungry look in his eyes.

"Show me," he went on, breathless. "Take me somewhere . . . some*when* . . . else."

"Um, okay," Roxanne said reluctantly. "Where do you want to go?" She paused, and then added, "Or when, I suppose I should say?"

Roxanne's father leaned forward expectantly.

"The future," he said. "The far future."

Roxanne stood, her chair legs squealing as they were pushed back across the kitchen tiles, and came around the table to stand beside her father. She reached out for her father. He slipped on his shoes, which he'd kicked off at some point during their meal, and took her hand.

He stood, and pushed his glasses up onto his nose.

They faced one another, their arms at their sides.

"Are you sure about this, Dad?"

Her father took a deep breath, and nodded.

"Okay, then. You should be careful, though, and stay right by my side. I'll leave the bridge open so we can come straight back if we run into any trouble."

Her father smiled, and nodded again, like a child being told Father

Christmas won't come if he doesn't go to sleep. She could tell that it didn't even occur to him that they could possibly run into trouble.

"All right," Roxanne said. She nodded, somewhat reluctantly, and her gaze flicked down to the bracelet on her wrist. "Sofia, we want to go to the far future." She paused, and glanced at her father for a moment before continuing. "England, somewhere near here, but a thousand years—"

"No," her father interrupted, shaking his head eagerly, a broad smile cutting across his hollow cheeks. "No, make it a million."

Roxanne looked at him a little askance, never having traveled half that far into the future, but nodded anyway.

"A *million* years in the future," she finished.

The bridge appeared with a noiseless flash of white light, a silvery ball hanging in midair between them.

"We only need touch the bridge, Dad, and we'll be translated through to the other side, whenever and wherever *that* is."

Roxanne's father raised his hand slowly, then hesitated, glancing down at the threadbare sweater hanging from his thin frame.

"Do you think I should bring a heavier jacket," he asked in deadly earnest, "or perhaps an umbrella?"

Roxanne suppressed the urge to smile. One step away from a trip a million years into the future, and her father was wondering if he'd catch a chill.

"Don't worry," she said, "if it's too cold we'll come right back, and if it's really nasty the Sofia won't let us through. Once or twice I've tried to go to places that were too hot, or covered in molten lava, or didn't have the right kind of atmosphere, and when I tried to step through I ended up right back where I started. I'm not sure how it works, but it seems that the Sofia's got some kind of safeguards built into it."

Roxanne's father nodded, relieved. Cautiously, he reached his hand forward again.

"Remarkable," he said, drawing fractionally nearer the sphere. "I'd first taken the images on the surface to be concave reflections of the surrounding environment, but I see now that we're actually seeing an inverted image of some other location. Are we seeing through—"

His fingertips touched the surface of the mirrored sphere, and as he winked out of sight, Roxanne reached her hand up and brushed the bridge.

"—to the other side of the portal?" her father finished, his voice trailing off as he got his first look at their surroundings.

Roxanne and her father stood facing each other, on the other side.

Around them, the twilight city buzzed with activity. They stood in a broad town square, perched atop a mountain of coral in the middle of a sapphire blue ocean. All around them, tall, slender people with a viridescent tint to their hairless skin just began to take notice of them.

"Remarkable, Roxie." Roxanne's father looked around, his eyes darting eagerly, taking in everything at once. "Just remarkable. Where are we?"

"Well, I only told the Sofia to move us through time, not space, so I'd assume we're somewhere in City Centre, Oxford, in the neighborhood of one million CE."

"Oh, but we must have moved a quarter of a mile upwards, at the very least, to judge by the sea level."

Roxanne shrugged, more concerned with the attention they were receiving from the locals than with the elevation.

"Look at those!" Roxanne's father was pointing upwards, eyes wide.

Overhead drifted strange creatures, tentacles and pincerlike appendages depending from large, gas-filled bladders. They floated along like zeppelins on the light breeze, looking like airborne jellyfish. The smallest of these was no larger than Roxanne's hand, while some of the larger ones were big as houses, with baskets of woven kelp tied to their pincers, in which green-skinned future people trawled nets in the crystal blue water.

The fishers in the jelly-zeppelins were just beginning to notice Roxanne and her father, pointing down and shouting in alien, liquid syllables. The faces were strange, with eyes large and black above their cheeks, their noses flattened to little more than slits, but Roxanne was able to read their expressions well enough. She recognized panic, and fear of the unknown, having seen it often enough before.

"The gravity is lower," Roxanne's father said, jumping up and down experimentally, flapping his arms at his sides. "That could account for the increased size of the indegenes, and the ability of those gas-creatures to stay airborne. Perhaps in the intervening millennia between our epoch and theirs, a substantial part of the Earth's mass was mined and sent off planet, or otherwise consumed, leaving the planet's gravitation substantially reduced."

The future-people on the ground, who had been at the edges of the wide square, cleaning unusual-looking fish, or drying out some variety of seaweed, or knitting into plaits some kind of fronds, began to rise to their feet, adults and children, all attention on Roxanne and her father.

"But what accounts for the green cast of their skin?" Roxanne's father said. "It could be that they have living within their circulatory systems or their epidermis some form of microorganism or flora, perhaps to aid the body in some symbiotic fashion by producing caloric energy through photosynthesis, turning ambient sunlight absorbed by the skin into fuel."

The future-people began to start towards them, keening in strange, high-pitched voices. Their teeth were long and fine, looking almost like bundles of hair, resembling nothing so much as the teeth of whales. The larger of the green people—whether they were male or female was impossible to say—brandished long poles with curved hooks on either end.

"It's time to go, Dad," Roxanne said, warily.

Roxanne's father was in the middle of theorizing about the use of the hooked poles that drew ever nearer, oblivious to any danger. The bridge, still open, hung in the air between them. Roxanne grabbed her father's arm, and then reached her other hand towards the bridge.

"We're going home," Roxanne said, touching the mirrored surface.

A flash of light, and Roxanne and her father were back in his living room. She still held his arm, and he swayed unsteadily on his thin legs, his eyes wide.

"I think you should sit down, Dad."

Roxanne's father gave her the briefest glance, smiled indulgently, and then turned and started from the room.

"Where are you going?" Roxanne asked, and her father stepped through the doorway into the hall. "The doctor said to limit your movements for another two weeks, and I think walking to the end of time just now more than used up your daily quota."

"Oh, screw that for a game of soldiers. We've got to get to my lab. All my notes and papers are there, and I'm sure that I'll be able to work up a statistical model of your device's operation in no time."

With that, Roxanne's father bustled out of the room, driving Roxanne before him, a manic gleam in his eyes. In that moment, he looked more alive than he had in years. She knew that eventually she'd have to let him go, that he couldn't last forever, that the illness would eventually win; but that was still off in the future, and for the moment, at least, they had all the time in the world.

Extract from Roxanne's Diary

Thursday, 26 Nov 1987

Dear Future-Self,

Okay, trust my dad to take anything and turn it into a big set of rules.

On the one hand, I'm glad that someone besides me finally knows about the Sofia, and I'm glad that it's Dad, cause he knows a lot about this sort of thing. He's helping me figure out all kinds of stuff I can do, and has some pretty solid ideas on how the thing actually works.

On the debit side, though, there's the fact that my dad is a scientist, and so everything with him is laws and guiding principles. The only problem is that he's taking a totally prescriptivist attitude toward this, when I'd much rather he took a more descriptivist approach.

For example, Dad's begun to write up a set of rules for time travel. All in my best interest, of course (note the sarcasm). Per Dad's chalkboard, they are:

RULES FOR PROPER TIME TRAVEL

1) DON'T LEARN YOUR PERSONAL FUTURE.
   Ignorance of the future is what makes Humans human. Animals live in the "Now," but only man can remember his past, and look forward to the future. Knowing in too great a detail what is to come robs us of this uncertainty, and we become machines, slaves to destiny.

2) DON'T TRY TO CHANGE YOUR PERSONAL PAST.
   We are the products of our own histories. The triumphs and tragedies of the passing days, from birth to death, are the things that make us who we are. To try to eliminate these, for temporary succor, runs the risk of changing who we are, possibly for the worse.

3) *DON'T MEDDLE IN THE DESTINIES OF OTHERS.*

When moving through time, you will often encounter individuals with whose histories you are familiar. There will be the temptation to tell them the difficulties ahead, or to help them avoid their troubles. The same prohibitions outlined in Rules 1 and 2 apply to others as well. To tell another too much of their personal future, or to change their pasts, would be to rob them of a bit of their humanity and irrevocably change their character.

Dad's only up to three laws, but I'm sure he'll think of more in time. I keep telling him that the point is probably moot, and that the Sofia doesn't seem to offer me the ability to change my own past, or to see my own future. As for messing with other people's destinies, this smacks of that Grandfather Paradox and Don't Step on the Butterflies silliness. If I could do that much damage to the world around me, I would have no doubt done it by now, if only through blundering around in ancient times in high school, chatting up Julius Caesar to try to improve my Latin scores.

Anyway, while Dad is busy working in his lab, I think I'll pop over to visit some friends in the States. It's Thanksgiving today over there, and I've never been one to turn down a good turkey dinner.

CHAPTER 4

THIS BOY

LONDON, 1988
AGE: 19 YEARS OLD

His name was Nigel Grant, and it made Roxanne ache just to look at him.

The professor was still prattling on at the front of the lecture hall, something about circles and squares, but Roxanne couldn't be bothered to pay attention. In her emotional calculus of the moment, there was little more important than Nigel, certainly not a survey course in "The History of Modern Thought," whatever that meant.

Roxanne had enrolled at King's College the year before, after moving back to England to be nearer her ailing father. When she'd revealed to him the strange powers of the bracelet on her arm, her father had insisted that she stay with him in Oxford so they could study its nature and workings full time. Roxanne, though, had different plans, and stood by her decision to study languages and history in London. She had grand schemes for what she might one day accomplish with the Sofia, schemes that would be impossible to realize if she was left ignorant and unable to communicate in some past epoch she might visit.

Thoughts of exploring the vastness of history, though, were all but forgotten in the first days of her second year at the college, when first she'd laid eyes on Nigel.

Weighed against a dark and brooding beauty like Nigel Grant's, the lure of history could only come up short. In the eyes of Roxanne Bonaventure, only weeks before her nineteenth birthday, the mystery of Nigel was without a doubt more compelling than any mysteries of the ages could ever be, the scales tilted inarguably in his favor.

She watched him now, while the professor droned on, seeing him much as she had on that first day, weeks before. Lounged in his seat at the far edge of the classroom, right up against the wall, one Doc Martens–shod foot crossed precisely over the other, his dark hair a delicately arranged mess and his eyes burning disinterestedly under perfect eyebrows, Nigel was the picture of everything Roxanne wanted from the world. The lecture seeming to hold his interest no better than hers, he flipped through a comic magazine, casually lingering over the pages.

The professor had said her name three times before she realized what he was saying. Startled, she almost fell from her chair as she swiveled around to face him. There could be no secret where her attention had been focused. She only hoped Nigel hadn't noticed. So far as Roxanne knew, the object of her attentions and potential affections had no idea she existed, and this was hardly the manner in which she hoped to announce her presence.

"Miss Bonaventure," the professor repeated, making a sigh of each syllable in her name. "Shall I repeat the question?"

"I—I'm sorry," Roxanne managed in response. "Yes, please, I was distracted."

"I think we can all see that," the professor answered, and then glanced meaningfully in the direction of Nigel Grant. "Most of us, at any rate."

Titters and giggles rippled across the room, and Roxanne was sorely tempted to open up a wormhole and disappear into the age of dinosaurs or somewhere.

"Erm," Roxanne said, her face burning red, unable to think of a suitable response.

"As I was saying," the professor went on, "the question before us today is this: What would a higher-dimensional creature look like to a three-dimensional being?"

It took Roxanne a few blinks to parse out his question. Scouring her brain, she dredged up a dim memory of the book they were studying: Edwin A. Abbott's *Flatland*, which she'd read in about an hour over the summer, wanting to get a jump on things. That was the old Roxanne, of course, from before the sight of Nigel had lifted the veil from her eyes and made her realize how many other more important things there were at the college besides the syllabus.

"Well," Roxanne finally answered, "it seems to me that this whole book was about just that thing, right? I mean, if you want to be accurate about it, then time is as much a dimension as breadth or width, and if that's the case, then the little square guy—"

"'A. Square,'" the professor prompted, folding his arms over his chest and regarding Roxanne with a resigned expression painted on his face.

"Right, so Mr. Square, in the book, clearly possesses two spatial dimensions and one of time, making him a three-dimensional being. What you meant to ask, I think, is what a higher-dimensional being would look like to a *four-dimensional* person."

The professor treated her to a somewhat dramatic sigh.

"Very well, Miss Bonaventure, point taken," he answered. "But for the sake of argument, and in order not to introduce confusion into my feeble professorial brain—as all of my notes follow Mr. Abbott's clearly primitive nomenclature and not your obviously more advanced schema . . ." He paused, a true showman. "Taking that into account, how would a higher-dimensional creature look to a three-dimensional being, assuming that you and I could be counted among that latter number?"

Roxanne shrugged.

"Beats me," she swanned back.

"Meatbags," barked a voice from the corner, which with a shiver Roxanne realized belonged to Nigel.

"Excuse me?" said the professor, threatening to bristle.

"I said meatbags," Nigel repeated. He closed the cover on his comic magazine, holding his place with a finger tucked between the pages, and pushed an errant lock of hair off his forehead with his free hand. "We'd be seeing three-dimensional . . ." He paused, and with a quick nod glanced over to Roxanne, who listened on with mouth hanging open. "Or four-dimensional, whatever . . . cross sections of a higher-dimensional being. Just like the Square bloke in the book seeing a 3-D sphere as a series of 2-D circles of different sizes, we'd see a higher-dimensional object as a series of 3-D objects." He paused again, and added for effect, "To put it another way, we'd be seeing bags of meat, maybe some hair, maybe some bones. Meatbags, right?"

"Well, then," the professor added, nodding in slow dawning admiration. "That's certainly a valid response, Mr. Grant. And I thank you for your participation, however brusque. Would that Miss Bonaventure—"

With that, the bell rang for dismissal, and whatever the professor might have hoped for Roxanne was simply added to the tally of the age's mysteries. As one, the class bounded to their feet, to the door, and out, Nigel taking an early and strong lead and Roxanne bringing up the rear, a persistent blush still rising on her cheeks.

Mere feet from the door, the professor following close behind, his lecture materials gathered in hand, it seemed to Roxanne as though the professor might want to finish his interrupted sentiment in some private conference. Carefully calculating, she was able to leave the room and get clear out of sight before he caught up, all without giving the impression she was running away.

Once she was well away from the lecture hall, the professor lost in her dust, Roxanne tried to catch a glimpse of Nigel on the commons, but he was nowhere to be seen.

"Remarkable," her father said, pushing his glasses up on his nose and whistling low between his teeth. A racking cough grabbed him, and as he sputtered, red-faced, he added, "Simply remarkable."

Only a day after her misadventure in The History of Modern Thought, Roxanne wasn't convinced the blush of embarrassment was completely gone from her cheeks. Her father, immersed in probing the bounds of reality, didn't seem to notice.

"Right, Dad," Roxanne answered, pulling a paper tissue from the box on the desk and offering it to her father. As he dabbed the spittle and disquietingly colored phlegm from the corners of his mouth, she sat back down, propping her chin on her hand with legs folded under her in the battered leather-upholstered desk chair. "Remarkable."

This Saturday, as on all the Saturdays in the year since she'd first revealed to him the abilities of the bracelet, Roxanne was up at Oxford in her father's fusty lab. For the last few weeks running, Professor Bonaventure had had Roxanne open temporal bridges into the past and future of the lab itself, treading lightly while testing for potential side effects.

"I mean it, Roxie," he continued, undeterred by the cough he couldn't seem to shake. "The implications are staggering. The time differential between the two mouths of the wormholes created by the device suggest the possibility for temporal-causality loops, were we to introduce some novel element in the past that might affect our current reality. But no matter how hard I try, it just doesn't seem to happen." He paused, and then chuckled. "Not that I'm trying to create a temporal-causality loop, mind you—not intentionally. Who knows? If we were to do so, perhaps we'd only succeed in unraveling the fabric of reality, ending the world as we know it completely and utterly."

"Right," Roxanne nodded, disinterested.

Her father insisted on calling it "the device," despite her insistence that "the Sofia" was the more correct name. He refused to anthropomorphize the thing, a point Roxanne had decided wasn't worth arguing.

"Right, indeed. I mean, just think about it, Roxie. We just sent a message back to ourselves, opening a wormhole to this time yesterday, instructing us not under any circumstances to open up a wormhole today. We know that the message was delivered successfully, as I stepped through myself and wrote on the blackboard, after making a note of the day and time. And yet today we find no message on the blackboard, no warning against sending the message back. There's only one satisfactory answer."

"The cleaning staff erased the board in the night?" Roxanne answered, drumming her fingers on the lab bench.

"What? No, of course not. I locked the door last night in anticipation of this experiment for just that reason."

"I was kidding, Dad." Roxanne rolled her eyes.

"Hmm? Well, in any case, the only possible answer is that, in moving forwards and backwards in time, the device is in some sense navigating through different worlds. By introducing some novel or random element in our own past, we don't affect our own present, but instead create some alternate present—a new line branching off from the altered moment. I can't say for certain without some additional experimentation, but it seems likely that what we're looking at is empirical proof of Wheeler's Many Worlds theory."

Roxanne bore down with the ballpoint pen on the yellow legal tablet in front of her, writing the name "Nigel Grant" again and again, feeling guiltily like a twelve-year-old schoolgirl but not really caring that she did.

"The truly amazing thing, though, is to take into account our findings of last month about the locality characteristics of the device. We know that the device, and by extension you while wearing it, can only exist once at any given point in space-time, right? So that you couldn't decide to travel back to yesterday and give our message to yourself, the Roxanne of twenty-four hours ago. The device can open the door, but if you try to step through, you end up right back where you started. Yes? But we know from past experience that you've been able to travel forward into more than one alternative timeline—or 'worldline,' I suppose we should say—and to return without incident to your starting position.

"That means that you yourself have the ability to navigate Wheeler's 'many worlds,' as it were, provided you start from a position on your initial temporal sequence—let's call it your 'baseline'—and work forwards. Traveling backwards, there will always be only one path, only one past leading to your relative present moment. From that moment forwards, though, there is a near-infinite variation possible, lines in which everything that might have occurred *does* occur."

"Uh-huh," Roxanne hummed, toying with the idea of spelling out "Roxanne Grant," but thinking that might be taking things a step too far.

"Say you were to see what might happen if you had a chicken sandwich today instead of a salad. You could open a wormhole an hour into the future, to around lunchtime, and then stop for a tasty chicken sandwich. Then it would be simply a question of following that line forward, either second-by-inching-second like the rest of us, or by leaps and bounds through the device's wormholes. You could see how the remainder of human history might progress, if you were only to eat a chicken sandwich today.

"Then, if you wanted to see how things might have been different with the soup instead, you'd only have to open a wormhole back into the past, to the hour before lunch. As you've already skipped over the intervening time between now and lunch, at no point in that hour were you and the device already present, so you aren't prevented by the locality characteristics from stepping through the wormhole. Then you choose the soup, and move with head held high into the future to see the changes wrought on mankind's tomorrows by this alternative choice.

"Of course, if you were to wait until *after* you'd already eaten the chicken sandwich to decide to change the outcome, without leaving an intervening period into which you could step, you'd never know what the world of soup might be like, as you'd never be able to access it. Once you've made a decision, the decision sticks, unless you've intentionally left yourself a loophole to abuse."

Roxanne was just about to break down and write "Mr. and Mrs. Nigel Grant" on the yellow pages when her father ceased his pacing and seemed for the first time all morning to notice her.

"Is something wrong?" he asked, stepping close and pushing his glasses up on his forehead. "You've seemed a bit . . . distracted?"

Roxanne answered without thinking, and regretted it immediately.

"It's this boy," she said, sighing dramatically.

"Well, that is . . ." her father began, obviously flustered. "A boy, is it? Hmm."

Roxanne bit her lip, and looked up at him. He looked positively terrified. Apparently, the thought of his daughter involved in any kind of romantic entanglement, potential or otherwise, was much harder for the senior professor to grasp than the obfuscated and hermetic theories he'd been yammering on about all morning.

"In your school, is he?" Professor Bonaventure finally asked, folding his arms over his chest.

Roxanne nodded.

"Not treating you badly, I should hope."

Roxanne shook her head.

"He doesn't even know that I exist."

"Ah," said her father, nodding slowly, "I see. So you're pining away, are you, Roxie? Hoping to capture his attentions?"

"Something like that. Look, it's nothing, really. Can we just not talk about it?"

"Whatever you want, of course." He stepped forwards, and laid a tender hand on Roxanne's shoulder. "But if you ask me, this boy is a fool if he doesn't go for you. You're such a lovely girl, with so much going for you, and he's daft if he doesn't see that. Just let him see who you are, use all of the advantages you have at your disposal, and if it's meant to be I'm sure you'll work it out."

Roxanne suppressed a cringe, but managed a weak smile. She found that the only thing worse than suffering her lonely torments in silence was suffering her lonely torments while getting relationship advice from her dad. Luckily, within moments Professor Bonaventure's attentions were back on the mysteries of the universe, trying to devise a way to test for the presence of Hawking radiation around the circumference of the Sofia's temporal bridges, and Roxanne was free once more to pity herself in peace.

The following Monday, back in class, Roxanne looked at Nigel Grant lounging in the far corner of the lecture hall and decided, once and for all, that he would be hers.

There was nothing else for it, she was convinced. Weeks and weeks had gone by, and she could think of nothing but Nigel. More specifically, she could think of nothing but Nigel and her together. At this rate, she'd soon be unable to think of anything else, and would forget to eat, forget even to breathe. It would only be a matter of time before her body was found in her sad little flat, desiccated and smelling of rot and pathetic desperation, undisturbed except for the delicate little teethmarks on the areas of exposed flesh where the neighbor's cats would have nibbled.

She hated those cats. Something had to be done.

Her father had suggested that she use all the advantages she had at her disposal. That seemed as good an idea as any.

It took some small bit of calculation on the pages of her yellow legal pad to work out the procedure, but by the time the morning classes were through Roxanne had it all planned out. Returning to her small flat near the campus, she changed into clothes more appropriate for a night at the pub, and dashed some food into the fishtank in the kitchen.

"Wish me luck," she told the fish, who didn't seem invested in the question one way or the other. She instructed the Sofia to open a temporal bridge to five days in the future. Taking a few deep breaths, Roxanne reached up and touched the mirror-ball surface of the wormhole.

Saturday.

Roxanne found Nigel sitting alone at the pub, just past sunset. He was sketching furiously in a pad laid on his knee, a pint of bitter at his elbow. With a confidence born of the sure knowledge that she was in a branching future she need never visit again, she found a seat next to Nigel at the bar and ordered a pint of Bass for herself.

"Evening, Nigel," she said, tapping him on the shoulder.

Startled, and looking a bit annoyed, he glanced up from his sketch pad.

"Oh," he said simply. "Hello." With an abbreviated nod, he went back to his sketching.

"I'm not sure if you know me," Roxanne continued, pressing on, "but we're in a class together—"

"Sure," Nigel answered, not looking up. "I remember."

Roxanne chewed at her lip for a moment and reminded herself that nothing she did or said could have any lasting consequence.

"Well, anyway," she went on, "it seems that I have this assignment for one of my other courses, and I have to interview a half dozen people before next week and assemble some statistical data, and I saw you sitting there and thought that perhaps you'd be willing to help me out, so that's why I sat down here next to you."

Reaching the end of her prepared statement, having drifted only marginally off her intended script, Roxanne paused for a much-needed breath. She'd not spoken more than two words running to Nigel since she'd first seen him, and this was proving more difficult than she'd thought.

"Oh," Nigel answered. "Well . . ." He left off, with the hint of a shrug, noncommittal.

"I'd pay for your time, of course," Roxanne added in a rush. "Say, by standing you a few rounds of drinks?"

With a casual motion, Nigel pulled his wallet from an inside pocket, inspected the contents to his satisfaction, and then set the sketch pad and pencil down on the bar.

"Fair enough," he said, still not meeting Roxanne's gaze, and finished off the last of his bitter in one go. "Another of the same," he called to the bartender with a snap.

Setting down the empty glass, he turned back to Roxanne.

"Fire when ready." He crossed his arms over his chest.

"Okay," Roxanne said, chewing the end of her pen nervously. "What is your favorite food?"

They spent the next few hours in the pub, Roxanne asking Nigel every question she could think of, Nigel providing his answers briefly at first, and with increasing detail as the evening wore on. In time, their interview became a conversation, Nigel in turn asking Roxanne about herself, her life, her likes and dislikes. Roxanne began to feel comfortable meeting Nigel's gaze, the conversation much more relaxed and unfettered by the third hour than it had been in the first.

She decided that this plan might really work after all.

∞

Friday.

Roxanne found Nigel at the bar, sketching. She recognized it as the same drawing he'd been working on a day later, though in a more skeletal form. The pub was fairly empty, only students and pensioners this early in the day. Still, with convincing bravado, Roxanne pulled out the stool next to Nigel's at the bar and ordered up a Bass.

When the drink had arrived, Roxanne casually sipping away the top few fingers, she glanced in a convincingly nonchalant fashion at the sketch Nigel was working on and nodded appreciatively.

"A bit like Shaky Kane, isn't it?" she asked.

Nigel looked up, a mixture of surprise and annoyance coloring his expression.

"What was that?"

"I'm sorry to interrupt," Roxanne answered. "It's just that your drawing there reminded me of a cartoonist I quite like, and I couldn't help mentioning it."

"Shaky Kane?"

"Why, yes," Roxanne said. "Do you know his work?"

"Know him?" Nigel set down his pencil and pad, and turned to face Roxanne. "He's only practically my mentor."

"Is that a fact," Roxanne answered, smiling.

Things went fairly well with Friday-Nigel, all things considered, until the question of which of Shaky Kane's comics Roxanne liked best came up. Roxanne provided her prepared answer, cribbed from the notes of her interview with Saturday-Nigel, but she fumbled a bit with the delivery, and Friday-Nigel became suspicious. When pressed on where she'd first seen the cartoonist's work, and on what other comics artists she admired,

Roxanne was on even less sure footing, and it quickly became apparent that she hadn't the foggiest idea what she was talking about.

Even this loss, though, Roxanne considered something of a victory, considering that she hadn't a clue who "Shaky Kane" even was. With renewed enthusiasm and confidence, she plowed ahead to her next try.

Thursday.

At the pub again, Nigel was at his accustomed seat. Roxanne found the seat next to him unoccupied yet again, and sipped casually at her Bass while watching the cricket game on the television over the bar.

"Bloody hell," she muttered under her breath, just loud enough to be heard by someone sitting near. "Why do they have this shite tuned in, when Arsenal's about to start playing at Derby?"

Roxanne managed to keep from glancing over at Nigel's reaction, but from the corner of her eye saw the sketch pad set down on the bar.

"Football fan, are you?" Nigel asked, and then added, "Hey, aren't you in one of my classes at the college?"

Roxanne smiled as wide as she dared, and casually turned to face him.

What Roxanne didn't know about football would fill a library of books, so it was hardly surprising that she'd be caught out in a lie. Still and all, it was a valiant attempt, made even more memorable by the fact that she'd managed to convince Thursday-Nigel he was picking *her* up initially, and not the other way around. When she'd been unable to name even one of Arsenal's players or coaches, though, and displayed an appalling ignorance as to the differences between American football and the proper English variety, Nigel had quickly lost interest and returned his attentions to his sketching.

Wednesday.

"God, what annoying crap this music is," Roxanne said, sliding into the stool next to Nigel's. "Why can't they play something good for a bloody change. Tangerine Dream, for a start."

"Hey," said Nigel, looking up from his sketch pad and waving the bartender over to order her a drink, "aren't you in one of my classes?"

Tuesday.

"Say, your name's Nigel, isn't it? Did you know there's an Ingmar Bergman film festival this weekend up at Cambridge?"

"What?" Nigel said, startled.

Monday.

"Nigel, my name's Roxanne, I'm in one of your classes at King's College, and if you buy me a drink I'd very likely go to bed with you."

Back at Nigel's bedsit, leaning against the wall and looking at the stacks of comic magazines and the Arsenal posters tacked on the wall, Roxanne began to feel a bit sick. Monday-Nigel was across the room, putting an LP of Tangerine Dream's live concert in Warsaw on the turntable, grinning irresistibly.

"I tell you, Roseanne," he said, brushing a lock of hair off his forehead. "I'd never have guessed you for a goer, back in class."

"Yes, well," she answered, not bothering to correct him.

She'd first approached Monday-Nigel convinced, finally, that she need only lure him with her feminine wiles, and that the stable long-term relationship she'd been hoping for would follow as a matter of course. Now, at his home, watching him leer at her in anxious anticipation of the unpacking of said wiles, Roxanne began to suspect it wasn't really worth it.

In the morning, would he be willing to tell her all about his favorite cartoonists, and why Arsenal was the best team on the planet? Would they go to obscure foreign films together, and eat curry takeout and visit secondhand record shops on weekends? Or would this be their only night together, the only time she'd brush moth wings against the flame of his brilliance, and then only silence?

And even if they did manage to forge the bonds of a lasting relationship out of this evening, would Monday-Nigel in the end be the man that Roxanne had dreamt of? Or would Roxanne even be the woman she wanted to be, having won him like this?

It was a great many questions, and to them all Roxanne had only one answer.

"Nigel," she announced, "I've changed my mind. So long."

Right there in the middle of Nigel's bedsit she opened up a temporal-spatial bridge to her own flat, a few hours in the past, to a point just after she'd left for the future.

Her fish hadn't quite finished their dusting of food when she arrived, only a few minutes of their objective time having passed for the subjective days of Roxanne's she'd been away.

The answer to all the questions she'd had, the thing she'd realized while looking at Monday-Nigel looking at her with lust in his eyes, was that she was thinking of someone else. Someone she'd approached just as herself, with no strategy or pretense, and with whom she'd been able to be the person she was when alone. A man who'd come to like her for who she was, and not for how well she played the part of his perfect woman.

Roxanne opened up a temporal bridge to Saturday and stepped through.

Roxanne found Saturday-Nigel at the pub, finishing up his sketch after their interview had concluded. From his perspective she'd just left a few minutes before, saying she'd got all the answers she needed. From her perspective, it had been days.

"Back so soon, are you?" Saturday-Nigel joked, raising his near-empty glass in a salute. "Thought you had somewheres to be."

"I changed my mind," Roxanne answered with a smile, and slid onto the stool next to his.

"What you mean is that you couldn't stand to be away from me, innit?" Nigel said, grinning devilishly.

"Something like that. Now, how about you buy me a drink for a change?"

"Delighted." Saturday-Nigel waved for the bartender to bring them another round. "Now, tell me more about this school you were at in America. Sounds bloody crazy, it does."

Roxanne smiled. She hadn't felt this relaxed in weeks.

"Fine," she answered, "but only to keep you from nattering on about Arsenal. Well, you see, I first went to America when I was ten, and I had no idea what to expect. . . ."

Extract from Roxanne's Diary

Dear Future-Self,

(And at what point do I stop being my present-self, and become the future myself? Has that already happened? Am I already her?)

Have been wrestling with the question of whether to tell Nigel about the Sofia or not. Dad says not to do so, but then I think Dad would be happier if he were able to keep the Sofia (and me, by extension) in his lab at all hours, until he'd ferreted out its every mystery and could publish the results to the world at large. Not that I'm convinced he ever will publish his results. I've begun to suspect that the reason he hasn't discussed the Sofia with any of his colleagues is out of some misguided attempt to shelter me. As though, were the world to learn of my abilities, I'd never be able to lead a normal life. As though growing up with a time machine permanently affixed to one's wrist didn't already preclude any chance of a normal life. But there it is.

In any case, I've more or less decided not to tell Nigel about the Sofia. It feels dishonest to keep him so in the dark, but I'm not sure if he (or our relationship, for that matter) could handle the strain of the disclosure.

As it is, things have proven surprisingly easy to manage. If I want to go off for a little exploring, all I need do is go into the next room, open up a bridge, and go wherever, and then on my return just make sure to open the bridge back to the split second after I left. I once spent a week in ancient Sumeria while Nigel was on the toilet, which is pretty funny, once you think about it. Perhaps he should eat more fiber.

My studies at university have proven invaluable. At night, it's up to Dad's lab to study physics, physics, and more physics, but during the days I haunt the King's College campus, studying every language they'll teach me, scouring history books to learn proper contexts, reading through the biographies of key historical figures, learning everything I can about the worlds that were and might once have been.

I suppose the biggest development in the last few months has been my new sleeping schedule.

With all the studying, and experimentation, and jaunts back in time, I found little time to rest, and it was beginning to wear on me. Nigel, my father, even some of my professors all commented on it. I was becoming a thin shadow of my former self.

It struck me eventually that there was no reason that I couldn't take advantage of the Sofia's abilities to get all the sleep I wanted. I could work around the clock if I wanted, so long as I popped off to some other era at some point in the day and got my requisite eight hours of sleep.

I tried to fit it into my schedule, and it works a treat.

I've kept my own flat, and Nigel's kept his, and between his late hours at the studio painting or down rehearsing with his horrible band, and my time spent up in Oxford with my dad, we only ever spend the nights together on weekends. That gives me my weeknights free, more or less. So I've got school all day, then it's a quick spatial bridge to Oxford, then back home to study through the night, then shortly before dawn I open a temporal bridge to this uninhabited South Pacific island at around the first millennium BCE. I've got it kitted out with a large tent, with a comfortable cot, portable generator, fresh water, and snacks. I can sleep in the tent, or in the hammock under the stars, wake up hours later rested and refreshed, and have a dip in the crystal blue Pacific waters before coming back to the present day to shower and dress for school.

The only nights I have to keep regular people hours are Friday and Saturday night, and even then I often sneak out of Nigel's bed in the middle of the night to pop back to my own island hideaway for a midnight swim and a few long hours' kip.

To be honest, I don't know how anybody else manages it, being stuck in the regular hours of the day and night.

My hours away are starting to add up, though, and it's getting to the point where I'm living several "subjective" weeks to everyone else's "objective" one. I think I'm getting older faster, in other words. Not too badly now, but I'm pretty sure I celebrated my last birthday a few months late, so far as my subjective calendar goes. So far Nigel hasn't noticed that my period seems to come once every week or two (as I've also developed the habit of taking off for the past whenever my flow starts again, so he won't get suspicious), but he's bound to catch on eventually.

Sooner or later I'm going to have to scrap the whole idea of keeping a daily diary altogether, or at least start figuring some other method of keeping track. Maybe if I just measure my own subjective days, wherever and whenever I am, and to hell with everyone else's calendar.

I've got to dash. I'm due at Dad's lab in about thirty seconds, and he doesn't like me to keep him waiting.

CHAPTER 5

TWO OF US

LONDON, 1991
AGE: 22 YEARS OLD

oxanne's mother was dead, to begin with. There was no doubt about that. But there was no one else that she needed, now that *he* was gone.

It was Christmastime in London, and Roxanne was in her small flat, drunk, unwashed, and miserable. And alone. Always alone.

Happy-sodding-Christmas.

Nigel was gone. That thought ran through Roxanne's mind over and over like a commercial jingle she couldn't shake, no matter how hard she tried humming some other tune.

Nigel was gone.

She could still feel him, his absence in the flat almost a palpable texture. Like the color of the miserable wallpaper, or the pattern on the warped linoleum. It was as though the flat had been redecorated in misery.

Who dumps their girlfriend of more than two years the day before bloody Christmas Eve? And he'd said *she* was cold.

And distant. And difficult to reach.

Roxanne drained the bottle of cheap plonk to the dregs, and screwed the top off another. It was her last bottle of what was optimistically (or euphemistically) labeled "wine," so she'd soon either have to pass out, or go out foraging for supplies.

Nigel had said she was cold in the center, like a frozen dinner pulled out of the oven too soon. Warm to the touch, but with a heart of ice.

The last bottle was half-drunk before Roxanne had even realized she'd started in on it.

What surprised Roxanne, perhaps even more than Nigel's departure, was that she'd not shed a single tear after he left. She'd barely even noticed—just had a bit more to drink and thought about how much freedom she'd have, now that Nigel wasn't around to worry about.

Now it was two days later. Now she'd noticed.

She *had* been distant, and cold, and difficult to reach—she admitted that now. She wasn't sure why she'd walled up and kept Nigel at arm's length. But she was feeling his absence now.

She was utterly and completely alone.

Well, there was always her father. He was always there for her, always ready with a hug or a kiss on the cheek. But he'd only wanted to talk about the intricacies of time travel and dimensional physics for the last few years, and Roxanne didn't have the strength for it. In some ways, it seemed like the mysteries of the Sofia had given her father a new lease on life, but at the same time, it could get dead boring talking only about time travel and the like.

Roxanne had few friends, and fewer she felt she could really open up to, and most of them were off for the holidays, vacationing or visiting family. It was just Roxanne, in her lonely flat, with a bottle of some cheap plonk (well, several bottles) and the gnawing pain of loneliness in her gut, and the sure knowledge that she would die alone.

It's not my fault, Roxanne decided, staring down the barrel of the last bottle. *I lacked a mother's love.*

Roxanne froze in place, a statue.

She'd lost her mother at such a young age. Barely five years old— just old enough to have realized there was a whole world beyond the back garden, her reality having consisted mostly of Roxie, Mummy, and Daddy up to that point. Barely moving in the larger world, and to have her mother ripped away at that crucial moment.

She'd started building the walls even then, all those years ago. It was hardly her fault that neither she nor Nigel could climb over them now.

If she'd known her mother, if she'd had a mother's hand to guide her, everything would have been different.

She could do it, she realized. It would be easy.

Roxanne had thought about going back a hundred times before, even talked about it with Father a time or two when the moment seemed right. But even after they'd realized there was no way she could futz with the flow of time, or erase history, or any of that science fictional nonsense, she'd known that it would be a bad idea. She'd buried her mother more than seventeen years before, and had spent the better part of two decades recovering from the loss. To go back, even for an instant, would run the risk of undoing years of recovery, barely healed wounds ripping open again, this time possibly for good.

But that was before Nigel, before Roxanne realized about the walls, and the lack of a mother's touch. Maybe some wounds *should* be reopened. Maybe that's the only way they ever really heal.

Roxanne tossed back the last of the wine, and dropped the empty bottle to the floor. She found her boots beneath the mess at the door, climbed into her jacket, and ran fingers through her ratty hair to straighten it. She hadn't seen her mother in a lifetime, after all, and would have to look her best.

Roxanne stood in the middle of the living room, listing from side to side like a boat in a heavy storm.

I shouldn't, said a small voice, somewhere in the back of her head.

"Screw it, I will," said a much louder voice, out loud.

Winking one eye shut to help her balance, Roxanne instructed the Sofia to open up a temporal bridge and, swaying only slightly, reached out and touched it with outstretched fingers.

∞

Roxanne stepped out into the cold of a London December, 1967. She thought it was Christmastime, but she couldn't be sure. She was still a bit tipsy, and her aim might have been a little off.

A scruffy-looking teenager with long hair, generous sideburns, and a leather fringe jacket went sauntering by.

"Hey, boy!" Roxanne called out, snapping her fingers noiselessly. "What's today?"

"What?" the boy replied with a disaffected sneer, flipping his greasy hair out of his face.

"Um, what's the date, my fine fellow?" Roxanne asked, trying for bonhomie.

"Piss off," the kid replied, flipping her the bird before turning and sashaying off.

Roxanne grinned sloppily. It certainly seemed like the Christmas spirit to her.

Christmas spirit. Christmas Spirit. The phrase repeated itself a few times in her head, antiphon to the persistent "Nigel Is Gone" chorus.

Christmas Past. Christmas Future. She'd come from the one to the other, like someone from a very special episode of a television sitcom nobody liked.

Roxanne was the Ghost of Christmas Future, come down long trains of years to get a glimpse of her mother's past.

Joy to the world.

The streets were more or less as Roxanne remembered, as they'd be in another twenty years' time, as they'd be in just a few more years' time, when Roxanne was old enough to notice things like that.

Her mum had just met her dad, if Roxanne's math and memory were correct. Her dad was finishing up his doctorate at Oxford, and her mother was living with her grandparents in Notting Hill. Roxanne remembered visiting her grandparents there, before her mother had died, before her grandfather and grandmother had died. They'd all died, or moved away, all of them, only Roxanne and her dad left in England now. But not *now*, not in 1967. In 1967, they were all still alive, in embarrassing hairdos and even more embarrassing clothes.

The drunk had started to fade a bit from Roxanne's eyes by the time she reached her grandparents' road, her steps a little surer than before, but she was still lit up with fire in her belly, and had hours and miles to go before she saw the town of Sober on the horizon.

It was cold, unconscionably cold, on the pavement across the street from her grandparents' blue door, and there were few out braving the winds. A cop down the street, a greengrocer on his way home from his market, a couple of kids kicking a half-deflated soccer ball, and Roxanne, still listing slightly side to side, working up the courage to ring the bell.

The blue door opened, and a woman Roxanne's age stepped out, wrapping a thick woolen scarf around her neck.

Roxanne stood struck dumb on the pavement for an instant that lasted an eternity.

She could see the shape of her nose in this woman's face, the line of her chin below a familiar mouth.

Roxanne tried to speak, and her voice crumbled to dust in her throat. There was a sharp pain deep inside that she'd not felt in years. Her eyes welled, and a choking sob rattled her hollow chest.

She couldn't do this. It'd been years, and she'd forgotten just how much losing her mother had hurt, back when she was small and defenseless, a fragile child. She felt herself devolving back into that fragile child again, emotions scraped raw and aching, just at the sight of her mother in the flesh. Or the woman who might be her mother, somewhere, somewhen. She'd avoided pictures of the woman for years, because seeing them always made her cry, and now Roxanne thought she could just walk up to her on the street?

Not hardly.

No, it wasn't her mother that Roxanne needed.

What she needed was another bottle.

Roxanne was lying on the ground, a rock pressing into the small of her back, a chill breeze blowing across her face. Her eyes were squeezed shut tight, while hammers sounded somewhere deep within her skull. Her mouth tasted as though something had crawled inside and died in some suitably horrible fashion. In all, she was feeling a bit . . . What was the word? Her grasp on vocabulary was failing her, it seemed.

But Roxanne was having trouble with more than her vocabulary, at the moment. Something to do with the pounding in her head, and the queasy feeling surging up from her toes.

She'd had a few drinks; she knew that much. At least a few.

Eyes still shut tight, most of her attention concentrated on suppressing the sense of sweaty nausea that seemed to well up from somewhere deep inside her, she pieced together what she could of the night before.

She hadn't wanted to hang around 1967. Too many painful memories. Or not memories, since she didn't remember them herself. What was it that you called a memory that's been handed down from one generation to the next? Was it still a memory, or was there some alchemical flash point where, in the telling, it became something else? A story, a legend, a myth?

In any case, it had started, innocently enough, with a few jars of mead in a Viking longhouse. From there she'd shared a few servings of kava with a group of Maori warriors, a few centuries before their first contact with Europeans. Then she'd necked more than a few cups of rice wine in some remote Japanese farming village, high on terraced steps, and chased it with rotgut in a saloon in the American West in the late nineteenth century. She started a bottle of absinthe with Toulouse-Lautrec in fin de siècle Paris, and finished it off with some goat herders on a mountain in Greece in the second millennia BCE, giving rise to myths of ambrosia, the nectar of the gods.

It was after getting into a drinking contest with a gang of Napoleonic-era British sailors on shore leave in a dingy Burmese dive—which contest Roxanne was reasonably sure she'd won—that things began to get a bit fuzzy.

Roxanne was in the middle of nowhere. Literally. A wide plain, with a few scrub brushes and outcroppings of rock, stretched out under a pale blue, cloudless sky. A bird wheeled over the far horizon—or rather, what looked like a bird, since from that distance Roxanne couldn't really be sure—but there were no other animals in sight.

Roxanne had no idea where she was, and worse, no inkling *when* she was. She'd always maneuvered through time and space relative to her starting position, giving the Sofia instructions to open a bridge to a point a century in the future, or a thousand feet to the north, and so on. If she didn't know where she was starting from, though, she'd have no idea where she was going. She had no clue whether she was in the future, or the present, or the distant past. She could travel blindly for subjective days, weeks, even months before she got her bearings and got back home.

Roxanne, her temples throbbing and her tongue thick and dry in her throat, scanned the distant horizon, considering her options.

"Well, this sort of sucks."

∞

She experimented, through the long morning, following the methods she'd learned from her father. Dispassionate, empirical, scientific. That was the way to solve a problem.

She started by walking in the direction of the rising sun, looking for water, or people, or anything but grass, sky, and rocks. After a quarter of an hour, Roxanne began to tire, and realized she had no business walking, not when she had a means of effortless travel bound to her wrist. She chalked this brief lapse in judgment up to the latent effects of the previous night's entertainment, and started traveling at speed.

She opened up a few bridges, moving in space but not in time. She'd jaunt a few miles in one direction, a few hundred in another, looking for people, or buildings, or animals. Anything that could help her figure out where and when she was. She guessed the African savanna, but it could just as easily have been some Pangaean plain, or some impossibly far-future grasslands. Without any point of reference, she was well and truly lost.

She traveled a few thousand miles in one direction, and found herself standing at the shore of some ocean, cool salt spray in her eyes. She traveled a few thousand miles back in the other direction, and found herself at the base of a mountain range. In another direction, desert, in another, more salt water, but still nothing to eat, nothing to drink, and nothing to suggest a time or place.

She thought about taking a quick trip a few hours into the future, to see if she recognized any constellations, but what she didn't know about astronomy was, well, everything.

Roxanne hopped back to her starting point: the wide grassy plain. The sun had risen to its zenith, and her shadow hid beneath her feet. Even with the aid of the spatial bridges prised open by the Sofia, her movements of the morning had worn her out, and Roxanne felt like she needed to rest. She sat on a level patch of ground, folded her arms around her knees, and rested her head. In a few minutes, in the warm midday sun, she was asleep.

In red-lidded darkness, curled in a fetal position on the hard ground, Roxanne slowly woke, hungry, hungover, and dehydrated. She opened bloodshot eyes, and looked out on the darkening plain. Pushing herself into a sitting position, she found bits of dirt and dried blades of grass stuck to the left side of her face, cemented in place by drool.

It was near sunset, and Roxanne's head was pounding harder than ever.

She thought about getting up and continuing her search, but she just didn't have the energy. She was exhausted and starved, without the will to keep moving. All she really wanted to do was sit there and cry.

So she did.

It began as a faint misting, her vision blurring in the fading late-afternoon light. Then tears welled from the corners of her eyes, and one by one streamed down to her jaw, leaving faint trails behind on grimy cheeks. Then the tears poured freely, and she began to sob, and she began to howl, and she began to scream.

Years of loneliness, from childhood on, ever and always alone. Motherless, sent away by her father, growing up among strangers on the far side of the world. Alone, always alone.

And just when all that seemed a thing of the past, when Nigel arrived out of the blue to rescue her, now he'd gone and Roxanne found herself alone again. Figuratively and literally, and in every imaginable sense. Alone.

Roxanne's head was ringing.

She flung herself on her back, arms and legs outstretched, and raged at the stars just winking in overhead.

"I've always been alone!" she shouted, cursing an uncaring universe. "I'll always be alone, and there isn't sod-all I can do about it!"

Her head was still ringing.

"Aargh!" She shouted a wordless howl of rage, damning the universe for being so unfair.

The ringing in her head continued, but changed pitch. At the end of thought, behind her boundless rage, Roxanne almost noticed something strange: now it almost sounded like singing.

"Why shouldn't I just curl up and die? Am I just *doomed* to be alone forever?!"

I am always with you, sang a voice in her head.

Roxanne stopped short, and sat bolt upright.

Had she finally gone mad? Wasn't hearing voices one of the early indicators? Or, worse yet, what if she'd been mad all these years, since that afternoon in the woods outside the Saint Anthony Academy, and she was only just now catching on?

I am always with you.

She might be mad, but there was something else at work. Roxanne knew that voice, though she was sure she'd never heard it before.

Instruct me.

It was a voice she remembered, but only vaguely, as though from dreams. Like a face glimpsed out of the corner of one's eye, familiar and completely unrecognizable at the same time.

"Who are you?" Roxanne asked out loud, not sure whether she wanted an answer or not.

Instruct me.

It came to her not in some slow, dawning realization, but in a rush, as though some dam in her mind had broken free. Roxanne realized that the voice she heard wasn't a sign that she was deranged. Not that she *wasn't* deranged, but the voice wasn't evidence for the prosecution. No, she realized that the voice had been hovering at the edge of her thoughts for years. It was the voice that whispered to her in her sleep.

"Sofia?"

Roxanne held her breath, and an eternity slipped past.

I am always with you.

"You can . . ." Roxanne struggled, unable to fit the thought into her head. "You can *talk*."

You instruct me; I act. You query; I answer. I am always with you.

Roxanne climbed unsteadily to her feet.

"Why haven't I heard you before?" Roxanne asked the empty air, looking all around her before thinking to look at her wrist. But the bracelet looked just as it always had, the lenticular jewel set in the band of silvery metal. "After all this time?"

You query; I answer. You instruct me; I act.

It made a kind of sense. Roxanne had never asked the Sofia to answer, and so it never had. She'd only given it instructions, which it had always followed.

"Sofia, can you . . . ?" Roxanne's voice faltered. She was still only half-convinced that she wasn't deranged, that she hadn't lost her mind in a California forest when she was eleven and wandered there still, carrying on conversations with the breeze.

Instruct me, came the answer, calm and soothing, the voice of an angel.

"Sofia, can you . . . can you take me home?"

You instruct me, answered the liquid voice, somewhere behind her eyes. *Home.*

The Sofia sang a soothing note that echoed in Roxanne's thoughts, and a temporal bridge irised open in front of her. On its mirrored surface Roxanne could see inverted the image of her ramshackle flat in London. In the future, in the past? Roxanne couldn't say, and couldn't care.

"Let's go home, Sofia," she said, and smiled.

Roxanne reached out with her left hand, the silvery band of the bracelet on her wrist picking up and reflecting the shimmering light of the silvery ball. She touched the surface of the bridge, and the two of them, Roxanne and the Sofia, were gone.

SECTION II

CHAPTER 6

A DAY IN THE LIFE

LONDON, 1998
SUBJECTIVE AGE: 29 YEARS OLD

The microscopic fibers of cosmic string material retracted into the housing of the Sofia, and the temporal bridge irised shut, returning to the probabilistic chaos of the quantum foam. Roxanne slumped down on the bed, fully dressed, her battered backpack falling with a muffled thud on the carpeted floor, and within seconds was already asleep. There was no better way, so far as she was concerned, to start off her birthday.

Having spent the last few weeks of subjective time on an extended trip down various worldlines, moving ever farther and farther from the world she knew, it was a welcome relief to return briefly to her own baseline. She'd been exploring, following a wild hair to learn what would have happened to the development of Earth civilization if man had not become the planet's dominant species. After so many long days spent in strange, often inhuman and just as often inhospitable realities, Roxanne had decided it was time for a break. When the Sofia informed her that she'd reached the last day of her twenty-eighth year, subjective time, the date of her twenty-ninth birthday in the objective time of her baseline seemed as good a point to stop as any.

She'd informed the Sofia to open a temporal-spatial bridge from the world of the hypochondriac birdmen to her bedroom at the Bark Place house in Bayswater, and crossed through right to the foot of her bed.

She snored, though there was no one there to complain, birdman or otherwise.

Roxanne woke late, almost noon, and after a quick call to her father up at Oxford to make dinner plans for later that evening, stripped out of her traveling clothes and took a long, hot bath. When she was pruned, fingers to toes, she climbed dripping from the bath, and toweled herself off in front of the mirror, noticing with dismay the increasing numbers of scars and bruises marring her once-smooth skin, to say nothing of the impact all of this subjective time was having on her once-trim figure. Whether she was more dismayed over her appearance, or over the fact that her appearance still mattered so much to her, she couldn't say.

The weather report on the television indicated that London was enjoying an unseasonably warm October day, so Roxanne lingered over her large wardrobe in the third-floor bedroom, picking out a completely impractical outfit. A light patterned skirt, reaching almost to her ankles, soft cotton sleeveless T-shirt with a V-neck collar, and a pair of sandals with straps crisscrossing over the tops of her feet. She looked herself over in the mirror, turning slightly to the left and right, letting the hem of the skirt shift back and forth rhythmically. If not for the wide-banded silver bracelet on her wrist, she might have been any other woman out for a stroll on the town.

This outfit wouldn't last five minutes in the worldline of the sentient dogs, she thought approvingly. *It's perfect.*

∞

Roxanne and her father had made plans to have dinner at the Royal China, not far from her Bayswater home. The dim sum at the Royal China put the other Chinese eateries in London to shame, and Roxanne knew from experience that she always ate more there than she planned. For lunch, then, something lighter.

A few blocks from her house was Inaho, a hole-in-the-wall Japanese diner, where she ordered the standard sushi box lunch with an order of miso soup. The fatty tuna tasted a bit off, and the miso wasn't the best it had been, but the eel more than made up for any shortcomings. Leaving an exorbitant tip, Roxanne headed towards the West End, and the shops along Oxford Street.

So much of her time, both subjective and objective, was spent in utter practicality. Sensible shoes, durable clothing, and protection against any number of contingencies. On rare occasions, such as today, she treated herself with impracticality, when she left behind the chore of being a strong independent woman and, for a brief moment, was just a girl.

At the third shoe store, Roxanne found a pair of pumps that would go well with the dress she'd just picked up for dinner. Practical concerns raised their ugly head at the fourth shoe store, where she saw a pair of ankle-high laced boots that seemed well made and durable, and just the thing for walking down innumerable variant timelines. At a leather shop, she found a new backpack to replace the one now lying at the foot of her bed back at the Bark Place house. After many journeys, it had finally been battered and scratched almost beyond recognition back on the worldline of the sentient dinosaur-men. As the cashier rang up the backpack, Roxanne realized that impracticality was slipping away from her, and she decided it was time for a bit of refreshment.

A short while later, Roxanne lounged beneath an umbrella-covered table in front of a little Oxford Street bistro, sipping a cup of tea and munching contentedly on a piece of chocolate biscotti. Dropping a few pound notes on the table, she wandered down the street, wondering whether to take in a show at the cinema before heading home to change for dinner, or whether she'd go and stretch out on the grass at one of the city's numerous parks. The question quickly became moot when she felt the sharp jab of what seemed to be a gun barrel between her ribs.

"Don't make a sound," came a rasping voice at her ear. "If you try to run or call for help, you're dead."

Roxanne let out a deep sigh. So much for a little relaxation.

Roxanne sat cross-legged on the rickety metal folding chair in the secluded back room, the only illumination from a bare lightbulb swinging on its cord overhead. Her would-be captor, odd gun in hand, paced the floor in front of her, the gun barrel trained on her heart.

Roxanne was hardly worried. Even if she hadn't learned enough martial arts training from her friend Sandford Blank and her cousin to snap the man in half at a moment's notice, the Sofia was there to protect her. Its crystalline intelligence, monitoring the chains of probability and possibility, would steer from any worldline in which she came to harm, unless Roxanne expressly ordered it not to do so. Which hardly seemed likely.

Not worried, Roxanne was by turns bemused, curious, and annoyed. Bemused at the man's sometimes outlandish mode of speech, and the disheveled look of his baggy trench coat and savagely buzzed hair. Curious about just what he was after, what he wanted, and what the strange gun he held in his thick-fingered grip was. And annoyed at the constant barrage of incessant, probing questions. She would play along just up until the point where she got bored. She had, after all, dinner plans to consider.

"Okay, I'll ask you again," the man snarled at her silence. "When were you born?"

"October eighth, 1969," Roxanne answered, her tone labored.

"And your name at birth?"

"The same as it's always been. Roxanne Bonaventure."

"And when did you purchase your house on Bark Place, Bayswater?" The man leaned in close.

"In 1861," she answered.

The man's lip curled back into a sneer.

"Look," she went on, "if I wanted to buy a fully restored, three-bedroom detached Victorian in that neighborhood in today's market, do you have any idea what it would cost?"

"I'm asking the questions here!"

"And doing a fine job of it, I want to assure you. Have you been professionally trained? You have the air of someone who took a correspondence class in interrogation."

"Look, you . . ." the man began. He stepped forward, bringing the barrel of his oddly shaped gun just inches from Roxanne's nose.

"Oh, for heaven's sake." Roxanne sighed, and then chopped the man to the ground. It took two moves to get him off his feet, one of them doing double duty to knock the gun from his grip, sending it flying up in the air, spinning end over end. Sandford would have been proud.

Roxanne caught the gun on its downward arc, and casually turned it on the man lying crumpled on the floor, holding his groin with both hands.

"That's better," Roxanne said, nonchalantly crossing her legs again. She'd never even stood up from the chair. "Now, let's try this from a different angle, shall we?"

The man looked up at her from under thick eyebrows, his eyes flashing.

"You'll get nothing from me," he sneered.

"Okay," Roxanne answered, and pulled back what seemed to be the cocking mechanism on the gun with her thumb.

"No, don't!" the man shouted, scrambling back. He held his hands up in front of his face protectively, shielding himself from the gun. "It might go off!"

Roxanne paused, and leaned forward with a wicked smile.

"That was my intention, after all," she said. She held the gun up in the light, inspecting it more closely. "What type of gun is it, anyway? I've never seen one like it in this worldline."

The man lowered his hands, and looked up at Roxanne apprehensively. As tough as he'd talked when he'd been the armed member of the party, with the situations reversed he softened rather quickly.

"It's an ice gun," he answered, his gaze downcast. "A compression firearm, it shoots a projectile of frozen water that melts in the target once the damage is done, almost completely untraceable."

"Wow," Roxanne said, marveling. "Can I try?" She pointed the gun directly at the supine man's forehead, her finger tightening slowly over the trigger mechanism.

"No, no, please," the man pleaded. "I wouldn't have hurt you."

"Well, we'll see," Roxanne answered. "Consider yourself on probation, with a review scheduled for just a few seconds from now. Your performance will be based on your answers to a few easy questions."

The man nodded, blanched.

"Before we begin, let's make sure you aren't hiding any other toys, yes?" Roxanne said. "Keep your hands where I can see them, and climb up on your knees, facing the wall."

The man did as she said. Once he was on his knees, she had him clasp his hands behind his neck, and patted him down. Satisfied there was nothing within his reach that might prove a problem, she stripped off his trench coat, and had him turn around to face her.

Beneath the trench coat, he was wearing a skintight one-piece gray bodysuit, formfitting and unfortunately leaving nothing to the imagination.

"Nice," Roxanne said, sarcasm dripping. "You'll have to get me the name of your tailor. I especially like the little booties." She gestured to his feet, where the bodysuit terminated in a socklike affair on each foot, treads on the soles.

The man looked down at his outfit, a little bewildered, as though it were the most perfectly ordinary thing in the world.

"Okay, question time," Roxanne continued. "First up, what's *your* name?"

"Pol," the man said, his voice low. "Pol Kenaston."

"Pol, huh? And why, Pol, were you so intent on dragging me away from my afternoon shopping, and asking me all these bloody annoying questions?"

"Well, that is . . ." the man called Kenaston began, his voice trailing off.

"Come on with it." Roxanne gestured with the ice gun. "You're on probation, I'll remind you. Now, this gear of yours, and your little spaceman suit there, suggests to me that you are not some garden-variety hooligan out for some fun, yes? This seems a more top-secret sort of affair, wouldn't you think? Some government spook show, perhaps? Or some rogue taxman out to collect on some perceived back taxes?"

The man looked up at her, his eyes narrowed, his mouth twisting into an amused sneer.

"Come on, I'm only mostly joking," Roxanne said. "But seriously, if you don't tell me who you're with, I'll test my marksmanship with your little James Bond number here on your forehead. And at this range, I don't suppose the quality of my marksmanship is going to make a world of difference to the target."

Kenaston sighed, defeated.

"The CDC," he answered. "I'm with the CDC."

"What's that, then?" Roxanne asked. "The Centers for Disease Control? I'm not any kind of viral vector, if that's your worry."

"No," Kenaston said. "The Chrono Defense Corps."

Roxanne blurted out a shotgun blast of laughter.

"The Chrono . . . ?" she began, but couldn't continue for her giggling. "Oh, that's brilliant. It's like something out of a damned Gerry Anderson puppet show. *'Chrono Defense Corps Is Go!'*" She paused, chuckling, and looked sidelong at Kenaston. "Wait, you're serious? Oh, dear."

Roxanne uncrossed her legs, and stood, pushing the folding chair back with a metallic squeal across the floor.

"Mr. Kenaston," she began. "Pol," she added in gentler tones. "I hate to be the one to tell you this, but that name is just ridiculous. Now I'm kind of sorry I made fun of your silly clothes." She paused, and then added, "You *did* know I was making fun of your clothes, didn't you?"

Pol Kenaston, agent of the Chrono Defense Corps, only groaned in response.

It was apparently the Bark Place house that had tipped them off. In her early twenties, subjective time, when she'd begun exploring time and the bifurcating worldlines in earnest, Roxanne had decided it best if she had a stable base of operations in the nineteenth through twenty-first centuries. After seeding some well-selected investments in the postwar American economy of the 1950s, she'd made a large cash withdrawal in the early 1990s, converted the currency into gold, and then brokered a deal in 1861 for a brand-new house, splendid in the High Victorian style. She hired a solicitors' firm in London to pay the regular expenses and taxes, visiting them a few times over the decades to ensure everything stayed aboveboard. From that point on, subjective time of course, she maintained households at several different temporal eras along her baseline, one in the 1890s, one in the 1940s, one in the 1990s, and so on.

Roxanne was hardly surprised that Kenaston's brothers-in-arms with the Chrono Defense Corps, whatever that would prove to be, had caught on that there was something not quite kosher about the woman at Number 9 Bark Place. She had never been careful about covering her tracks, after all. Why bother? With the world continuously branching countless times every picosecond, every possibility made manifest in some variant line, it hardly mattered if someone in one worldline caught on that she wasn't what she seemed, as there'd be countless other worldlines where no one ever got a clue.

The notion that meddling in the past would somehow interfere with the present was malarkey. Roxanne had learned that in theory as a child at her father's knee, and proven it time and time again in the years that followed. If she were to travel back in time to 1889 and strangle Adolf Hitler in his cradle, she'd succeed only in introducing a new series of branching worldlines, but would do nothing to affect all of the remaining lines in which she *didn't* strangle the infant Hitler. Likewise if she traveled back to the height of the Roman Empire, and set off a nuclear bomb at the palace of Julius Caesar, it wouldn't mean that the rest of history would be distorted; it would only mean that there would be new worldlines featuring a radioactive Rome, branching off orthogonally from the baseline.

The only thing Roxanne couldn't do, she knew, was affect her own past. The Sofia was unique in all the branching worlds of the Myriad, existing only in one worldline at a time. Alone among all of the objects and artifacts, particles and people in the universe, the Sofia could follow only one chain of possibility, the crystalline intelligence at its core selecting from the countless possible worlds at every passing instant. It might open a door to the past, or to the future, but could never visit the same place and time twice.

Likewise, since first she'd been given the Sofia by the mysterious crone in the woods, all those years before, Roxanne was unique in the Myriad. There were other variant Roxannes, of course, but only those originating before the bracelet was placed on her wrist. From that point onwards, Roxanne did not bifurcate with the rest of reality, but followed a straight and steady path to the future.

This meant, Roxanne and her father had theorized, that in every other worldline spawned into being, Roxanne and the Sofia alike suddenly winked out of existence. There were countless worlds and realities in which she suddenly ceased to be. The implications of that were staggering, and not something on which Roxanne chose to dwell. Nevertheless, taking all of that into consideration, the possible difficulties of a house being owned under her name for the course of centuries was a trivial concern at best.

Pity, then, that Pol Kenaston and his friends didn't seem to have quite the same grasp of temporal mechanics as Roxanne.

"So let me get this straight," Roxanne concluded, gesturing with the ice gun at the man crouched on the cold, concrete floor. "You and your mates have found some sort of time machine, but somebody else found it first, or after you, and in any case you're worried that other people are going around mucking up the flow of time."

Kenaston nodded.

"And this magic time machine of yours was just dug up in Antarctica, right? You lot didn't invent it?"

Kenaston nodded again.

"Well, this I have to see," Roxanne said. She stepped towards him, menacing with the gun. "Where is it?"

"It's more than a day to fly there," Kenaston snarled back, having recovered some of his accustomed composure. "And you're nuts if you think the CDC is going to ferry you there in their private jet."

"I can arrange my own transportation, thank you," Roxanne replied. "And I intend to be back well in time for dinner. I'll only ask you once more, and I want coordinates. Where is it?"

Kenaston treated her to what she was sure he thought a steely glare, and then rattled off a pair of numbers, latitude and longitude. Down at the bottom of the world, from the sound of it, not far from the South Pole.

"And it's underground, you say? How deep?"

Kenaston shrugged.

"Twenty feet," he guessed. "More or less."

"That'll do," Roxanne answered. Keeping the ice gun trained on him in her right hand, she raised her left hand to her face, bringing the jeweled face of the Sofia inches from her nose. It wasn't necessary, but Roxanne felt a bit of theater was in order.

"Sofie, you there?" she asked out loud, equally unnecessarily. She and the Sofia could converse silently, in her mind, but she wanted Kenaston to understand just what he was dealing with.

I am always with you, came the liquid voice of the Sofia in her thoughts.

"Sofie, I need to take a little trip. Open a spatial bridge, same temporal values as our present location," she said, and then rattled off the coordinates Kenaston had supplied.

Roxanne's arm tingled as the Sofia went to work. A microscopic cosmic string fragment, suspended in a five-dimensional superfluid, rotated into the 4-D hypersphere of space-time fractionally, sending pinpricks shooting from Roxanne's wrist. The Sofia, scanning the quantum foam filling the space just in front of Roxanne, calculated the probability of an infinitesimally small naturally occurring wormhole linking the dim back room with the coordinates Roxanne had indicated. Going through a million calculations in a blink, the crystalline intelligence of the Sofia found the appropriate probability state just a few feet to Roxanne's left, and snaring the wormhole threaded it with microscopic tendrils of the cosmic string material. The negative energy characteristic of the cosmic string fibers stabilized the wormhole, holding it in place and widening the aperture, creating a bridge between two points on the 4-D surface of space-time. At one end was the room where Roxanne stood guard over her erstwhile captor, at the other end the mysterious cavern of which Kenaston had spoken.

The whole operation took less time than an eyeblink, but Roxanne marveled at the process as she always did. It had taken years for her and her father to theorize a rough approximation of the Sofia's workings, but it still seemed half magic and half miracle to Roxanne all the same. She'd give anything to learn where the Sofia had come from and who had made it. It was a bitter irony that of all the doors the Sofia could open, the one place it could not go was into its own past. That door was closed to Roxanne forever.

Kenaston sat on the floor, slack jawed, staring up at the spatial bridge hanging in midair over him. It looked something like a mirrored glass ball, but on closer examination one could see inverted on its spherical surface the image of the world beyond the bridge's far terminal. A dozen rectangular shapes, ringing a large open space.

"Okay," Roxanne announced, after pausing for the appropriate dramatic effect. "After you."

At the point of the ice gun, she nudged Kenaston to his feet, and then marched him the short distance to the spatial bridge. As soon as he came into contact with the spherical surface, with his eyes screwed shut and his face a rictus of terror, he winked out of view. At that precise instant, the inverted image on the bridge's surface altered, a miniature Kenaston now seen beyond, standing at the center of the ring of shapes.

Roxanne clucked her tongue and gathered up her shopping bags. As interesting as this was, she would have to hurry if she was going to make dinner on time.

Roxanne stepped through the bridge into the cool air of the Antarctic cavern, informing the Sofia to retract the cosmic string threads and let the bridge fall back into its probabilistic state in the chaotic quantum foam.

Kenaston was hurrying towards the opening on the far wall, a slight gap between two of the towering rectangular shapes.

"Hold on," Roxanne called, bringing the ice gun to bear. "I've not grown tired of your company just yet."

Kenaston, shoulders slumped, turned and walked slowly back to Roxanne's side.

Roxanne did a slow circuit of the room, passing each of the shapes in turn. They resembled rectangular boxes of reflective space, not too different from the surface of one of the Sofia's bridges; but where Roxanne's bridges showed images of the tunnel's far end, these boxes reflected back the light of the room. Roxanne paused by one of the shapes and caught sight of her reflection. She shivered in the chill air, and shook her head at her thin skirt and open sandals. The world conspired against her impracticality, it seemed.

The boxes themselves, like giant coffins made of flawless mirrors, were about ten feet tall, five feet wide, and a foot deep, twelve of them arranged with five-foot gaps between around the circumference of the circular space. Their appearance reminded Roxanne of something, but it took her a long moment to remember what it was.

"Visser wormholes," she finally said, snapping her fingers and turning to Kenaston. "You said these . . . what did you call them?"

"Forever Doors," Kenaston replied, a bit sheepishly.

"God help me," Roxanne said. "Okay . . . 'Forever Doors.'" She grimaced to say it, and had to pause before she continued. "You said that they are grouped in pairs, and if you step through one you'll come out at some set period in the past or future at the door immediately adjacent."

Kenaston nodded.

"The largest differential between doors is twenty-five thousand eight hundred years," Kenaston added, "but don't think that'll be enough to hide you from us. Go through one of these Doors and we'll have every agent of this era on your tail."

"Twenty-five thousand eight hundred years," Roxanne repeated, ignoring the rest of his grandstanding. "The precession of the equinoxes."

Kenaston's eyes widened, despite himself.

"Yes," he admitted reluctantly. "It took our boys a while to figure that out."

"I'm hardly surprised," Roxanne replied casually.

"The Eternity Chamber—" Kenaston began, before Roxanne's responding bark of laughter cut him off. He composed himself and continued. "The Eternity Chamber was first discovered by an American with the Amundsen Expedition. He got separated from the rest of the party during a whiteout storm, and stumbled into a fissure in the tundra. Working his way farther into the fissure to escape the storm, the ground beneath him gave way and he fell into"—he indicated the room with a wave of his hand—"this."

"So if you're so concerned about people mucking about in time—which, I remind you, is nonsense—" Roxanne said, "why don't you have someone guarding the doors? Or at least some surveillance equipment?"

"Cameras and other electronic gear don't work right in here," Kenaston explained, "and when agents have tried to spend extended time down here they end up . . . funny in the head. Some sort of radiation bleeding off the doors, our lab boys figure."

"Okay, but why aren't you shouting for help?" Roxanne asked. "No base camp up above?"

"We tried it back in the 1980s," Kenaston answered, "but it attracted too much attention from flyovers between McMurdo and Vostok, and didn't really stop rogue time travelers slipping past our defenses into the chamber. Not many people know about the Eternity Chamber, but those that do usually try to use it for their own ends. Anyway, now we just keep our guys stationed at the various Antarctic outposts, just a short hop from the Chamber for operations or maneuvers."

"'Maneuvers'?" Roxanne parroted. "Christ, if you could only hear yourself." She paused, calming herself, and then went on. "Look, all I want to know from you is who built these things, and why."

Roxanne had been looking for evidence of temporal technologies on a hundred thousand worldlines for years of subjective time, and had never come near even a hint of it. This was the first she'd heard of a successful experiment, much less what seemed to be six of them.

"We—that is . . ." Kenaston began awkwardly. "We don't know," he went on, his shoulders slumping even farther. "We've been able to dope out the mechanics of the Eternity Doors, with the help of the guys in our labs. Visser—who's one of ours, by the way—confirmed the suspicion that these were artificially created wormholes. The differential between the wormhole mouths suggests near–light speed technology."

"The Twins Paradox," Roxanne said, nodding. "You snare one end of your wormhole, drag it in a big circle at relativistic speeds; and when you're done, the time-dilation effect has meant that less subjective time has passed for the traveling end than passed objectively for the static end."

"Yeah, that's about it," Kenaston answered. "But as to who did it, and why, we don't know. We can only travel back to the moment the first Door was opened, so to speak, and our agents who've done so have only found the empty room, just like you see it now."

"So who did it?" Roxanne repeated. "Who built it? You must have some theories, if you've been using the things all this time."

"Well, based on the technology needed to construct the things, and the time frame involved, the CDC figures that there was either some lost prehuman Earth civilization, or else some extraterrestrial civilization that stopped by to build it. And based on the architecture of the structure, and the dimensions of the Doors, we figure they had to be at least twice the size of modern-day man. Our historical experts started calling them the 'Archons,' and the name stuck; but beyond the fact that they must have existed, we don't know anything."

"So it would seem," Roxanne said. She shivered slightly in the cold air, and wished that she'd thought to bring along Kenaston's trench coat. "All right," she continued, "it looks like I've got all out of you I'm going to get, yes? And I've got a dinner date tonight, so I don't have any time to waste. So let's finish things up, shall we?"

Dramatically, Kenaston fell forward on his knees, and stretched his arms out to either side, his head back, eyes closed.

"Do it quickly," he said, his voice grave. "I deserve that much."

"Phht," Roxanne blurted. "I'm not going to kill you, you damned moron. What do you think I am?"

Kenaston opened one eye, squinting at her.

"You're not?" he asked.

"No, of course not. I'm not a monster, you know. You inconvenienced me, sure, but that's hardly a killing offense. In strict Old Testament style, I plan only to inconvenience you." She strolled around the room, counting off the doors. The twelve, all together, represented six pairs of Visser wormhole mouths, with a set time difference between each pair.

"So, the longest time difference is twenty-five thousand eight hundred years," Roxanne continued, casually, "with the remaining five diminishing by factors of twelve from there, right? So the next is twenty-one fifty, the one after that is one eighty, and so on."

Kenaston nodded, one eye still squeezed shut.

"So if I were to send you back, I don't know, a quarter of a million years to this exact spot, it might take you a while to get back, wouldn't it?" She paused, smiling wider. "Even after you work out the right combination of jumps to get you back to roughly this point, you'll have your work cut out for you. A lot of jogging back and forth between doors, I should think."

"But . . ." Kenaston began. "That could take hours . . . days, even."

"I'm sure," Roxanne answered. "You can always go up top and warm up some snow with your hands if you get thirsty, but I imagine you'll have to hurry if you don't want to get too hungry. I'll place a call to that base—McMurdo, was it?—and let them know you're out here and need a pickup. They should be here by the time you get back."

"You wouldn't," Kenaston breathed, eyes opening wide.

"Sure, I would. What difference does it make to me if people find out about your little magic time machine? I told you already, it won't make any difference. I'll just hop the tracks to a worldline where nobody knows and live my life out in peace. Besides, the more people know about this thing, the better the chance someone will figure out what your 'Archons' were up to. Who knows? Maybe I'll take the time to head back there myself, one of these days, and see what I can see."

Kenaston climbed slowly to his feet.

"You're crazy," he said, holding his hands before him protectively, looking towards the exit.

"Nope," Roxanne answered, and in her thoughts whispered a series of commands and coordinates to the Sofia. "Just hungry, and running late for dinner."

There was a flash of light, and a temporal bridge opened up in the empty air between Roxanne and Kenaston.

"I'll keep your gun, if you don't mind," Roxanne said. "I think it's kind of cute." She gestured with the business end of it, just to show how cute. "Now, start walking. You've got a busy day ahead of you."

She nudged Kenaston forward, until he came into contact with the bridge and winked out of sight. Roxanne left the temporal bridge open momentarily, amused to see Kenaston refracted in miniature on the sphere's surface, stranded in the year 500,000 BCE. Then, at a thought, the Sofia retracted the fibers and closed the bridge, extruding them again immediately to open a spatial bridge back to Roxanne's Bark Place house.

Roxanne had just enough time to get through, showered, and dressed in her new dress and pumps before her father arrived. She just remembered to call McMurdo base before heading out the door. She figured it was the least she could do.

The dim sum at the Royal China in Bayswater was indeed the best either of them had tasted, and Roxanne and her father both agreed that it was well worth the trip.

Extract from Roxanne's Journal

Subjective Age: 29 years, 8 months, 10 days

After several subjective days of repeated attempts to locate the "Archons," I'm finally admitting defeat. After freezing my white ass off in several millennia of Antarctic cold, I'm done with it.

I've gone back to what the wankers in the "CDC" consider the starting point of the "Eternity Chamber"—the moment at which the Visser wormholes were snared and arranged—and as near as I can figure, the whole thing sprang up out of thin air. One minute there is nothing but solid rock and ice, straight down, and back for untold millennia, and the next minute the whole arrangement is there, complete and functional. It's as though it was just dropped into place, prefabricated, from somewhere else entirely, but neither Sofie nor I can work out how, or when, it was done.

I'm tempted to drag in some of the finer minds I know to puzzle it out, but with the lack of evidence, I don't think they'd do any better than I. That, and the fact that a field trip consisting of me, my cousin J. B., my dad, and Sandford would be an unwieldy bunch, to say the least.

CHAPTER 7

NOWHERE MAN

LONDON, 1893
SUBJECT AGE: 30 YEARS OLD

Outside, the gently swirling flurries of snow blanketed the streets, but as the temporal bridge irised shut behind her, Roxanne Bonaventure found the bedroom on the third floor of the Bark Place house warm and inviting. It was the work of a few minutes to get a fire going behind the grate, which nudged the temperature up a few more degrees, and then it was out of her soiled traveling clothes and into some appropriate period garb.

It was just before dawn, Saturday, December 30, in that calm lull between Christmas Day and New Year's Eve. Roxanne had last been in the period a few months ago subjective time, enjoying Christmas in high Late Victorian style, and with the lingering holiday cheer in the air, intended to spend a few relaxing days in a more sedate age. She'd ring in the new year with old friends, catch up on some sleep, and then continue her travels down the branching worldlines of the Myriad.

Her fingers still somewhat numb from the frigid air of the ice age she'd just left, she found it a much more difficult task than normal to manage the fasteners and stays of the Victorian dress and boots. She'd just worked her way into the heavy fabric of the dress, the last latch in place, when there came a knock at the bedroom door.

Roxanne bristled for a brief instant, expecting trouble, before realizing who it must be. The only person it could be.

"Yes, Mrs. Pool," she called through the door. "What is it?"

Mrs. Pool, a stout working-class matron of the era, had been employed as the day maid at Number 9 Bark Place for the last five years, objective time. Five days a week she arrived precisely at dawn, and worked the house from roof to cellar until almost dusk. She was paid well—there was no question about that—her employer Miss Bonaventure paying at least three times the going wage. And so far as she was concerned, Miss Bonaventure was there every morning when she arrived, and there every evening when she left, provided she wasn't out on the town on some adventure or other.

Through the good graces of the Sofia's crystalline intelligence, Roxanne always maintained a strict schedule when visiting the period. In later eras, domestic staff were much more lax about their employers' habits, and thought nothing of a single woman who disappeared for days at a time. In the 1890s of Victoria's London, though, such things were still frowned upon, and Roxanne had learned from experience in earlier decades how disastrous the effects of her accustomed habits could be. In Victorian times, then, she lived as a Victorian woman, tailoring her sensibilities to their closest period-specific roles. This meant, in the most general sense, that she be seen to be a decent, upright citizen.

It was a matter of ease to accomplish, once she got the hang of it. She made a habit of leaving the period late at night, after Mrs. Pool had gone home for the day, and whenever she wanted to take a break and chose to return, she'd simply open a temporal bridge to the morning following her last visit. Though months or years might pass in her subjective time, so far as Mrs. Pool and the rest of Victorian London were concerned, Roxanne had only been gone a matter of hours.

"A messenger with a card for you, miss," came the rough-hewn tones of Mrs. Pool through the sturdy oak door.

Roxanne, settling the dress on her frame, crossed the thick rug, and unlocked the door.

"Good morning, Mrs. Pool," Roxanne said warmly, her tone precise and practiced.

"Morning, miss," the day maid answered, smiling easily. She held out a calling card. "This come for you, just a few moments back."

"Thank you," Roxanne answered, taking the card.

The front was featureless, flat white and unmarked, but on the back were written five words, in a precise hand, as regular as if they'd been typeset:

MISS BONAVENTURE, WE ARE NEEDED.

"Will you be wanting breakfast, miss?" Mrs. Pool asked. It was hardly counted among the standard duties of a day maid to act as cook as well, under normal circumstances, but given her salary the older woman never hesitated to offer.

"No, thank you, Mrs. Pool," Roxanne answered. "I'm afraid I may be busier than I expected."

The streets of London were far too cold and snow covered for Roxanne to use her bicycle, as was her usual habit. Instead, she flagged down a hansom cab outside her front door, and climbing in instructed the driver to take her to Number 31, York Place, Marylebone, just a dozen or so blocks to the north and east. To the home of Sandford Blank, consulting detective.

The ride, which in the late twentieth century could have been accomplished in little more than two minutes, barring traffic, took closer to a quarter of an hour through the snow and slush, but the extended duration gave Roxanne a chance to better reacquaint herself with the rhythms of the period. She'd first set up shop in the late 1880s in her midtwenties, subjective time, largely out of a desire to see firsthand the world of Arthur Conan Doyle, Charles Dickens, and Robert Louis Stevenson. It was while at the Saint Anthony Academy that she'd developed an early passion for Victorian fiction and history. When a short while later she'd discovered the nature and workings of the Sofia, one of her first thoughts was that she'd have the rare opportunity to visit the places of her imaginings in person. As was so often the case, though, the realities of the situation proved far different than she could ever have dreamed in her fantasies.

It was after a year or two of objective time, around the beginning of the 1890s, that she first came into contact with Sandford Blank, and suddenly faint slivers of her childhood fantasies began to encroach on reality. Blank was like something from a Victorian penny dreadful, a figure of pulp fiction made real. That he was one of the most impressive individuals Roxanne had ever encountered, in any era or worldline, only tended to add to his mystery.

A slow half-smile crept across her lips as the cab approached the curb in front of Number 31 York Place, and tipping the driver handsomely she stepped gingerly down into the slush and muck. She had covered only half the distance between the curb and the house when the front door swung open violently, a tall gray figure in a bowler hat stalking out into the still-faint morning light. In one hand he carried a silver-topped cane, in the other a rolled-up newspaper.

"Splendid, Miss Bonaventure," the man declaimed, crossing the distance to the hansom cab in a few long strides, slapping the newspaper against his leg. "You've hired us a cab. Come along now, don't dawdle. We've got some distance to cover before we're through."

He threw open the cab's door with a flourish, and then waved Roxanne back in.

"Good morning, Blank," Roxanne answered with a smile, miming a quick curtsy before mounting the step on the cab's side. "And how are you today?"

"No time for idle banter, my dear," Blank answered, climbing in after her. "There's business in Richmond, and we've been called up to look into it."

"Business? What sort of business?"

"Our sort of business, Miss Bonaventure," Blank replied, allowing himself a tight smile. "Strange business."

Blank called out an address in Richmond, a suburb just to the south of the city, and then settled back in his seat for the long ride. He was dressed in his typical gray—suit coat, waistcoat, trousers, and hat all a uniform shade—with his only concession to the inclement weather being a gray topcoat tossed over the ensemble. As they rode along the bumpy roads, he slapped periodically at his knee with the rolled-up paper, face already screwed tight in fierce concentration.

"And where, if I might ask, are we bound?" Roxanne asked, molding her speech patterns as near as possible to the period norm. So far as Sandford and her other Victorian associates were concerned, she was one of the New Women, a precursor to the liberated twentieth-century feminists, but still and all there were limits to how far beyond the standard roles she'd be allowed to wander.

"To the home of a Simon Travaille," Blank answered, "a scientist of some repute and an expert in the subject of physical optics."

"And do I take it, by your firm grip on the thing, that this periodical has something to do with the matter at hand?" She indicated the rolled newspaper in his grip.

"No, I'm sure you'll learn all you'll need to assist me when we arrive, Miss Bonaventure," Blank answered. "This . . . this obscenity" —he smacked the paper against his knee more forcefully in way of punctuation—"is only another in a continuing series of slanderous attacks upon my person."

"Oh, I must say I'm intrigued." Roxanne reached out, and pried the newspaper from his hands. She unrolled it, and saw that it was the sixth issue of something called *The Halfpenny Marvel*. "May I ask what this humble little penny dreadful contains that has so set your nerves on fire?"

"This!" Blank fairly shouted, and reaching over tore the paper open to one of the inner pages. There, beneath a crude drawing of a man in a bowler hat, was a story entitled "The Missing Millionaire."

"Do you see?" Blank went on. "I've only just now coerced Doyle to leave off writing that damned parody of me he's been peddling these last few years, and now this jackanapes comes along to fill the void, not two weeks later."

"'Sexton Blake,'" Roxanne said in admiring tones, reading aloud the name of the principal character. She recognized it immediately, and stifled a laugh. She didn't even have the heart to tell Blank about Doyle's decision to revive the other character, years later. "Oh, this sounds intriguing."

"Damnation." Blank glowered. "At least Doyle had the good grace to learn the details of my cases before bowdlerizing them beyond recognition. This feckless hooligan hasn't even the decency to do that, but cuts pure fiction from whole cloth, and steals some small degree of credibility by attaching it to my reputation."

"Well, Blank, it hardly says 'The Adventures of Sandford Blank,' now does it?"

"Oh, a child could recognize the similarities," Blank shot back.

"My dear fellow," Roxanne answered, "if you asked me, I'd say that a child himself was the author, if the mangled syntax and style is any indication."

"Ppth," Blank sputtered, his customary sound when he considered a conversation at an end.

Roxanne, grinning devilishly, spent the rest of the ride reading aloud from the paper, dramatically acting out all of the roles, paying special attention to the part of the bowler-wearing consulting detective. Blank sneered in silence, pretending to be fixated by the snowflakes drifting slowly to the ground outside the hansom cab's fogged windows.

"Mr. Caruthers?" Blank asked when the slight, bald-headed man answered the door. The house was fairly impressive, one of the grander in a respectable neighborhood. The impression of the interior beyond the open door was one of warmth, comfort, and above all wealth.

"Yes," the little old man at the door answered, uncertain. By his manner and dress, he was a servant of some stripe—a valet or butler.

"I am Sandford Blank," Blank replied. From the pocket of his waistcoat, he drew out a calling card, white and featureless on both sides. "My card," he said, handing it to the man.

The servant, Caruthers, took the card with a confused look on his face, but after glancing from it to Blank and back momentarily, the confusion melted, to be replaced by an expression of understanding and trust.

It was a talent that Roxanne had seen Blank use any number of times. He'd spent some time in the Orient in his youth, it was rumored, which would account both for his abilities with the martial arts and for his trusted retainer and manservant Quong Ti. His experiences in the Far East, though, it was sometimes suggested, gave Blank a great many more advantages than was normally assumed. He had the odd talent of being largely forgettable; that is, anyone who spent any amount of time with Blank, after a short absence following, tended to find themselves unable to recall any distinguishing details about his appearance. They could describe him only in the most general of terms, remembering that he was tall, well muscled, and favored gray in his choice of dress, but could not recall the shape of his nose, or the curve of his chin, or the quality of his voice. Likewise, on first meeting him, after initial suspicion or confusion most tended to accept his word as golden, and to answer any question put to them. That he had no official credentials, despite the frequency with which the police, the Crown, and others relied on his abilities, did not seem to affect the valuation strangers placed on his authority. Whether these qualities or abilities were the result of some sort of Oriental mesmerism, neither Roxanne nor anyone else could say for certain.

"Are you with the police?" Caruthers asked, stepping forward and motioning Blank and Roxanne to enter. "I've already spoken with the man from Scotland Yard last night."

"No, Mr. Caruthers, I'm not with the Yard," Blank replied, shaking the snow from his topcoat and gliding past the servant down the hall, Roxanne in his train. "Though on many occasions, such as this one, I'm called upon to assist in unusual cases. This is my associate, Miss Roxanne Bonaventure."

"Pleased to meet you," Caruthers said automatically, bowing slightly to Roxanne before closing the door behind them. "This way, please," he added, leading them into the smoking room.

"Is Simon Travaille in at the moment?" Roxanne asked, taking a seat on the divan in the smoking room and trying to work out exactly why they had come.

"No, miss," Caruthers replied, taken aback. "Mr. Travaille isn't here at all."

"And where is he, then?" Blank asked, as though he knew the answer.

"That's just the trouble, sir," Caruthers answered. "Just like I told the man from the police. Mr. Travaille has just flat disappeared, and I think I know who done it."

"Mr. Caruthers," Blank said, arranging himself on a high-backed chair, "do please sit down while we talk. Having you hovering over me like that is making me nervous."

Caruthers's eyes widened, and he looked from Blank to the available chairs nervously. It was obvious he'd never sat down in the room before, and Roxanne wasn't sure if the idea had ever even occurred to him to try.

Slowly, Caruthers inched over towards a stool, the most uninviting and uncomfortable-looking offering in the room.

"That's it," Blank urged, waving his hand up and down before him. "You can do it."

Holding his breath momentarily, Caruthers allowed his hindquarters to close the remaining gap to the stool's surface, and with a sigh of relief was off his feet.

"Splendid," Blank said, applauding softly. "Now, if you could just recount for us the events of the last twenty-four hours, just as you did for the police, hopefully we can be of some assistance."

Caruthers nodded deliberately, and began his tale.

It seemed that his employer, Simon Travaille, was something of an eccentric, to put it kindly. Forever working on some strange project or other, or else playing some elaborate hoax on his friends, Travaille, it appeared, had always been something of a trial for his loyal retainer Caruthers. Over the course of the last months, however, things had taken a strange turn, with Travaille spending more and more time in the seclusion of the laboratory he'd had constructed at the rear of the house, hardly visiting the rest of the house at all. The only exception to this self-enforced hermitage was the weekly gathering of writers, editors, scientists, and gadflies that assembled at the Richmond home every successive Thursday. The cook, Miss Trent, typically earned her week's wages in that single night, preparing food for anywhere from a half dozen to a dozen hungry gentlemen, as opposed to the boiled eggs and toast of which Travaille usually demanded his menu consist.

This Thursday past, December 28th, Caruthers had seen Travaille retreat into his laboratory in the early-morning hours, remaining in seclusion there until well after his Thursday-night guests had gathered in the smoking room. Caruthers had thought nothing of it, his employer's habits having a tendency to shift and alter as the months and years passed.

Thursday night progressed as it always did, the laughter and smoky voices of Travaille and his guests drifting back to Caruthers at his post in the kitchen, whiling away the hours in the delightful company of Miss Trent. Finally, the guests departed, and Travaille had returned to his laboratory.

The following morning, Friday, a frequent guest of Travaille's weekly gatherings appeared at the door. A writer of some kind, Caruthers thought, the man seemed agitated about something, and demanded to see Travaille at once. Caruthers, thinking little of it, showed the man to the smoking room, and then went back to inform his employer that a guest had arrived. Travaille responded to the knock on his locked laboratory door with a muffled shout, and answered that he'd be out in a moment. Caruthers returned to the smoking room, informed the guest that Travaille would be only a moment, and then returned to his duties.

A short time later, Caruthers heard his employer exit the laboratory, join the guest in the smoking room, and then could hear the two men talking in low but heated tones. After about a quarter of an hour, by Caruthers's reckoning, he was upstairs tending to his employer's wardrobe when he heard the noise of the laboratory door being slammed. After another quarter of an hour or so, Caruthers went back downstairs, and found the guest in the act of exiting the front door.

The guest seemed flustered, his gaze darting back and forth guiltily, and after a prolonged and awkward silence he turned back and rushed up to Caruthers.

"Has your employer come out this way?" the guest asked, or something to that effect, Caruthers reported.

Caruthers replied that no, so far as he knew, Travaille had neither left by the front door—the only exit now that the laboratory had been built over the rear of the house—nor had he come up to the first floor. Likewise, Caruthers assured the guest, there was no exit from the laboratory itself, save back into the house, the only windows being too narrow and high for any easy exit.

"He must have disappeared," the guest replied briskly, or so Caruthers recalled, and then hurried from the house, leaving Caruthers behind in an empty house with a mystery. In the hour that followed, Caruthers searched the house top to bottom, as well as the surrounding grounds, and found no sign of Travaille. He did, however, find Travaille's camera missing, as well as several small objects of some value that had always been kept in visible locations in the smoking room.

"And it is your impression, Mr. Caruthers," Blank asked, summarizing, "that this guest had some hand in the untimely disappearance of your employer Travaille?"

"Yes, sir," Caruthers answered, nodding slowly. "Yes, it is."

"And this gentleman's name?" Roxanne asked.

"Something like . . . West, perhaps?" Caruthers answered. He thought for a moment, his wrinkled face distorted with concentration. "No, Wells, that's it," he finally added, triumphant. "H. G. Wells."

Roxanne's breath caught in her throat, and Blank only smiled a knowing smile.

Flagging down another hansom cab, the pair of investigators turned south again, heading even farther from the inviting warmth of their homes at the city's center. Blank provided the driver an address in Sutton, some considerable distance from London proper.

Roxanne had to bite her lip to keep from saying too much to Blank too soon. She cherished her association with the man too much to reveal the nature of her existence to him at this point, and was sure any untoward revelation about knowledge of future events would certainly hamper their relationship. Instead, as she so often did, she allowed him to steer the course of their discussions.

"You seemed to recognize the name of this Wells fellow," she asked, leading. "You wore that same queer smile you so often do when you hold cards the other players haven't seen."

"Too true, Miss Bonaventure," Blank answered with a smile. "I had the bulk of Caruthers's story from a contact at Scotland Yard late last night, and made some inquiries as to the habits and character of this man Wells. He's a writer of some stripe, having penned two textbooks published this past year, as well as a string of articles on a variety of topics, most for the *Pall Mall Gazette*. A short visit to the offices of the *Gazette* this morning revealed that Wells lives in Sutton, with his wife, Isabel. I thought we might call on him there, and see how he responds to Caruthers's charges."

"Seems perfectly reasonable," Roxanne answered.

"Naturally." Blank smiled.

The scene at the Wells' household in Sutton, when they arrived, was hardly what they might have expected. In the lingering afternoon sun, no lights were seen burning in the windows of the house, and no smoke curled up from the chimney. Blank knocked repeatedly at the door, and was stymied when no one answered. In his exasperation, he took to shouting through the door and into the windows, demanding to know whether anyone was in.

It was the neighbors who finally answered. The man who appeared on the front steps of the house adjacent, put out at having his evening meal interrupted, curtly informed Blank and Roxanne that the Wellses had quit their Sutton home and moved on.

Blank pressed the man for more information, peppering him with questions until more details were forthcoming.

Finally, with the aid of the neighbor's well-informed wife, the over-the-garden-wall gossip seeming to travel faster than telegraph,

Blank and Roxanne were informed that the Wellses *had* indeed moved on, but to separate locales. The Mrs. Wells, tearful and with regret, had gone on to Hampstead, to stay with relations, while the Mr. Wells had flounced off to London alone. Continuously helpful, the neighbor wife even had a forwarding address for Mr. Wells in London, in the events that any parcels or post arrived for him at the Sutton address before the post office had updated its records.

Blank thanked the two neighbors profusely, and with a spring in his step he and Roxanne again climbed into the hansom cab and began the long ride back into London.

That evening, returning late to town, Sandford and Roxanne enjoyed a relaxing dinner at his York Place home, and then whiled away the evening chatting in his first-floor sitting room. Near midnight, Roxanne returned home to Bark Place, and after pushing all thoughts of the possible crimes of the young Mr. Wells from her mind, settled in for a long, refreshing slumber beneath heavy down quilts.

The next morning, the sun sparkling on the night-fallen snow, Sandford and Roxanne convened at his Marylebone residence, and set off at a stroll to Number 7 Mornington Place, just a few blocks away.

Arriving at the steps of the building, a lesser light in a barely respectable district, Blank knocked forcefully on the frail wooden door, tapping the foot of his cane on the ground. When a young woman answered the door, he was startled, and stepped back to check again the number over the eaves.

"I'm terribly sorry," Blank said, doffing his hat. "I'm afraid I was misinformed. I was looking for a Mr. Herbert G. Wells?"

The young woman, perhaps not yet in her twenties, chewed nervously at her lip for a moment before answering. From the flat beyond the door, Blank and Roxanne could hear the sound of voices raised in agitation, male and female, and of feet stomping back and forth.

"Yes," the woman finally answered in a quiet voice. "Bertie lives here. He lives here with me," she added, apparently trying for a more forceful and determined tone.

"Really?" Blank asked, his voice liquid and running. "And who might you be?"

"I might ask you the same," the woman replied, placing her hands on her hips. "A stranger who arrives uninvited at my door, asking questions."

Looking close, Roxanne thought that the redness around the woman's eyes suggested recent tears, but couldn't be sure.

"How terribly rude of me," Blank replied, and produced one of his cards. In less than a minute, he'd won the young woman over to his side, as he'd done with so many others in the past.

The woman, introducing herself, was a Miss Amy Catherine Robbins, an erstwhile student of the former teacher Wells, with whom she was reportedly in love. Wells, Catherine was quick to add, had left his wife, Isabel, behind to live with her in the city, and there was nothing anyone could do to stop them.

"Oh, my dear," Blank assured her, "we wouldn't dream of interfering with the course of true love. Is there any chance that Mr. Wells is here at the moment?"

Blank craned his head around, trying to see beyond Catherine into the flat. The tumult within seemed to have intensified, escalating to a chorus of voices shouting after Catherine to return, and asking who was at the door.

"No," she said, shaking her head sadly. She paused, and with apprehension added, "But he'll be back shortly."

"Splendid," Blank sang, and taking Catherine by the arm slipped past her and led her back down the hallway into the flat. "Then we can wait for him together. Oh, look at my manners. Miss Robbins, this is my associate Miss Bonaventure." By this point, he'd dragged the somewhat dazed and unresisting Catherine well out of reach of the door. "Miss Bonaventure, if you'd be so good as to close the door."

Roxanne nodded with a smile, and following him in closed the door behind her.

The commotion within the flat proved to be something of an impromptu family reunion in progress. Besides the young Miss Robbins, there was her mother, the respectable widow Mrs. Robbins, up from Putney, who'd brought along with her a ragged assortment of a half dozen male Robbins relatives, all with a singular purpose. It appeared that the decision of the young Miss Robbins to take up housing with the still-quite-married Mr. Wells was not a popular one among the Robbins family, and the present contingent had assembled on the home at 7 Mornington Place to make their feelings on the matter clear.

Of the assembled, Mrs. Robbins was by far the most outspoken.

"It just isn't right, Mr. Blank," she explained, once Blank had worked his peculiar introductory mesmerism on her. "She's too fine a lady to be mixed up with the likes of him, and what future is there in it, I ask you? Why, I have it on good authority that after seeing to the financial affairs of his poor, betrayed wife, Mrs. Wells, that this Wells character has no more than one hundred pounds in the bank. Not a pfennig or farthing more."

"And what good authority would that be, Mrs. Robbins?" Blank asked.

"Why, that of the bank manager himself, whose first cousin is married to a Robbins, my own nephew."

"That would certainly seem a reliable source," Roxanne put in.

"Quite," Blank said.

"And at the top of it all," the Widow Robbins continued, her tone growing ever more dramatic, "now he's in some sort of trouble with the law. Oh, Catherine, you just can't stay in this den of iniquity; you simply can't. Come home with me to Putney, finish up your schooling, and find yourself a respectable gentleman."

"Yes, Catherine," came a ragged chorus from the assembled Robbins men. "We'll see to your dear 'Bertie,'" one chimed in menacingly.

"You don't understand," Catherine pleaded, walking the fine wall separating tears and rage. "None of you do. Bertie has grand plans, he's told me. And we won't have to worry about money a bit."

Blank smiled, his attention piqued.

"Grand plans, are they?" he asked. "Have you any idea what those might be?"

"What's all this about?" came a new voice from behind Sandford, and the focus of the room's attention shifted away from Catherine to the newcomer.

Roxanne turned, and saw him there. He was more or less the man she'd seen in so many photos back in school, but with subtle differences. The longish mustaches were there, and the precisely parted hair, as well as the tweeds and a ratty scarf; but his cheeks were more sunken than they'd be later in life, his eyes darting and timid. This was a man setting the first footfalls on the road his life would follow, unsure where the path would lead, and not the more assured man of later years who'd look back on his career and accomplishments with pride.

"Oh, Bertie," Catherine swooned, and rushed to his side.

"Mr. Wells, I presume," Blank said, miming a bow from the neck up.

"Come on, boys," one of the Robbins men said, and stepped forward to lead his brothers and cousins in the charge.

Roxanne bristled. She was sure that Blank's pugilistic skills were equal to the challenge of six angry men, as were her own for that matter, but this was hardly the sort of Victorian civility she'd come to expect of the era, and hardly the relaxation for which she'd hoped.

"Now, then, gentlemen," Sandford cautioned, stepping between the advancing Robbins men and the hapless and wan Wells tensing defensively in the entryway. "There's no reason for things to take an ugly turn."

"I don't know, Blank," Roxanne said with a smile, sizing up the Robbins in the lead. "I'd say that they already had, from the looks of him."

The lead Robbins snarled, and balling his hand into a fist cocked his arm back for a blow.

Blank casually thumbed the silver handle of his cane, which came loose from the wooden shaft, sliding up to reveal an inch of wicked steel within.

"Now, now, Blank," Roxanne said, stepping in front of him. "I hardly think it's quite as dire as all that."

The lead Robbins, his momentum already carrying him forward, looked aghast at the thought that the blow intended for Blank might land instead on this flower of Victorian womanhood. He needn't have worried. The man's fist just inches from her face, Roxanne sidestepped, ducking the blow, and drove a tight fist into the soft flesh of the man's armpit. The Robbins man, squealing in pain, doubled over, collapsing onto the hard and dusty floor.

"See?" Roxanne called back over her shoulder. "It just requires the delicate touch of a woman's hand."

"In the rubric of comparative strengths of pens, swords, and hands," Blank answered, stepping forward to stand at her side, and drawing the full length of his sword-cane from its wooden concealment, "I will choose the sword in virtually every case."

The five Robbins men still standing looked from their moaning brother to the pair of investigators watching them casually, and drifted back to the corners of the room with practiced casualness. Mrs. Robbins, aghast equally at the boorish behavior of her kinsman on the floor, and at the startling behavior of Mr. Blank and Miss Bonaventure, could only gape, mouthing wordlessly.

"I think, at this juncture," Blank announced, punctuating the remark with a flourish of his sword-cane, "that matters could best be handled with smaller numbers."

"I agree," Roxanne answered in a singsong voice.

"Any objections?" Blank asked, his glance surveying the room, taking in the pair of young lovers cowering by the door, the bewildered and enraged widow, the man still moaning on the floor, and the five men ranged around the walls. "Splendid. Then I suggest we remove all unnecessary elements from the conversation, so as to more quickly pierce"—he gestured again with the blade—"the heart of the matter."

Blank turned to Mrs. Robbins, and in a courtly maneuver offered her his arm.

"Mrs. Robbins, it has been a distinct pleasure making your acquaintance, but I think it best we part company at this point. Gentlemen," he called over his shoulder, leading the Widow Robbins to the door, "if you'll follow me?"

In less than a minute more, only Blank, Roxanne, "Bertie," and Catherine were left in the flat, the Robbinses gone and the door locked firmly behind them.

"Now then, Mr. Wells," Blank said, turning on the younger man. "To business, and strange business at that."

"I admit it," Wells confessed, when the question had scarcely been put to him. "I did steal some trinkets and baubles from Simon's home, as well as a mineralogical sample of some interest. But I tell you I had nothing at all to do with his disappearance."

"Do you credit it, Miss Bonaventure?" Blank asked, his gaze fixed on the young writer. "A man confesses to one crime to prove himself innocent of another."

"Stranger things have happened," Roxanne answered warily. She was unsure either way, of Wells's innocence or guilt.

"I'm sure they have," Blank answered casually, "but not frequently." He brushed his pants legs straight, and sat up in his rickety chair. "Very well, let's start with the simple facts. Mr. Wells, you admit to stealing valued items from the home of a man you count among your closest friends. Why?"

Wells swallowed hard, and shot a longing glance at the young woman sitting by his side.

"As I'm sure you know," the young writer finally began, in serious tones, "Catherine and I are just starting out together, and financial compensation for my writing assignments is hardly what one might call exorbitant. As Mrs. Robbins told you, after seeing to my wife Mrs. Wells's needs, I was left very little capital with which to begin our new life, and when faced with the opportunity to supplement my income with a few minor items from Simon's home, I couldn't resist the temptation." He paused, averting his eyes, and added, "Besides, I hardly think Simon will miss them, considering where he's gone."

"Well now, that has certain ominous overtones, don't you think?" Blank asked jauntily. "And where, if I might ask, has Mr. Travaille gone, in your opinion?"

Wells rubbed at his lower lip with an ink-stained finger, considering his answer. He looked to Catherine, who with large eyes looked back only with love and support. Finally, swallowing a few times in preparation and taking a deep breath, Wells continued.

"To the past, one assumes," Wells answered. "Or the future. One of the two—it hardly matters which."

Roxanne looked on wide-eyed. She'd suspected as much from the beginning, but could hardly credit the suspicion. It was simply too unbelievable.

"I'm sorry, Mr. Wells," Blank said. "I may not be as clever as the next man. I'm afraid I'll have to ask you to clarify that."

Wells began to rise to his feet, and Blank jumped off his chair first, gripping his sheathed sword-cane firmly. Wells sank back onto his seat, frightened.

"I only wanted to show you," Wells began. "That is, I can explain. . . . It's all to do with that mineralogical sample I told you about. You'll see."

Blank considered the matter for a long moment, and then nodded.

Wells climbed to his feet, and under Blank's careful watch retrieved a valise from the sparsely furnished bedroom adjoining the sitting room. Returning to his seat, Wells opened the valise on his lap, and withdrew a half dozen or so small valuables, the booty of his impromptu raid on Travaille's home. Finally, he drew out a small object wrapped in a cloth handkerchief embroidered with the initials "HGW."

"This," Wells explained, carefully unwrapping the handerkerchief to reveal what seemed a small hunk of quartz, "is chronium. It is the element of time."

Blank reached out his hand, demanding the small sample. Reluctantly, Wells handed it over. Once Blank had inspected it the object was handed over to Roxanne. She looked at it closely, and had the Sofia scan it for any radiation or unusual qualities. To her surprise, she found that the Sofia could barely register the existence of the object, and was completely unable to identify it.

"Simon told me," Wells continued, "that he'd recovered this from a meteorite that fell in Horsell Common south of London some years past, and that he had spent the years since investigating the strange properties of the material. He claimed, and I could scarcely believe it at first myself, that when an electrical charge was sent through the element, that it rotated into the fourth dimension, leaving the normal flow of time behind."

"The fourth dimension?" Roxanne asked, trying to recall the status of higher-dimensional theory in this era.

"I recall a series of books and papers on the subject by Charles Hinton," Blank said distractedly. "But do you mean to tell me that this stuff, this little bit of sparkle, will travel in time with the application of electricity?"

"That was Simon's contention," Wells answered, his attitude resolute, "and several experiments which he carried out in my presence convinced me of the theory's validity. It was this strange temporal quality of the stuff that led him to term it 'chronium,' after the Latin—"

"Yes, yes," Blank said, interrupting, waving him silent. "I'm sure that none of us requires a lesson in linguistics at this point. What experiments, precisely, did Mr. Travaille perform which convinced you of his claims?"

Wells took another deep breath, and straightened up defensively.

"Travaille constructed a time machine, a vehicle for traveling backwards and forwards in time at will."

Roxanne was baffled, and fairly enraged. It was all faintly ridiculous, the idea that Wells, whom she'd so admired since childhood, would pass off his fictional notion of a time machine to excuse some potentially horrible crime, perhaps even murder, or worse. She narrowed her eyes, glaring daggers at the young man, biting her lip to remain silent.

"That is, you must admit," Blank said in measured tones, "a difficult concept to accept."

Wells laughed nervously.

"Oh, I assure you," the young writer answered, shaking his head, "I felt exactly as you when Simon first told me. It wasn't until he showed me the effect in action that I believed him."

"Showed you?" Roxanne blurted out, almost shouting.

"I share my associate's concern," Blank added. "How did he show you?"

"By sending a sample of the chronium forward in time, or back, he wasn't exactly sure which." Wells paused. "He used the bulk of his supply in the construction of his time machine, using two rods as control mechanisms: one for traveling forward, the other for traveling back. This little bit was the only piece left over from the construction."

"I think we've heard enough—" Blank began, and started to rise to his feet.

"Wait, wait," Wells pleaded, his eyes welling. "If I proved to you that the chronium can in fact move freely in time, you would have to believe that I had nothing to do with Simon's disappearance, right?"

Blank nodded reluctantly.

"Wait here," Wells shouted, and leapt to his feet. He rushed back to the small bedroom, and returned with a small mechanical device, all wrought iron and gears, with a handle on one side and a pair of copper wires trailing from the other.

"This is a portable electrical generator which Simon gave me some years past," Wells explained. "He used it to effect any number of hoaxes on his Thursday-night guests, but had no use for it when he procured a larger and more efficient model. If you'll allow me. . . ." He set the portable generator on the floor, and reaching forward snatched the piece of quartzlike material from Roxanne's grasp. Without further preamble, he carefully wrapped the first of the copper wires around one end of the object, the second around the other. Then, setting the wrapped object in full view on the bare floor, he knelt down beside the generator, taking the crank handle in hand.

"Watch carefully," Wells instructed his disbelieving audience, his young lover included. "It will begin to fade slightly, and then will disappear from view entirely as it rotates ana or kata into the fourth dimension."

"Ana? Kata?" Blank repeated.

"I'll explain later," Roxanne assured him, her nineteenth-century theoretical mathematics and physics coming back to her.

"Watch it, now," Wells shouted, cranking the generator's handle faster and faster, the noise of the machine reaching a crescendo as it went.

"This is ridiculous," Roxanne muttered. Wells was obviously well informed on the current theories, but this little sideshow was beneath him, surely. What could he hope to gain?

Before Roxanne's disbelieving gaze, there was a quick spark, and a snap, and then the quartz material of the "chronium" did indeed appear to fade, becoming slightly more transparent, the grain of the wood floor visible through it. Roxanne's eyes opened wide, and she leaned in for a closer look.

Suddenly, there was a popping sound, and the wire-wrapped object simply vanished from view. The two copper wires fell flat on the ground, severed as cleanly as if by a pair of shears.

"There," Wells said, out of breath and jumping to his feet with a look of triumphant zeal in his eyes. "I told you. It has traveled somewhere in time, to history past or futurity unknown."

Roxanne goggled, and could think of nothing to say.

"In that case," Blank answered casually, rising to his feet, "I think we're done. We'll leave you in peace, Mr. Wells, Miss Robbins. Come along, Miss Bonaventure," he said, strolling towards the door. "Our work here is through."

Roxanne trailed after, her mouth hanging open.

That night over dinner Roxanne kept quiet, in silent communion with the Sofia. She pinged it again and again for anything it might have registered about the disappearance of the "chronium," but it came up empty with every iteration. She racked her brain trying to work out how Wells might have hoaxed the thing.

"Why, Miss Bonaventure," Blank finally said, breaking the silence, "I believe you've hardly touched your soup. It'll have gone cold by now, you know."

"Sandford," Roxanne said, using his Christian name in an odd flash of familiarity, "I must admit that I'm baffled. You can't possibly believe that Wells caused that little bit of rock to travel in time, can you?"

Blank smiled back at her.

"Roxanne," Blank answered, sounding back her familiar tone, "as I've told you time and again, there is an explanation for everything that happens in this world of ours, a theory which best fits the available facts. Yes?"

Roxanne nodded reluctantly. When she'd first heard the nineteenth-century consulting detective so closely echo her own father, she'd been amazed.

"Well, in that case, the theory which best fits the available facts, all of the available facts, is that Simon Travaille did in fact master the science of traveling in time, and that Mr. Wells, while admittedly a thief, was innocent of any wrongdoing surrounding Travaille's disappearance. No other theory comes close to working so neatly as that."

Roxanne glowered, unwilling to accept something so obviously wrong. Chronium couldn't possibly exist, she knew, because no era or worldline she'd ever visited had ever seen such a thing, and the chances were astronomical against such a thing occurring only in one branch of the Myriad. Only the Sofia, she realized, met that standard. And herself. That brought her up short.

"After all," Blank added, interrupting her train of thought, "I'm sure Wells will make some good of this." He uncorked a bottle of wine, and poured them each a glass.

"There's no reason to prosecute for the theft," Blank went on, "since Travaille has no estate to press any charges, but perhaps Wells has walked away from this experience with more than he imagines. Who knows? Perhaps in a few years, Wells will write his own account of this strange business, and make something of a name for himself." He paused, and raised his glass in a salute.

Roxanne looked sidelong at Blank, wondering for the thousandth time just how much he suspected about her life, and just who he had been before they'd met.

"Who knows indeed?" Roxanne answered, raising her own glass in response. "Stranger things have happened."

Extract from Roxanne's Journal

Subjective Age: 32 years, 3 months, 5 days

God, but Nostradamus is an ass. Misquoting me left and right, and without a single attribution.

Man Who Saw the Future my ass. More like Man Who'll See Me Punching His Bloody Big Nose.

I should have learned not to get drunk in the sixteenth century. It always seems to end badly. That century, from beginning to end, is nothing but trouble. But still I go, hunting down possibilities. I'm still forever trying to find some verifying proof of other time travelers or time-traveling mechanisms. I've been convinced for years that the woman who gave me the Sofia was myself at an advanced age, but have yet to develop a credible theory as to where my older self obtained the Sofia in the first place. It can't simply be that I gave the Sofia to myself who would grow up and give it back to my younger self. That's a closed, timelike loop without any entry or exit point, and unsustainable. Perfectly acceptable for a work of pulp fiction, but untenable in real-life application.

But my every attempt to ferret out other time-sensitive or time-active individuals seems to end badly. There's the useless puppet-squad of the Gerry Anderson time-cops, Chrono Defense Corps Are Go!!, but they're no help. They are no better than a Cargo Cult, a few witless children who stumbled across a powerful artifact they can neither comprehend nor properly control.

I decided to take a chance on the sixteenth century—which seemed to be full of mystics, prophets, and visionaries—thinking that surely among this collection of wild-eyed seers looking into the future mists there must be someone with a clue as to time's mysteries.

No such luck.

Da Vinci, though more or less charming, was an old fart with rotting teeth and chronic halitosis, who just seemed to have an innate knack for anticipating technological innovations, particularly if they were of the gruesome and violent nature. Thank God the variant Leonardos on most worldlines had the good

graces to destroy their most destructive designs and prototypes, or the Renais-
sance (and the rest of Western civilization, for that matter) might very nearly
have been snuffed out long before it had truly begun.

Montesi, visionary lyric poet unknown in most worldlines, turned out to be
a shameless hack who had the good fortune to have an ear for rhyme, and a
weakness for the grape that engendered some truly impressive hallucinations.
The futuristic cityscapes described in his longer poems, and remembered as clas-
sics on some truly remarkable Italian-dominated worldlines, were really just
the product of too much wine and a few loaves of past-due bread. Having eaten
at his table, and having a bit of his wine for myself (to say nothing of some
well-aged bread), I saw a few visions of my own.

But Nostradamus, who supposedly could see the future, turned out to be the
greatest fraud of them all. A quack physician barely making his rent payments
from deluded peasants when I met him, he insisted I stand him a few rounds of
drinks down the pub before he'd answer any questions, and when he'd got me
good and sauced he started pumping me for information. When I finally sobered
up, I realized he was a no-hope loser, with nothing to tell me that I couldn't read
off the label of a bottle of lager, and left him to it. When, on returning home, I
chance to glance through his "prophecies" again to see for myself what all the fuss
was about, I saw that he'd done nothing but quote my drunken ramblings, out
of context and without even giving me credit, in his torturous verse

That's it. If I'm ever back in the sixteenth, it's nothing stronger than water
for me.

CHAPTER 8

ANOTHER GIRL

LONDON, 2004
SUBJECTIVE AGE: 35 YEARS OLD

Roxanne Bonaventure paused in the middle of the street, looking up. A whistling had come across the sky, and she wondered if this might not finally be the end of the world.

On the sidewalks on either side of the street, in the shadows of shops' awnings and on bus stop benches, others paused in their tracks and looked up. These were people familiar with the notion of living in the last days. But there was no real fear or excitement on their faces; they had long since become used to the idea.

Roxanne didn't see the car coming until it was too late. She turned, holding her left hand up before her, as though to ward off a half ton of steel and plastic, and the crystalline intelligence of the strange jeweled bracelet on her wrist took care of the rest.

Roxanne Grant thought she saw a woman in the middle of the road, but when she blinked and looked again, there was no one there. A whistling sound came from overhead, and Roxanne wondered absently if this might not finally be the end.

Roxanne Grant saw the woman in the middle of the road. She blinked, and looked again, and for a brief instant was sure that she was looking at herself, looking back at her. She blinked again, and the woman was gone. A whistling sound came from overhead, and Roxanne wondered absently if the end might finally have come.

Roxanne Grant saw the woman in the middle of the road. Her grip on the steering wheel tightened, and she let out a startled gasp. The woman was every bit a mirror image of Roxanne herself, the O of shock on her face a reflection of Roxanne's own expression. Roxanne braced herself for the inevitable impact, and closed her eyes.

The impact never came. When she opened her eyes, the woman was gone. Roxanne drove on through the city, hurrying home to Nigel. She was sorry they'd ever fought, but she'd make it up to him.

Roxanne Grant saw the woman in the middle of the road. She tightened her grip on the steering wheel, but it jerked and bucked in her hands, turning sharply to the left of its own accord. With a deafening squeal, the brakes locked, and the car plowed into the side of a newsagents. Dimly, over the tumult, Roxanne heard the sound of whistling from the skies overhead. When the car had finally come to rest, Roxanne checked herself for any serious injuries, and finding none, looked back to the road to see what had become of the woman. She was gone.

Where had she gone? She had looked exactly like Roxanne, to the smallest detail. Roxanne had never believed in ghosts, but was beginning to seriously consider the possibility. When a doppelgänger appears from nowhere and nearly manages to kill you, cynicism is typically the first casualty.

Roxanne Grant checked herself for injuries, and found none. With a painful crick in her neck, she looked over to the road, to see herself walking towards her. She was sure she was in shock. That was the only reason for a phrase like that to make any sense. Herself walking towards her. Then she disappeared. The one walking, not Roxanne Grant sitting in the car. She wished Nigel was there to hold her, just before she decided it was best she lose consciousness for a while.

Everyone makes new worlds by their choices. Each decision brings into existence new realities with every passing moment, new worldlines bifurcating out into the Myriad. Reality is defined by probability, not impossibility, and anything that could happen, does, but somewhere else.

Roxanne Bonaventure knew this better than anyone. She alone could travel the roads of probability, and see firsthand the effects decisions could have. Roxanne was unique in all the worlds of the Myriad, existing only in one worldline at a time. While everything else in existence—every person, particle, and planet—split and resplit with every passing picosecond, nearly exact duplicates spilling out and creating new worldlines, Roxanne followed a solitary path.

The Sofia, the strange artifact bonded permanently to her wrist, could exist in only one point in space and time along a worldline at any given instant, and could never occupy the same point twice. Roxanne, since she'd first been bound to the Sofia when she was eleven years old, had walked a lonely road. With every step she took, every branching possibility she followed, whole worlds sprang into existence in which Roxanne and the Sofia simply ceased to be. Roxanne had learned long ago not to think too much about the impact her sudden disappearance might have had on those around her; it was simply too large a concept to carry around in her head.

She worried about it still, even against her better judgment. What bothered her most was the thought of those she might have left stranded in other worlds or times. Though she typically traveled alone, she had on rare occasions taken others with her through bridges to other eras, to other worldlines. If she was correct, and at every instant a near infinity of realities sprang into existence in which she simply ceased to be, did that mean that there were worldlines in which her traveling companions had just been abandoned? One minute they were talking to Roxanne, or climbing a mountain, or fighting Nazis, all the while enjoying the adventure, and the next instant Roxanne had vanished, leaving them alone with no way ever to return home.

On those nights when she couldn't sleep, these were the thoughts that haunted her.

Roxanne Grant craned her neck painfully towards the window, and watched the woman approaching the car. She was practically Roxanne's mirror reflection. The mirror-Roxanne walked tentatively to the side of the car, and bending down looked into Roxanne's eyes.

"Are you all right?" the mirror-Roxanne began, and then paused. Raising a hand to her mouth, she added, "Oh, dear," before she promptly disappeared.

Roxanne Bonaventure hadn't been paying attention crossing the street. It was all her fault, and if not for the Sofia, that would have been an end to all her adventures. Fortunately for her, the crystalline intelligence had identified the impending accident as a threat, and steered Roxanne down a chain of tortured and improbable probabilities that avoided any injury to her.

In the majority of worldlines branching off from that decision point, the car cruising down the thoroughfare at a safe speed would have caught Roxanne in midstride on its bumper, in most cases pulling her under one of the two front wheels, in a slightly smaller percentage sending her flying over the hood of the car and smashing into the windshield, and in a small percentage sending her bounding into oncoming traffic in the opposite lane. The worldline the Sofia chose to follow, selected from all the bifurcating options of the Myriad, was the one in which the car's brakes developed a rare and catastrophic mechanical failure, resulting in the brakes locking and the steering wheel jamming hard to the left.

Of all the possible worlds she might have inhabited, then, Roxanne found herself in the one in which the late-model compact had just veered suddenly off to the side of the road, jumping the curb onto the sidewalk and smashing into the side of a newsagent's. Faint plumes of gray smoke ribboned up from the abused tires and brakes, steam pouring out from underneath the hood, and from the direction of the engine came the faint ticking noise of a totaled car breathing its last gasps.

"Oh, dear," the mirror-Roxanne said, and Roxanne Grant couldn't help but agree.

"I like that jacket," Roxanne answered, absurdly, before she passed out from shock.

"I like that jacket," the woman in the car said, before losing consciousness.

The whistling came again across the sky, and Roxanne Bonaventure involuntarily flinched. The plane passed overhead, flying perhaps a little low but steadily, and seemed to satisfy with its normality the other passersby on the street, who immediately returned to their business.

Roxanne waited by the car until the emergency services arrived, and then waited back in the shadows while the car was towed away and the paramedics gave the driver a quick and somewhat cursory examination. Roxanne couldn't help but notice the admiring looks the people on the street gave the aid workers, and the haggard expressions the latter wore. This was a worldline that had seen its share of emergency.

It wasn't hard for Roxanne Bonaventure to understand what had happened; accepting it, though, was another matter entirely.

Roxanne had been on another one of her rambles. Part exploration and part vacation, these rambles had come to occupy much of her free time over the past years. Roxanne had gotten into the habit over the years of roaming the worldlines of possibility whenever the mood struck, most often finding realities of a certain genus or species to study, worlds of similar origins and outcomes. She might want to explore the possibilities of an Earth dominated by some nonmammalian species, and spend months of subjective time exploring worlds of dinosaur-men, of fish-people, of civilizations of intelligent birds. Or she might explore all the possible roads leading to a single destination, finding all paths that led mankind to adopt matriarchal societies, or numerical systems other than base-ten, or to prize some abstract personal quality besides physical beauty. She would make notes of her travels, noting parallels and points of divergence, and then file them away on returning to her baseline.

Someday, Roxanne intended to compile a definitive study of societal development. She knew that such a work would never have an audience, that in fact she most likely could never show it to another living soul, but still the project consumed her energies. As the notes accumulated in a hidden basement room of her Bayswater home, Roxanne began to feel a bit foolish, thinking there was perhaps something obsessive or even neurotic about her habits, but she was always quick to dismiss these fears. Other people might spend years on family genealogies that no one outside of their relatives would ever see, if even they did, and no one thought them neurotic obsessives. Her work was a "family tree" of sorts, after all, but one in which the branches represented bifurcating worldlines of possibility through the Myriad, and not nieces, nephews and cousins.

It was one of these extended rambles through related realities that had brought Roxanne to this pass.

Roxanne had been searching out the nature of war.

When the paramedics had done with her, Roxanne Grant managed to find her cellular phone in her purse, and called home.

"Nigel, honey, it's me," she said. "Yes, I know I'm late, but I've had something of an accident. No, I'm fine, but I'm afraid the car isn't. Yes, pretty much totaled, I'd say, but the wrecker has hauled it off and is supposed to call us with an estimate in the morning. No, I'm fine, really. Is Diana there with you? Good. No, don't come pick me up, I'm quicker getting a cab home from here. I'm sure. Really, I'm fine. I'll be home soon. Okay, dear. See you then."

Roxanne rang off, and dropped the phone back into her purse. She looked at the skid marks on the pavement, and the broken bits of glass and plastic that marked the place her car had been. She wondered, for the hundredth time in the last few minutes, who the woman she'd seen had been.

"I'll be home soon," Roxanne Bonaventure heard the woman say into the phone. "Okay, dear. See you then."

She watched as the woman paced the marred pavement, like a chalk outline of the car's corpse, and then walked to the curb to hail a taxi. If she was going to speak to her, Roxanne would have to do it now.

Roxanne Bonaventure's own baseline had known almost ceaseless war for the past seventy years, in all but name. Since the end of the Second World War, there'd been scarcely a day that hadn't seen armed conflict in one corner of the globe or other. Perhaps it had always been that way, and it was only the advent of worldwide communications that made the condition so noticeable, but Roxanne couldn't help but feel that something was wrong. This couldn't be man's natural state, she was sure.

The only thing that separated her base worldline from other, more martial realities was the scattered nature of the conflict. While the nations of the civilized West had been involved in minor skirmishes over the decades, or protracted military engagements on foreign soil, there had not been an all-out war fought on the native soils of the United States or Canada in over a century, or in England or western Europe since the 1940s. There had been random attacks, terrorist plots and bombings, and even gunfire exchanged on occasion, but *war* was always something that happened to other people, somewhere else.

So Roxanne had set out to find a world as much like her own as possible, which differed in this one respect: the nations she thought of as home had known armed conflict, and recently. England. The United States. Under siege, in contemporary times, and still bearing the scars. How would things be different?

What she'd failed to consider, as this world branched off from her own at a point before the Sofia was bound to her wrist in 1980, was that there would be another Roxanne living in it, one whose path diverged from her own before she first set foot on her solitary road.

Roxanne Grant tried and failed to wave down three taxis in a row. It was getting dark, and as inviting as this quarter of the city was in daylight hours, she had little desire to haunt it by moonlight.

A guard unit rolled up the middle of the street, the heavy treads threatening to crack the pavement, and blocked traffic in both directions. Nearly a decade after the last war, and they still hadn't worked out a better system than that. Someone should design a smaller tank, for pity's sake. Just big enough for one person, say, and narrow enough to fit on the sidewalk.

That was a laugh. Like Daleks, rolling down the pavement, a member of the Home Guard pedaling away furiously, announcing through built-in speakers, "We are the masters of Earth, please step aside."

Roxanne giggled in spite of herself. Fetching her pepper spray out of her bag, she started up the street to the next intersection to try for a taxi again.

Roxanne Bonaventure saw the woman pull the spray canister out of her purse, and decided to change her approach. She'd intended to walk right up and tap the woman on the shoulder, but given the strong possibility that she'd catch a mouth- and eyeful of pepper in the attempt, it was probably wiser to try a more subtle approach.

"Roxanne," Roxanne Bonaventure said aloud, stepping out from the shadows. "Roxanne!" she repeated, louder and a bit more forcefully.

The woman turned, startled, and raised the spray canister up like a ward against danger. She saw Roxanne slowly approaching, and froze solid.

"But . . ." the woman began, sputtering. "You're . . . me?"

Roxanne smiled, and nodded.

"Sort of," she answered, with an apologetic shrug. "Can I buy you a drink and try to explain? I have loads of questions for you."

This was a worldline in which, at a moment of bright promise, things went utterly dark. A linchpin decision, made one way in the world Roxanne had known as a child, made another way here, that created an entirely new future.

In the fall of 1979, sixty-six American citizens were held hostage in Tehran, the capital of Iran. Jimmy Carter—at the advice of his national security advisor, Zbigniew Brzezinski—ordered a covert rescue mission. In the world of Roxanne's childhood this mission failed, the US helicopters crashing into one another in the desert before they could ever reach the target, and the hostages released without a shot fired as soon as Carter had left office, a ploy by the Iranians to discredit and embarrass the outgoing president.

In this reality, the mission was a relative success, and the hostages were rescued, but at a high price: fully a third of the troops sent on the mission were killed in action, and a dozen of the hostages were fatally wounded in the process. In retaliation, the Iranians took another fifty Americans still living in Tehran hostage, and scattered them throughout the Iranian countryside.

Back home in America, Cyrus R. Vance had already resigned his position as secretary of state, his post filled by Edmund S. Muskie. Carter, however, with the perceived success of the hostage rescue mission, was riding the crest of a wave of resurgent popularity. At the advice of Muskie and Brzezinski, Carter ordered another rescue invasion, this one an overt invasion and declaration of war, with the backing of Congress.

This second invasion, however, was not nearly as successful. The Iranians had retrenched, and hidden the hostages well. The Iranians, under siege by the invading Americans, turned first to their fellow Arab states for support, and then to the Soviet Union.

Israel, meanwhile, threw its lot in with the United States, followed by Britain, France, Canada, and a string of other Western nations.

De facto, and almost by accident, a Third World War had begun.

They sat across a low table in a pub near King's College, Roxanne Grant and the woman in the mirror.

"I haven't been here for years," Roxanne said, trying for casual and just barely missing. She rubbed at her neck with the fingers of one hand, and glanced around the large, smoky room. Not much had changed.

"Me neither," the other woman answered, and smiled.

"Hmph," Roxanne grunted. "Well, I suppose not."

If she was honest, Roxanne Bonaventure would have to admit that she was cheating. Only a little bit, though, and in the interests of time. She'd been through this kind of scene before, and things always turned out the same in the end. She was just editing the flow of things a bit.

When faced with the impossible, or at least the improbable, people always went through three stages: shock, denial, and acceptance. Intractably, these steps were always followed, however short or long the individual stages might be.

To save herself the nuisance of hours spent convincing this variant of herself of the reality of the situation, she instructed the Sofia to nudge its way down the chains of probability to find a string of circumstance in which the other woman was much more willing to accept the strangeness of their situation. Everything that could happen did, after all, and so there was bound to be a worldline in which someone could accept coming face-to-face with an alternate version of themselves without too much psychic trauma.

"So you're me, but from another dimension?" the variant-Roxanne asked, running a finger along the top edge of her pint glass and mulling things over.

Roxanne hadn't been back to the pub in years, both subjective and objective, but it was exactly as she remembered. Even decades of protracted war and repeated invasion, it seemed, could not stymie the spirit of a good pub.

"More or less," Roxanne answered, taking a pull of her own glass.

"Is this some kind of *Star Trek* thing, then?" the woman went on, leaning forward on her elbows. "So that things are reversed in the world you come from? Good is evil, evil good, that kind of thing?"

"No, no," Roxanne answered with a slight laugh. "Just slightly different. England wasn't invaded in the eighties, for a start, and there were no World Wars Three and Four."

"Oh," the variant-Roxanne said simply. She seemed to think for a minute. "That . . . that must be nice."

"No," Roxanne said with a touch of regret. "Just slightly different."

The Third World War had lasted a few years into the 1980s, and when the allied Western powers finally prevailed, there was something resembling peace for a few years. Then, as usually happens in these situations, those fires not completely doused in the last war fanned higher again, and by the beginning of the following decade another world war was in full swing, with the cast of characters altered just a bit.

Both the United States and England had survived and, in the end, repelled several invasions, and the mechanisms put into place for the protection of the nations and their citizens continued into peacetime. Normalcy was eventually reached, after a fashion, but the specter of war continued to hang over the people, daily grim reminders of what had happened, and what might yet happen again. Ruined husks of high-rises shadowed the metropolitan areas of New York, Chicago, and London for years, and even now, almost a decade after the cessation of hostilities, the Home Guard that had been instituted during the crises still patrolled the London streets daily, enforcing the law and watching for possible signs of aggression.

London was a less-colorful city than it once had been. The forced evictions of foreign nationals and recent immigrants during the Fourth World War, when more stringent antiterrorism and civil defense bills had been passed by both houses of Parliament, had left the population perhaps feeling a little more secure, but almost certainly more homogenous. Much the same thing had been tried in the States, to disastrous effect. The riots still sparked in larger American urban centers to this day, American citizens of foreign birth desperate to protect their property and liberties, their terrified neighbors eager to root out sedition, and the authorities in the middle left unsure how many freedoms could be sacrificed in the name of liberty before the whole thing became a hollow sham.

Roxanne Grant felt oddly at home with this strange woman, who looked so like her and yet had lived such a different life. In their brief time together, the

woman, this other "Roxanne," had told her such amazing stories that she scarcely knew how much of it to believe. She should believe it all, she supposed, every word of it, anything being plausible after you'd accepted the existence of other dimensions, but it was still too much to get her mind around. Time travel, other worlds, alternative realities, and an endless procession of variants. But not of Roxanne—the other woman made that clear. It was only because their paths had diverged before the whatever-it-was had been placed on the other woman's arm that Roxanne even existed; if the split had come later, Roxanne and her entire world would have just ceased to be.

That was reason enough for another drink, if anything was.

"So I lived the rest of the Third War in America, with my cousin and his family," the variant-Roxanne explained, "and came back to England once the war was over. My father was in a London hospital after the war, because of injuries he'd got during the Occupation, so I ended up living here in London, studying medicine at King's College so I could be nearby. I was a sophomore when he died." She paused, a cloud of pain drifting over her features, and Roxanne felt the urge to reach out and take the other woman's hand in her own. Then the moment passed, and it was too late. "It was soon after that I met Nigel. He was studying at the college on a Home Guard grant, on the officer's track, and he was the most beautiful man I'd ever seen. I was lonely, and maybe a little wounded after losing my dad, and Nigel was just there for me. You know? Well, we ended up getting married right after the outbreak of the Fourth War, just before he had to ship out. He came back six months later, short a leg but otherwise intact. I was already seven months pregnant."

Roxanne listened as a life she'd never lived unfurled before her eyes. This variant of her had lived a life that she could hardly imagine, had suffered through pains and terrors far beyond anything Roxanne had ever dreamed possible. And yet, at the end of it, she was able to look back on horrific tragedies without breaking, or to remember the brighter moments during a nation's darkest hours with a fond smile.

"You have children?" Roxanne asked, eyes wide.

"Just 'child,' I'm afraid," the variant-Roxanne answered, and fished an accordion of photos from her purse. "After his injuries, Nigel couldn't. . . . Well, Diana was the only child we could ever want, anyway. She's enough of a handful on her own."

The variant-Roxanne opened up the folds of plastic to a particular photo, and held it up for Roxanne's inspection. It showed a young girl, eleven going on twenty, standing on the edge of a gray-sanded beach, a fishing net in one hand and rod and reel in the other, with giant rubber boots on her feet. In the net flopped what seemed a giant fish, and the little girl was beaming with the biggest, happiest gap-toothed smile Roxanne had ever seen.

"She's her mother's daughter," Roxanne said without thinking, and then laughed.

"That's what our Nigel says, anyway," the other Roxanne answered, and joined in the laughter.

It was getting late. Nigel had rung her cell phone twice, wanting to make sure she was okay, and when he'd asked where she was and with whom, Roxanne Grant hadn't been sure how to answer.

The other Roxanne, who'd been so many places and seen so many things, had lived a life that Roxanne Grant could scarcely have dreamt of, and yet, at the end of it all, this mirror-image woman seemed to be missing something vital. Was it that she was lonely, and walked this strange and dangerous universe alone? Or was it something else?

Roxanne couldn't be sure. All she knew for certain was that, whenever she mentioned her husband Nigel, or brought out pictures and stories of Diana, a strange faraway look would flash over the other Roxanne's face, if only for an instant, and then she couldn't help but feel sorry for her.

It was getting late. Roxanne Bonaventure knew that the other woman would have to be getting home, and she herself would either have to leave or find somewhere to stay the night before curfew. The Home Guard was already on patrol, and it wouldn't do to be caught out on the streets after hours.

She couldn't help but feel sorry for the variant-Roxanne. Oh, she was making the best of a bad situation, to be sure, and should be commended for it, but Roxanne could hardly imagine. Living through not one, but two major wars and waves of invasion, suffering through the loss of a father, the crippling of a husband, and an unplanned pregnancy? Roxanne wasn't sure if she herself would have held up under the strain. Well, she would have, it was obvious, had she started at the right time, but still. She wouldn't want to give it a try now—not for all the money in the world.

The pair of Roxannes settled up at the bar, made their way outside, and waited at the curb for a taxi.

"Would you want to, I don't know, come home with me?" the variant-Roxanne asked, uncertain. "I'm not sure what I'll tell the family, but I'm sure we could come up with something. I know we have loads more to talk about."

Roxanne chewed at her lip, seriously considering the offer.

"No, I don't think that'd be such a good idea," Roxanne answered finally. "Too many . . . weird emotions."

The other Roxanne nodded.

"Yeah, I know what you mean," she answered.

A taxi pulled up to the curb in front of them, idling noisily.

"Well, this is me, I guess," the variant-Roxanne said. "How's that for strange days, eh? A car crash and a double from a *Star Trek* alternate dimension, all in one day."

"Welcome to my world," Roxanne said through a smile.

The variant-Roxanne opened the rear door of the taxi, and then paused, turning to face Roxanne. An odd, puzzled silence followed, and then Roxanne and her variant took each other in an awkward embrace. Hugging like sisters, they settled together as though they were one person split into two, being finally restored.

"You be careful, okay?" one of them said as they huddled together.

"You, too," said the other, with a voice cracking more than she would have expected.

They pulled apart, and held each other at arm's length for a long moment. Then, with a lopsided smile, the variant-Roxanne turned and climbed into the taxi. As the car pulled away, Roxanne instructed the Sofia to open a bridge back home to her baseline, and she stepped through.

Can't help but envy her, each Roxanne thought, in unison across the Myriad, as they stepped across the threshold of their homes, *but I wouldn't trade places, not in a million years. I'm just glad to be home.*

A whistling came again across the sky, and somewhere worlds ended, and somewhere new worlds began.

Extract from Roxanne's Journal

Subjective Age: 35 years, 11 months, 20 days

On a lark, I've gone back to visit my old South Pacific island refuge, site of so many blissful hours of sleep, solitude, and swimming. I'd not been back for years, subjective time, but returned to a point just after I'd last visited, back in the days of Nigel, and late-night studying, and messy, furtive lovemaking in his dingy bedsit.

The Polynesian explorers who would one day find this island and make it their home named it Kovoko-ko-te'maroa, *which meant in their native tongue "The Land Where the Earth Rises to Kiss the Sky." Which was all well and good for the Earth and the sky, but there wasn't much in the way of kissing going on while I was there.*

Still, I spent a few days there, back in the first millennium BCE, sunbathing and skinny-dipping, and sleeping out under the stars.

In the end, it all got to be a bit too familiar, and a bit too uncomfortable. Settling back into those same routines of my youth, I began to imagine that I was that age again, that I was Past-Self Roxanne, just relaxing before returning home to studies, and experimentation, and more furtive lovemaking with Nigel.

I don't have any room, nor any time (ironically) for anything so messy as a relationship, and am thankful I've managed to escape entanglements this long. Still, under the clear canvas of stars, beside a sparkling ocean of night, it occurred to me that it might be nice, at some point, to have someone to whom I could return, at the end of a long journey.

But if he exists, anywhere in the many worlds of the Myriad, I haven't met him yet.

CHAPTER 9

GOLDEN SLUMBERS

LONDON, 1936
SUBJECTIVE AGE: 36 YEARS OLD

Roxanne Bonaventure stood in the shade of the sheltering oak, Atalanta Carter at her side. They were hidden from the view of those wandering the lanes of Kensington Garden, not least of which the man and woman pushing the pram along the edge of the Long Water.

The man and woman neared the marble fountain of the Pumphouse, and paused to peer in on the occupant of the carriage. They lifted the infant out, cooing like lovestruck doves, and seemed to strike a pose—father, mother, and child—a portrait of familial bliss suitable for framing.

"Bugger," Atalanta Carter snarled. "We shouldn't have come here."

"Come on, now, Adda," Roxanne answered, resting a sympathetic hand on the other woman's shoulder. "You've seen what you wanted to see. Let's go."

Atalanta sighed, and smoothed her rough skirts over her thighs.

"Not yet," she said softly, reaching up and resting her own hand on Roxanne's. "Just a minute more, and then we can go."

"All right," Roxanne replied in a quiet voice, nodding.

The two women stood together, hiding in the shadows, looking at a life neither of them was likely ever to know.

Accompanied by Roxanne Bonaventure, Atalanta Carter had long months before left an England rainy, gray, and cold. From Plymouth by steamer through the Straits of Gibraltar to the North African coast. From Alexandria to Cairo to Asyût by rail. From Asyût backtracking north forty miles on horseback along the Nile to Tell-el-Amarna. To Tell-el-Amarna, and the ruins of Akhetaten, City of the Sun's Horizon.

It was a large sandy plain bordered on three sides by the mountainous cliffs, on the fourth by the eastern shore of the Nile. The ruins stretched over an area measuring more than two thousand by one thousand meters, encompassing remnants of brick houses, a large gate and enclosing wall, and the traces of avenues and streets.

Most travelers passed the region by without a second glance, eager for the splendor of Luxor and the Valley of the Kings to the south, but the site had always held a particular fascination for Atalanta. Even the British team who had conducted the most recent excavations were now gone, sent off to other posts, other chances for riches and glories. Funded by the Egyptian Exploration Society and under the direction of J. D. S. Pendlebury, they had abandoned the site after the Egyptian government introduced new regulations regarding the division of antiquities. No longer able to haul back half his finds to England, the chances of a quick fortune unearthed now denied, Pendlebury had found himself with fewer eager contributors back home. Atalanta had made her own arrangements with the Egyptian government, though, and wasn't about to turn away yet.

The ruins at Tell-el-Amarna stood silent now, as they must have done for three millennia. Though most Egyptologists agreed that the site had given up its last secrets, Atalanta felt otherwise. There were answers here to questions still unasked, and she would be the one to find them.

Roxanne Bonaventure had accompanied Atalanta Carter to the region twice before, though never to the ruins of Akhetaten. If Roxanne's enthusiasms for this site in particular were somewhat cooler than hers, it hardly seemed to bother Atalanta. Having worked and traveled for so much of her life in solitude, Atalanta was grateful for the company. In Roxanne, she'd found a true companion, someone in whom she could confide, and with whom she could be herself without reservation. With the memories of her treatment at the hands of family and would-be colleagues years past still tender in mind, this small blessing was enough justification for her.

With Roxanne's help, and the native laborers she could afford with the moneys supplied by her mysterious London-based benefactors, Atalanta was convinced that this would be the trip in which the ruined city would give up its final secrets.

Akhetaten had been erected in antiquity to the glory of the Sun God by Akhenaten, the heretical pharaoh who had driven out the animal-headed gods of Egypt and instituted, for one brief flourishing moment, the world's first monotheism. He instituted the singular worship of the Aten, or sun-disk, which he claimed was the source of all life and prosperity on the Earth. Within little more than a decade, Akhenaten was dead, succeeded by a boy-king more easily swayed by the priests of the old guard. History was made to forget the heretic who had led Egypt astray, to forget how he had died, and then, to forget even that he had lived. The capital moved back to Thebes, south near the Valley of the Kings, and the City of the Sun's Horizon was given up to the desert sands.

It was thousands of years before Napoleon's army stumbled across the ruined city, millennia in which the brief reign of the sun god Aten was forgotten, but in the decades that followed the rediscovery the blank pages of history were slowly written in. Now, Atalanta was sure, the final lines could be written. The question of how the heretical pharaoh had come to leave behind the faith of his fathers, and to what end he finally came, would at last be answered.

There was a small part of her that looked forward to the day when she could march into a meeting of the Egyptian Exploration Society, bathe in their adulation after presenting her momentous findings, and wait for them to offer her a seat in the Society, finally and at long last. She'd spit in their faces, and tell them just where to stick their vacant seat. The insufferable prigs.

Roxanne Bonaventure, in her thirty-six years of subjective life, had survived untold dangers, thrived in the most inhospitable environments imaginable, and proved the equal of any challenge that came her way, but there was one thing she simply could not abide: sand in her underwear.

Roxanne hated the desert, hated it with a passion that went beyond all reason. To her way of thinking, sand was the reason for human advancement. The human urge toward civilization was simply an excuse to develop urban areas so that no one need ever sit down in sand again. Beaches she saw as a necessary evil, acceptable only as a means to an end; but a desert, with no ocean to justify the nuisance, was almost literally intolerable.

Only for Atalanta would Roxanne have agreed to climb on the back of a horse, of all things, and ride through desert lowlands to the middle of nowhere. Now, with grains of sand working their way into still-unhealed saddle sores, she found herself wondering if even her childhood idol was worth the trouble.

She'd first found out about Atalanta shortly after she learned to read. She couldn't have been more than seven or eight, and she'd found a box full of books and papers in her father's closet. She didn't work out what the "Ex Libris Jules Bonaventure" written in the front of the book meant until sometime after, but her father told her that everything in the box had belonged to her grandfather, and that she was welcome to any of it. The book was the only thing that interested her.

It was the biography of a woman named Atalanta Carter, who'd been born in 1900 at the end of one century, or the beginning of another, depending on whom you asked. The book had painted Atalanta's early life in only the broadest of strokes, but even at her tender age Roxanne understood the unspoken details well enough. Atalanta's father was the son of a noble family dating back to the age of William the Conqueror, and had a seat in the House of Lords, immeasurable wealth, and vast estates. The only thing he ever wanted from life was a son and heir to whom he could leave it all. When his wife, who had so far failed to produce male offspring, died as a result of complications related to Atalanta's birth, Atalanta's father took it as a sure sign that he was being punished by God. Borrowing a classical reference for his only daughter's name, he entrusted her to the care of a string of nannies and governesses, found a new bride after a suitable period of grieving, and set about trying to produce appropriate progeny. By the time his second child, a son, was born four years later, Atalanta had been all but forgotten.

A ghost in the family home, Atalanta spent her childhood drifting from room to room, reading voraciously or else wandering the family estates, climbing trees, riding horses, and getting muddy whenever possible. Her father's only wish for her was that she grow up a respectable and proper lady, marry sufficiently well to reflect favorably on the family, and above all escape notice.

As soon as she was able, Atalanta left the family home, determined to avoid becoming respectable or proper, to escape marriage at all costs, and above all to be noticed.

∞

They'd arrived at Tell-el-Amarna late in the afternoon, the sun hanging fat and red on the western horizon, and found their accommodations waiting for them.

The Egyptian Exploration Society had been at the site for some fifteen years, carrying out excavations every summer, and had developed some degree of infrastructure. They had constructed semipermanent housing for the staff on-site: rough wooden shacks that would, in time, be swallowed up by the desert sands just as the ruins of Akhetaten had before them. In the meantime, however, Roxanne and Atalanta were not above using the EES's castoffs for their own.

In the days that followed, Atalanta would hire up a party of locals to act as workers, and designate one of the laborers experienced with European archeologists to act as foreman. Tonight, though, she and Roxanne would relax, conserve their energies, and simply enjoy being for a moment in the shadows of history. For most of her adult life, Atalanta had been unable to escape the siren call of things lost and forgotten.

She'd been just twenty-one years old when she bluffed and bullied her way into an archeological expedition to Egypt, to Thebes and the Valley of Kings. Lord Carnarvon had rightfully objected that she had no skills, no qualifications, and no measurable assets to offer the operation. However, owing to some tenuous familial relation and his general good nature, she was able to convince Howard Carter to plead her case, and she was accepted as a member of the team.

She was there that day in November when Howard first broke through the second sealed door into the tomb of Tutankhamen, and had waited in the passageway with Carnarvon and the others while Carter squeezed into the burial chambers. When she'd first seen for herself the wonderful things that Howard had been the first to glimpse, which no one had laid eyes on in over three thousand years,

Atalanta knew that she had found her true calling. There could be no other life for her than this.

"Look, Roxanne," Atalanta said, pointing up to the starlight-dappled sky. "A shooting star."

"Must have missed it," Roxanne answered, craning her neck around.

"Hmm." Atalanta sipped her brandy from a tin cup. "An auspicious sign, do you think? Or should we be worried?"

It was just after sunset, and Roxanne and Atalanta sat on camp stools around a sputtering fire, talking infrequently, enjoying the silence of the dead city just beyond the camp.

"Hard to say, Adda," Roxanne answered with a smile.

There came a low rumbling noise in the near distance, far-off thunder. Had it been another year, Roxanne would have thought a jet airliner was passing overhead.

Roxanne was roused from a restful sleep by the cold steel of a rifle barrel prodded into her ribs. In the dark confines of the rough cabin, she looked up to find a man in the uniform of a Nazi soldier standing over her.

"Stand up," the soldier barked in thickly accented English. "Quickly. And I will shoot."

"I'll assume, for the moment, that you mean that you'll shoot if I *don't* stand up quickly," Roxanne answered casually, climbing to her feet. She'd dropped off to sleep fully dressed, the brandy and the cool night air taking its toll. "Do you mind if I put on my boots?"

Behind the solider with the rifle was another, carrying a lantern. Neither could have been much older than eighteen. They glanced at one another, a bit nervously Roxanne thought, and conferred in low

German whispers. They were jackbooted thugs, unaccustomed to people who refused to cower in fear at the sight of them.

"You will put on boots and come with us," the soldier with the rifle finally ordered, bristling and trying to look menacing.

Roxanne was sorely tempted to open up a temporal bridge to the last ice age and push the pair of them through, but curiosity got the better of her. She'd go along with them, just long enough to see what this was all about, and then take the appropriate steps. The Sofia would always intervene were anything, or anyone, to threaten her safety.

In the company of her two escorts, Roxanne was led to a larger structure that the previous expedition had used to store findings out of the elements. Atalanta was already there, tied to a chair and held at gunpoint by a soldier in an ill-fitting uniform. She was being questioned by an older man with a dueling scar on his lip. He wore the uniform of an officer in the SS, with dainty wire-rimmed glasses perched on his nose.

"Morning, Adda," Roxanne said, pulling up a chair as though she were joining them for tea. The nervous young guard who'd escorted her quickly bound her hands behind her, fastened securely to the chair. "What's all this about?"

"I'm still trying to make it out myself," Atalanta answered, trying to match Roxanne's casual tone. "As near as I can tell, these gentlemen are insane."

"Sounds about right," Roxanne said, sizing up the officer.

The SS officer held a pair of leather gloves in one hand, which he slapped into the palm of the other like a comic opera villain. Roxanne wondered if he'd practiced the motion in front of a mirror, or whether it came to him naturally.

"Very amusing," the officer said, hissing like a snake. "The much-vaunted English humor, keeping your upper lips so very stiff. Amusing. Though I would have assumed that two women all alone in the desert, with no escort or protection, might practice a little more care when welcoming uninvited visitors."

"I don't recall welcoming you, sir," Atalanta sneered.

"True," he answered. "But still, here we are. I must admit that we were surprised to find anyone at all. It was our understanding that the English had left this site some months ago. We had expected to find the location uninhabited, and yet here you are."

"We hadn't expected you either," Roxanne answered with a shrug. "Do you mind telling us why you're here? You've got about two minutes, and then I'll start getting bored."

"We wouldn't want that," the officer said humorlessly.

Roxanne couldn't help but smile. He had no idea how much he didn't want her to get bored. She doubted this jumped-up melodrama villain and his stooges would last too long against saber-toothed cats and woolly mammoths. Or should she go straight for velociraptors and *Tyrannosaurus rex*? So many choices.

"Allow me to explain," the officer continued. "My men and I were sent here on the personal orders of the Führer to secure the area. In one day's time, our archeological staff will arrive to supervise new excavations. Your presence here was not accounted for, but presents no special challenge. You will either prove yourselves useful to us in the next twenty-four hours, or I will have my men shoot you. What use they make of your bodies, either before or after you are shot, will depend entirely upon the degree of your cooperation."

The officer paused for dramatic effect, and again slapped the gloves into the palm of his hand.

"I leave you to consider your options," he announced. "Good evening."

The officer ordered the soldier in the ill-fitting uniform to stand watch over the two women, and then motioned for the others to follow him. When they had gone, Roxanne turned to Atalanta.

"All right," Roxanne said in a low voice, "I admit it, I'm intrigued. Now I have to find out what the hell is going on."

∞

Roxanne was trying to work out how best to dispose of their jailer when the soldier gave them a wink, and in a refined British accent told them, "Don't worry. I'm here to help."

It was not a development Roxanne had anticipated. When the soldier revealed his name, she felt as though she'd wandered into someone else's story.

"My name is Bonaventure," the man in the ill-fitting Nazi uniform explained, slinging his rifle over his shoulder and beginning to untie Atalanta's hands. "Major Jules Bonaventure of the RAF, seconded to the Ministry of Intelligence." When he'd freed Atalanta, he went to work on Roxanne's bonds. "I managed to, shall we say, incapacitate one of the captain's men just before they reached your camp, and took his place. Cutting it a bit close, I admit, but I suppose it's all worked out in the end."

Roxanne's mouth moved, but she found that she had nothing to say.

"In the end?" Atalanta said sharply, standing up and rubbing at her wrists, working feeling back into her bruised joints. "And is this? The end, that is?"

Her hands freed, Roxanne rose unsteadily to her feet, and turned to regard their rescuer with a confused expression on her face. What the devil was her grandfather doing here?

"So far as you ladies are concerned it is," Jules Bonaventure answered, taking hold of his rifle. "My first priority is to get you two safely out of here, and then return and settle the Boche's hash. Come on." He turned, and made for the door.

"Just a moment, Major," Atalanta said firmly, planting her feet and putting her hands on her hips. "I've been working this site for the past two summers, and have invested a great deal of time, money, and energy in the organization of this expedition, and I'm not about to be driven off by a group of gun-wielding lunatics."

"Hsst," Jules hissed, jerking his head towards the partially opened door. "A bit quieter, if you don't mind, unless you'd like to carry on this conversation accompanied by a hail of gunfire."

"What are these reprobates after, anyway?" Atalanta went on, lowering her voice only marginally. "What at Amarna could possibly interest thugs like these, or their blasted Führer?"

"The Aten," Jules answered, stepping forward and taking Atalanta by the elbow. "The sun-disk of the heretic pharaoh. The Nazis believe that it was a power source of some kind, and that if anyone is to uncover it, that it should be them."

"I *am* in the wrong story," Roxanne muttered, shaking her head.

"Quiet, now," Jules ordered, and dragged Atalanta unceremoniously toward the door. "If either of you makes a sound, you won't have to worry about the Germans, because I'm just as likely to shoot you myself."

Jules slipped outside, checking that the way was clear, and then urged the two women to follow. They went, reluctantly, out into the dark Egyptian night.

Once they were out of earshot of the camp, Jules Bonaventure related what he knew of the Germans' intentions, at the women's insistence.

In the early years of the twentieth century, the Deutsche Orient-Gesellschaft, a Berlin-based expedition led by Ludwig Borchardt, had conducted extensive excavations at Amarna. Their findings had been primarily of a scholarly nature, consisting largely of clay tablets inscribed with Akkadian cuneiform, similar to the so-called Amarna letters found by earlier expeditions. These Amarna letters were essentially records of courtly life, duplicates of correspondence sent to and from the pharaoh at Akhetaten, and the like. The importance of the tablets found by Borchardt could not be known until a full translation had been done, but all indications were that these too would be fascinating to historians of the period, and of little interest to anyone else. Besides these findings, and work done to fully map out the extent of the ruined city, the only other discovery of note had been a cache of sculptures by the court artist Thutmose, including a painted limestone bust of the pharaoh's wife-queen Nefertiti, which had caught the imagination of all Europe when exhibited later in Berlin. Hitler himself had later looked upon the bust, and insisted that he would one day build a grand museum of Egyptology in Germany, and enshrine at its heart the Nefertiti bust. Hitler declared that Nefertiti had been a true Aryan beauty, suggesting by extension that the pharaohs themselves were of suitable genetic stock.

When the clay tablets Borchardt unearthed were later translated, though, some small number of them were found to differ significantly from the rest. Like the earlier Amarna letters, the bulk of Borchardt's discovery had turned out to be correspondence to the Egyptian pharaoh from vassal states and ambassadors abroad, informing him on the state of international affairs, and most often requesting the support of his military, which the pharaoh Akhenaten seemed unwilling to share. Some of the tablets, however, were revealed to be meditations on the sun-disk, the Aten of the pharaoh's new-formed religion. The Aten, so these tablets claimed, gave the pharaoh Akhenaten "life" and "dominion" over the whole world.

The Germans were well aware of reproductions of palace and tomb wall carvings made primarily by British Egyptologists such as Howard Carter and Sir Flinders Petrie. These showed Akhenaten and the royal family basking in rays from a circular disk high overhead, from which radiated lines of power terminating in stylized human hands. The hands held the symbol of the ankh, representative of life, as well as other symbols suggestive of power and domination. In some of the carvings, the people of Egypt were shown to be worshipping the pharaoh Akhenaten himself, as he worshipped the Aten. The suggestion was clear that the pharaoh received some special power or privilege from the sun-disk, and that the people benefited secondhand.

Most of the information included in the Borchardt tablets was familiar to the British and other Europeans, but in the political climate of Germany following the world war, strange notions took root and flourished. While other Europeans were content to view talk of a sun-disk proffering life and dominion to the king as poetic license, the Nazis became convinced that the Aten was some sort of power source. In their conception, Egypt was at one time ruled by a pure strain of Aryan conquerors who had mastered some unknown force to bend a subject people to their will. That the pharaoh had died, and his city had been left forgotten, then, meant only that the mongrel enemies of the Aryans had managed to cheat and defeat him somehow, and had razed the city to the ground out of fear and jealousy. Lost, though, had been the secret of the Aten, and the nature of the power it had bestowed upon Akhenaten and his wife Nefertiti.

Hitler was convinced that the power of the Aten was real, and that he would have it for his own.

The trio of Atalanta, Roxanne, and their rescuer Jules Bonaventure worked their way north along the line of arid cliffs. With a cloudless sky overhead and a full moon hanging against a canopy of stars, they needed no lantern to light their way. Moving through the black-and-white landscape, they spoke still in low voices, the sounds carrying across the sandy shores and out over the swift-moving Nile.

"So you're some sort of spy?" Roxanne said, still bewildered, when Jules had finished relating the story of the Nazi interest in the mythical Aten. "But I thought . . . that is . . . I'd read somewhere that you were an aviator." She would have kicked herself, had she been able. She'd still not gotten over the shock of running into one of her ancestors in such strange surroundings, and in the company of a woman she considered one of her dearest friends, and hadn't thought first before blurting out facts about her grandfather's life that a woman in her position was unlikely to have known.

"I'm not sure where you might have read that," Jules answered warily. In the low light, Roxanne could just make him out, narrowing his eyes. He was only a few years older than she at this point in his life, in his early forties at the most. "But you're right. I'm a spy only by circumstance. Before all else, I'm a flier."

Jules climbed to the top of a ridge, a few yards ahead of the two women, who both soldiered on without complaint despite scrapes and bruises.

"Come on," he said, calling back to them and waving for them to join him. "I'll prove it to you."

Beyond the ridge, in a low-lying wadi, a dry riverbed sheltered on both sides by the high cliff walls, stood a squat-bodied, broad-winged plane. Even in the dim light, Roxanne could see that there were no propellers at the nose or wings, but instead what looked to be fat turbines suspended beneath the wings at either side of the fuselage.

The trio scampered down the side of the wadi to the plane, kicking up clouds of gray dust, Jules in the lead. Reaching the plane first, he reached out and touched the underbelly of the lift body gingerly, tenderly, almost like someone patting a favorite house pet.

"What the devil is it?" Atalanta said, walking around to the far side.

"The DCX-1, Developmental Craft X-1," Jules explained proudly, "an experimental jet-propelled aircraft developed by the engineers at the Royal Aircraft Establishment." He paused, and then added, "I call her *Duchess*."

"I'll be damned," Roxanne said softly. She hadn't known jet engines were developed this early.

"This is only her third trip out of the hangar, to be honest," Jules went on. "I was working with the boys down at the RAE, tightening up some loose ends after our first two trials, when word came down from the Ministry of Intelligence that they needed someone who could get to Egypt in a matter of eyeblinks. They'd just intercepted a communiqué that spelled out the Nazis' plans for this Aten thing, and wanted someone on the ground before the Germans were able to dig it out. It was a close call, I'll tell you. The turbines almost seized up over Gibraltar, and that would have been the end for all of us, I imagine, but I managed to pull her out and wing it the rest of the way."

"Remarkable," Atalanta said, looking on Jules with newfound admiration.

Roxanne looked at the two of them, her grandfather and the woman she'd admired since childhood, and understood. This had all happened before, in the past of her baseline. Her grandfather had met Atalanta Carter in Egypt, and some sort of bond had developed between them, with the only tangible evidence of the encounter a dusty biography her grandfather had cherished the remainder of his life. But what was between the two of them? How close had they become? If she interfered too much, affected the actions of the other two, she would only succeed in creating a new branching worldline, and might never know what Atalanta and her grandfather had meant to each other.

She wanted desperately to know, wanted to learn what sort of connection had been lost and forgotten.

"My first priority now is to get you two to safety," Jules went on. "I could fly you to Cairo, and the tender mercies of the English ambassador, but then I'd run the risk of the Germans completing their mission in my absence. I suppose I could radio for assistance, and a boat could be here to pick you up by tomorrow night at the latest."

"Whatever you decide to do with us," Atalanta answered, "you must look after the site. If these Germans are as fanatical as you've said, God only knows what kind of damage they might do to the ruins. I don't know if you believe all this rubbish about the Aten being some magical device, but I don't, and I'm afraid that should these madmen discover that they're wrong, they may cause irreparable harm to any artifacts still remaining undiscovered."

"Well, to your point," Jules answered, "the intercepted communiqués did order the archeological team to arrive with a considerable amount of explosives."

"You see!" Atalanta said. "That's what I was afraid of. Please, Major," she pleaded, "you must stop them. Or else let me try. I'll not have the work of years destroyed in a day by these hooligans."

Atalanta had drawn near Jules when delivering her impassioned plea, and now rested a hand on his arm. The contact was brief, but in that moment their eyes met, and something seemed to pass between them.

"You'll be all right here?" Jules asked, his tone surprisingly tender.

Atalanta nodded in response. Roxanne didn't even have to speak; it was as though she'd become invisible to the pair of them sometime in the last few minutes.

"I'll go, then," Jules said, stripping off the German soldier's jacket he wore. "I'll radio for a pickup for you ladies, but with any luck, I'll be back here before the boat arrives and we can all leave together." He reached up into the plane's cockpit, and drew out an ammunition belt. "Don't you worry; I'll have this mess settled in no time."

Dawn broke over the wadi, and Roxanne found herself faced with a pair of mysteries. What was the truth behind this Aten that the Nazis sought? And what had developed in time between her grandfather and Atalanta?

The first question was easily answered. She had only to hop back a few millennia; see the city and its pharaoh in their original, pristine state; and determine whether or not he had some secret power at his disposal.

The second question would prove somewhat trickier to solve. To learn the answer to it, Roxanne would have to restrain her curiosity, try not to interfere, and see what developed.

Roxanne had never revealed to Atalanta the truth about her circumstances, nor anything about the Sofia and the abilities it granted her. In order to solve the riddle of the Aten, then, she would need a few minutes of privacy in which to generate a bridge to the past, and to open up a bridge back to the relative present when she was through.

It was at times like these that Roxanne understood what Clark Kent must have gone through, always needing to find a handy phone booth before he could save the day. Unfortunately, in the dry wastes of the Egyptian hinterlands, there were few phone booths to be found.

"I'll be back in a minute, Adda," Roxanne said, while Atalanta sat in the shade of the DCX-1's wing, looking expectantly in the direction Jules Bonaventure had gone. "All of this excitement has played havoc with my digestion, and I'm afraid that I need to attend to it immediately."

"Go ahead," Atalanta answered distractedly. "I'll be here."

Roxanne turned, and scurried up the far side of the wadi.

When she was safely out of sight over the ridge, she ordered the Sofia to open a bridge to a location a few miles south of their current position, some three thousand years in the past. The bridge irised open, snared from the surrounding quantum foam, its reflective surface glinting in the brilliant morning sunlight. Roxanne reached out, brushed its surface, and went through.

1300 BCE, and Roxanne found the city abandoned to the desert, the shapes of houses and temples left standing softened by the dust and sand slowly reclaiming the land. It would sleep in this strange half-life, a dead city, for three thousand years, until the dawning of the modern age. She opened a bridge to a decade earlier, and stepped through.

1310 BCE, and the city stood in ruins. The soldiers of a later pharaoh, on orders to excise the blight of the heretical Akhenaten from the face of Egypt, had demolished the larger buildings, and hauled off the precious cut stones to fill more traditional temples and tombs elsewhere. Roxanne moved on.

1320 BCE, and the City of the Sun's Horizon, Akhetaten, was a ghost town. Wandering the periphery of the city, keeping out of sight, Roxanne caught glimpses of the last stragglers. They were people with nowhere else to go, those too closely tied to the detested Akhenaten to be received elsewhere, courtiers of a forgotten court, priests of a hated religion.

1330 BCE, and Roxanne watched as the boy-king and his sister-bride, successors to the pharaoh Akhenaten, were led in a processional from the city down to the banks of the Nile. They would abandon the city of Akhetaten and relocate to Thebes, the traditional home of the Egyptian crown. At their side, watching over them closely, was the vizier Ay, who would one day seize the reins of power for his own.

1335 BCE, and Roxanne watched as the pharaoh Akhenaten and his queen waved down at the populace from the palace's Window of Appearances. They tossed down gold necklaces to curry the favor and allegiance of the soldiers and prelates who held the people in line with truncheon and flail. The people of the city groveled in the dusty streets, trembling in fear.

1340 BCE, and the rot had begun. Roxanne listened from the shadows of the palace walls as the pharaoh Akhenaten issued his latest decree. Egypt would have no god other than Aten. The military would enforce this edict, effacing all outlawed references from temple, tomb, and sanctuary from Memphis to Thebes. Any mention of another god, whether specifically by name or just by use of the hieroglyph for the plural "gods," was to be eradicated, even when it occurred in names, including that of Akhenaten's own father. The people were confused, and afraid. They would later hear stories of soldiers setting fire to villages, ransacking temples, and burning sacred animals, stripping the priests of other gods naked and beating them, or worse.

1342 BCE, and the city was in full flower. A new Utopia, a

kingdom made heaven on Earth. The people rejoiced in the establishment of the new capital with a celebration that lasted for days, draining countless wine jugs, carpeting the new-made streets of the city with flowers, singing the praises of the god incarnate, Akhenaten. The pharaoh, receiving their worship, conducted his thrice-daily oblation in the open-air temples to the sun-disk Aten, that he might receive life, dominion, and wisdom.

1345 BCE, and the pharaoh stood at the center of a barren desert bay while the royal retinue waited with the barges at the shore. Not yet Akhenaten, he still bore the name his father had given him, Amenhotep IV. Roxanne watched, and the secrets of the Aten were at last made clear. Disgusted, she turned away, and opened up a bridge back to the wadi, the jet plane, and Atalanta.

Atalanta was gone.

Roxanne had been away, in objective time, less than a moment, the bridge of her return irising open almost immediately after the departure bridge had closed. In that brief span, though, her companion Atalanta seemed to have disappeared. In the loose sands at the base of the wadi, in addition to the three sets of tracks leading from the direction they had come toward the plane, there were now two sets returning to the ruined city to the south.

Atalanta had gone after Jules.

Roxanne gathered up some supplies from the cache in the plane's cockpit—a string of canteens, some dried food, and a blanket— and set out after Atalanta.

Roxanne lost the trail in the rocky cliffs, the track marks disappearing as soon as the loose sands ended. She followed for a few hours more, trying to catch one of the two, but as the sun climbed to its zenith, and the air grew stifling and hot, the chances that she would join them before they reached the ruined city became increasingly remote.

"Screw this for a game of soldiers," Roxanne said aloud, and opened up a bridge to the ruins, a few hours into the future. She'd take a shortcut, and meet them at the end of the road.

Roxanne stepped out onto the dusty track that was all that remained of the royal road of the city of Akhetaten. She found there a strange tableau, a moment between actions, almost as though it were frozen in time.

Jules Bonaventure was on his knees, battered and bruised, his lip cut and bleeding generously down his chin. The SS officer stood over him, a pistol-wielding hand held at the upswing of an arc. The two Nazi soldiers stood close by, their weapons ready. A few yards off, hidden from their view behind the ruins of a temple, stood Atalanta Carter, a large-barreled pistol clutched in a two-handed grip.

Roxanne didn't even want to blink, afraid something might happen that she would miss. Should she interfere? She could easily dispose of the three Germans, if the need arose. Or should she wait, and see what happened next?

The question was not hers to answer. Without warning, Atalanta Carter stepped out from behind the temple ruins and pointed the pistol unswervingly at the SS officer.

"Hey!" Atalanta shouted, and just as the Germans turned to look, she fired off a flare that hit the SS officer square in the chest.

Jules must have been as startled as the Germans, but he didn't allow that to slow him down. Lunging up off his knees, he plowed into the nearer of the two soldiers, battering him to the ground. He grabbed on to the soldier's rifle, one hand on the stock, another on the barrel, but the soldier refused to release his hold. Pushing and pulling the rifle between them, struggling for control, the two men wrestled furiously on the ground, kicking up clouds of dust.

As the two tussled on the dusty ground, the remaining soldier was caught in an instant of indecision, looking from the woman with the smoking pistol, to the officer writhing on the ground in flames, to his comrade wrestling with their prisoner. That moment of indecision was all the advantage Jules required.

With one hand swinging the barrel so that it pointed at the standing soldier, Jules let his other hand slide up the stock to the trigger guard. The soldier with whom he wrestled realized in the last instant what he planned, but it was too late. With his thumb, Jules depressed the trigger, and a booming shot rang out.

As the standing soldier slumped, collapsing lifeless to the ground, the soldier wrestling Jules lost his focus for an instant. Jules rammed forward, banging his forehead off the soldier's nose, and the struggle was over.

The two soldiers incapacitated, Jules staggered to his feet and swung the barrel of the rifle towards the writhing form of the SS officer. The officer was desperately trying to strip off his burning jacket and shirt, shrieking like a banshee.

Roxanne decided it was time for her to enter the scene. Screwing the cap off one of the canteens, she rushed to Jules's side, and doused the flames as best she could. The officer would be scarred, but he would at least live.

Atalanta joined them, the still-smoking flare gun in her hands.

"I thought I told you ladies to wait by *Duchess*," Jules said, shouldering the rifle and wiping the blood from his chin with the back of one hand.

"And aren't you glad we didn't?" Atalanta answered, smiling. "Well, hello, Roxanne. Glad you could join us."

"I almost didn't make it," Roxanne answered. She pointed to the officer absently. "He's gone awfully quiet, hasn't he?"

"Shock, more than likely," Jules explained. "He'll have second- or third-degree burns over his whole torso, I should expect, and in the face of that kind of pain, the brain tends to lock itself down for protection."

"So this was your big plan, was it?" Atalanta asked, indicating the two soldiers, one dead and one stunned insensate, and the prostrate form of the burned officer. "Is this how you spies usually handle matters?"

"Well, I'd planned to wait until the archeologists arrived to make my move," Jules answered, "but Heinrich here stumbled on me unawares, which somewhat forced things to progress unexpectedly." He indicated the flare gun, and smiled at Atalanta approvingly. "Nice trick there. Though I wonder what would have happened if either of these gentlemen had returned fire. Only one shot per load on those things, you know."

"I did know, actually," Atalanta replied. "But I was sure you could come up with some solution if the situation presented itself. So, what now?"

"Well, I'd be for leaving," Jules said, rubbing tenderly at his bruised neck, "but I'm afraid that my orders are to prevent the Germans from securing this Aten thing, and that means I'll have to wait until the remainder of their party arrives this evening."

"I shouldn't worry about that, if I were you," Roxanne cut in. "There's no such thing."

Both Atalanta and Jules turned to look at her.

"How can you be so sure?" Jules asked, eyes narrowing.

Roxanne wished she could tell them. Wished she could explain how she'd gone back to ancient times, and seen the strangely featured pharaoh standing alone on the sands, plagued by muscular tics, frothing slightly at the mouth, caught in the grips of some form of epileptic fit, his temporal lobe seizing. He'd fallen on his back, staring up at the sun burning high overhead, in the same sort of position as the officer now lying in shock at their feet. When the pharaoh had recovered his senses, he'd called his queen and followers from the royal barge to his side, and had explained to them the details of his vision. He'd hallucinated that his father Amenhotep had become the sun itself, and that in death his father had now given him the approval he had never given in life. They would build their new city here, consecrated to the image of the sun, to forever remember the event.

There was no Aten, no secret power source, no hidden key that would give the Nazis the ability to defeat all enemies. Like the Nazis' own leader back in Berlin, Akhenaten had not been divine. He'd been only a man, plagued by all-too-mundane madness, who went on to infect an entire people with his insanity. The madness of Akhenaten had burned in the end down to ashes; the madness of the Nazis' leader would burn for years yet, catching up all of Europe in its flames.

"I . . . that is . . ." Roxanne began, searching for some explanation that would satisfy the others.

"She's right," Atalanta interrupted, laying a hand on her shoulder. "The Aten itself is a myth, and is not the issue at hand. What matters is preserving the Amarna site against these vandal hordes."

"What if the matchstick there were to regain consciousness," Roxanne offered, "and radio to his team with orders to return to Berlin?"

"Yes," Atalanta answered, clapping her hands together. "He could say, I don't know, something like—"

"He could say a British team already at the site had done excavations in the region they intended to investigate," Jules said, interrupting, "and that they had found no evidence of any kind of physical Aten."

"If they went for it, we could continue our work here uninterrupted," Atalanta said. She paused, deflating, and added, "But you'd have to convince him to say it."

"I wouldn't go quite that far," Jules answered. "After all, we have their radio gear, their pass codes and call signs, and I'm a fair hand at mimicry, if I do say so myself."

"Oh, Major," Atalanta fairly shouted, and grabbed him in a tight embrace. "I could kiss you!"

Jules beamed, returning her embrace, and then a cloud seemed to pass over his features. He pulled away, holding Atalanta at arm's length.

"I, erm, that is," he stammered, flustered. "That is to say, I'm sure that my wife will be happy to have me home. We are expecting our first child any day now, after all."

"Wife?" Atalanta repeated.

"I . . ." Jules began, and then broke off. He took Atalanta by the shoulders, looking into her eyes. "Let me add, which is to say, I want you to know . . ." He paused, and then said simply, "Atalanta, you are a most remarkable woman. Would that I had met you a lifetime ago."

Roxanne stood looking at the two of them, standing at arm's length, staring into each other's eyes without saying a word. Another tableau. She *had* walked in on someone else's story, and this was where it ended.

It hadn't ended there, after all, though it might as well have. The Germans were convinced by Jules's performance on the radio that there was no reason to journey from Cairo, and had promptly boarded a plane back to Berlin. At the site at Tell-el-Amarna, though, Atalanta had found that the SS officer and his soldiers had ransacked and despoiled her supplies, presumably after discovering their escape. Jules had stayed with them, Roxanne and Atalanta, until the local authorities arrived, both to help guard their German prisoners, and to ensure that the archeological team from Berlin did not in fact arrive.

In the two days before the Egyptian authorities managed to send a crew to take charge of the officer and the surviving soldier, Roxanne looked after their injuries and kept careful watch over them, armed with their own rifles. Their injuries were serious, but not severe, and they would survive long enough to be arrested by the authorities on charges of "intent to deface national antiquities." While Roxanne kept her eyes on the Germans, Atalanta and Jules were left to their own devices.

When the authorities arrived, Jules had their assurances that the two Germans would be held incommunicado for several months before being allowed to contact their superiors in Berlin, which would give Atalanta ample time to complete her excavations.

It was another day before fresh supplies arrived from Asyût, and Jules refused to quit the camp until the ladies were appropriately provisioned. Roxanne spent the long hours of that day and night down by the banks of the Nile, watching the waters of history roll by. Atalanta and Jules found their own diversions.

When the supplies had been stocked away, and the fellaheen were on their way back to Asyût, it was time at last for Jules to leave.

Roxanne gave her grandfather a comradely handshake before leaving him alone in the company of Atalanta. He'd never even learned her last name, and it didn't appear that Atalanta had told him. Neither of them had taken much interest in her, these last seventy-two hours.

When Jules had gone, trudging up over the ridge towards the wadi where his plane *Duchess* sat waiting, Roxanne had drawn near Atalanta, and put an arm around her shoulder.

"I don't know that I'll ever see that man again," Atalanta said, a far-off quality in her voice. "But I doubt that I should ever be able to forget him, or this strange sort of holiday we shared here together."

Roxanne wasn't sure exactly what had gone on between the two of them, and when she was honest with herself, admitted that she didn't really want to know. Whatever it was, it had been between them only.

"I can assure you, Adda," Roxanne said, holding her friend tighter, "that he won't be able to forget you either."

Months later, back in London, Atalanta had suggested to Roxanne that they take a stroll over to Kensington Gardens. It was only after arriving, and seeing who else was enjoying the fresh air, that Roxanne suspected her friend's motives.

"He called on me, after our return," Atalanta explained, looking at the man and woman cooing over the pram. "Only to say that he couldn't see me again. He had his family to consider, he said. He just couldn't leave them."

Roxanne had no response to give, save to take her friend's hand in her own, and squeeze it tightly.

"He mentioned coming here with his family sometimes," Atalanta went on. "He said that when he was here, he couldn't imagine Egypt actually existed. That he almost couldn't believe the man he'd been in Egypt had actually existed. He said that it was like some sort of dream, half-forgotten on waking, that haunted him all through the day, but to which he could never return."

Atalanta fell silent, and Roxanne squeezed her hand tighter.

"Come on, now, Adda," Roxanne repeated, pulling Atalanta away from the scene. "Let's go. There's nothing for us here."

Atalanta sighed, and straightened up.

"You're right," she answered. "Let's go."

The two friends turned back towards the bustle of the city, and walked away, leaving behind them a life neither of them was ever likely to know.

Extract from Roxanne's Journal

Subjective Age: 37 years, 6 months, 15 days

I've been lately testing the limits of probability: the old saw that, given an infinite number of possibilities, anything that could happen would happen. I've begun an attempt to verify this theory for myself.

If anything that could happen would happen, in the many worlds of the Myriad, it stands to reason that any world, civilization, or individual of which one could conceive must, by definition, literally exist. So long as nothing in that conception was counter to the laws of physics or probability, then any imagined reality was actual reality, somewhere.

I began simply enough. Cherished works of fiction from my childhood, if containing nothing fantastic, would be the first place to look.

I began with Jane Austen's Pride and Prejudice. *Though perhaps a little unlikely, there was nothing in the plot or characters' backstories that was literally impossible, so by the terms of my hypothesis such a reality had to exist somewhere.*

It took longer than I'd expected, a few weeks of fruitless searching, but in the end I found it. The world of Elizabeth Bennet and the dashing Mr. Darcy, or one near enough to matter. It was hard to fathom, but as I stood watching from the sidelines, the story of their complicated courtship and eventual union played out before my eyes, just as I'd imagined it years before.

Then I moved on Kurt Vonnegut's Mother Night, *and the movie* Casablanca, *and the mysteries of Hercule Poirot. Even a version of* Charlotte's Web, *though naturally the animals couldn't talk, and the little girl Fern was doubtless schizophrenic, imagining the barnyard creatures were answering her.*

I began to wonder if there wasn't something of the Uncertainty Principle at work here, at least in its popular conception. That the very act of my searching for these worlds somehow brought them into existence. It was hard to imagine that these realities had always existed, unobserved (as it were), but duplicating in every respect fictions I had known.

I became particularly confused when encountering, in reality, fictionalized versions of things I'd myself experienced, and people I had known. To see Arthur Conan Doyle's Sherlock Holmes in the flesh, while knowing full well that Doyle had based his stories on the flesh-and-blood Sandford Blank, was a bit too much to conceptualize.

I wonder now, though, if I've not limited my researches overmuch. I've restricted my explorations to works with a high degree of realism, those which do not break any of the established rules of science.

Suppose, though, that even the rules of science themselves were just as malleable. Worldlines branching away in the early picoseconds of the big bang, where the laws of physics developed in slightly different ways, could give rise to a whole host of even more fantastic realities.

It's hard to imagine it, but by this logic there might be, somewhere out in the Myriad, far, far removed from any line I've ever visited, a world where a little blonde girl could chase a white rabbit in a waistcoat and vest down a hole into a separate dimension of reality. Where vanishing cats and hookah-smoking caterpillars are every bit as real as all the other creatures of fiction I've so far discovered.

Pity, then, that I can't venture that far, that to make the attempt would mean I'd have to step through a temporal bridge into the very furnace of the big bang itself. The Sofia might open that door for me, but there is no way she'd let me walk through.

So much for worlds of "if" and "maybe."

CHAPTER 10

WAIT

LONDON, 2007
SUBJECTIVE AGE: 38 YEARS OLD

Roxanne's father had been ill for a long time, and despite endless batteries of radiation treatments and chemotherapy and every experimental procedure they could find, in the end the cancer was finally winning.

Roxanne stayed by his side, reliving the painful memories of losing one parent while facing the grim reality of losing the other. She scarcely slept, keeping vigil with him, wanting to spend every possible moment with him.

Then, her father's condition worsened, and he died.

It was while making the funeral preparations that Roxanne decided.

The funeral parlor was a place of cold, clinical comfort, with dim lights over her father's open casket in the viewing area, and severe, straight-backed chairs arranged around the mortician's desk. The embalming and dressing process had left Roxanne's father looking like a wax replica of himself, his cheeks rosy apples of simulated liveliness, a faint smile fabricated across the rictus of his mouth.

This will not do, Roxanne decided.

The mortician was going on about burial options, now. Having suffered the indignities of having to select a suitable coffin in her grief, she was now forced to select interment.

The evil that men do is often . . . something something, Roxanne couldn't help think, distantly remembering some play from high school or from trips to Elizabethan England. *But the good is often interred with the bones.*

Her father's bones. Her father's bones, which had become the skeleton for this wax replica straight from Madame Tussauds, which might at any minute open its wax eyelids and rise up, golemlike, from the tasteful brass and black veneer coffin the mortician had steered Roxanne into selecting.

This will not do.

She had lost her mother, so early, so young, and eventually come to terms with the pain of that loss. She'd once tried to undo that wound, traveling to the past and to other worldlines to find a living mother, but it was too late. The damage had been done.

Not this time.

The pain so fresh, the wound so open and raw, there was no reason Roxanne couldn't try to undo the pain. Undo the tragedy. She didn't have to accept this fate. Wasn't she the mistress of space and time? What was beyond her reach?

Without even bothering to answer the mortician's last, dangling question, Roxanne rose up from the straight-backed chair, opened a temporal bridge to the future, and stepped through, leaving the mortician alone with the wax statue of her father.

In the second decade of the twenty-first century, Roxanne found a battery of natural cancer fighters that had shown proven results in several years of clinical testing. A combination of genistein, which suppressed the formation of blood vessels in cancer tumors, and antioxidants, which reduced mutation rates in cancer cells by suppressing free radicals, the treatment was available in a liquid form, to be administered over the course of a week.

Roxanne returned to her baseline a matter of months before her father would die, to a day when she'd been off exploring some worldline or other. Off adventuring, leaving her father alone to die by inches.

Not this time.

Locking up the Bark Place house, she went to stay with her father in Oxfordshire. She insisted on cooking all his meals, and in particular insisted on fixing his morning tea.

Roxanne's father, who had been looking weaker for months, was glad for the company, and though he politely observed for a few days that his morning tea tasted funny, after a week of having Roxanne visiting he began to feel much, much better.

Roxanne stayed with her father for months. They played chess in the evenings, and went for long walks in the afternoons, and her father insisted that Roxanne tell him all about the places she'd traveled, the times and worlds that she had seen.

Having lost her father, Roxanne now had him back again, and didn't ever want to leave his side.

Then, her father's condition worsened, and he died.

Roxanne didn't bother with the funeral this time. The treatment had given her father at least three additional months of life. Moving in the right direction, but not yet there. Complications had arisen that the antioxidants and genistein were not equipped to prevent.

In the early days of the twenty-second century, Roxanne located a genetic protein inhibitor, administered orally, that blocked the production of defective proteins by the cancer gene, preventing the farther spread of diseased cells.

Traveling back now a few months farther still, to when her father had been a little stronger and she had been off exploring the Myriad, Roxanne locked up the Bark Place house and went to visit her father.

Roxanne's father was glad to have her to visit, but politely pointed out for the first few days that his morning tea didn't taste quite right, and that the new toothpaste Roxanne had bought for him tasted absolutely horrible. After a couple of weeks with Roxanne in the house, though, he began to feel much better.

In the six months that followed, Roxanne hardly left his side. In the late afternoons they'd rent videos of all the movies her father had missed seeing, having spent all his time in the lab, all those years. In the mornings they'd read the paper, racing each other to see who could complete the crossword and the jumble first.

Roxanne was happy, but felt uneasy. Would these last treatments be enough? Her father seemed strong and healthy, but there was always the possibility of something amiss.

Then, her father's condition worsened, and he died.

In the twenty-third century, Roxanne found an immune-system enhancement agent that created monoclonal antibodies that specifically targeted the proteins found on the surface of the cancer cells.

After the first three weeks of Roxanne's visit, her father began to feel much better, though he could hardly stomach the tea, the sugar on his grapefruit tasted horrible, and there was something terribly wrong with his new toothpaste.

Roxanne and her father went through old photo albums for hours, sat wistfully in front of the fire on cold nights, played Scrabble and Cluedo and a dozen other old games gathering dust up in the closets.

But always Roxanne was vigilant, keeping watch for some signs of disease, of the onset of symptoms.

Then her father's condition worsened, and he was about to die.

Roxanne's father was laid out in bed, his breath rattling in his lungs, his skin stretched and pale.

Roxanne sat by his bedside, her thoughts preoccupied.

In her last trip to the twenty-third century, to get the protein-inhibitor treatment, she'd read about some promising work with angiogenesis and telomerase blockers that she was anxious to try. As soon as her father died again, she would travel back to the future, pick up new treatments, and then return to a point sometime last year to try them out.

Roxanne was tapping her toes, absently chewing on her lower lip, holding her father's thin, bony hand in one of hers.

"Let me go," her father said, in a raspy voice.

Absently, Roxanne let go of her father's hand, and leaned back in her chair.

"No," her father said, shaking his head slightly on the pillow. "Let me go."

Roxanne turned, and looked into her father's watery eyes, and with a painful shock understood his meaning.

"No," Roxanne answered in a small, far-off voice. "I can't."

Roxanne's father looked at her for a long time, his expression pitying and sad.

"How long have you been doing this?" he asked, and then was interrupted by violent, racking coughs. He wiped pink-flecked spittle from the corners of his mouth. "How long have you been sneaking me treatments, but still watching me die?"

Roxanne opened and closed her mouth, but couldn't bring herself to answer.

"This isn't the first time, is it?" he went on. "You've done this before, God knows how many times. But it never works, does it? I'm never cured."

Roxanne choked back bitter tears, and shook her head.

"No," she said softly. "Never for very long."

Her father's eyes welled up.

"Oh, my poor girl," he said, his voice wavering. "This does you no good, you've got to know that. You've lived with me dying by inches in front of your eyes for how many subjective months? Years, even. While I've just suffered over, and over, and over. This is why you don't use the Sofia to cultivate a timeline of your own." He coughed into his hand, but kept on. "You've forgotten the first rule, that you can't let these abilities of yours prevent you from being human. Living life moment to moment is what defines humans. Animals live only in 'now,' and only man can remember his past, and look forward to his future. If a human lives without any uncertainty about what tomorrow brings, then she's no longer human, but a machine."

Roxanne reached out, and took his hand in hers again.

"Don't let yourself lose your humanity while trying to keep me here," he said, straining. "Let me go."

Roxanne, tears streaming down her face, bit her lip. She shook her head, and held tight to her father's hand.

Through the long night, his condition worsened, and in the morning he was dead. Roxanne never left his side.

SECTION III

CHAPTER 11

TOMORROW NEVER KNOWS

LONDON, 2012
SUBJECTIVE AGE: 43 YEARS OLD

Roxanne Bonaventure had lived forty-three years of subjective time, and felt every hour of it in her bones. Keeping track with the passage of objective time in her baseline, stopping in for fits and starts between voyages to past, future, and the absolute elsewhere, she managed to celebrate her birthday subjectively and objectively at the same time. It was five years, local time, since her father had passed away, so rather than visit her cousin J. B. in California, or drop in on any others among her small circle of friends, Roxanne spent the early hours of October 9, 2012, alone, in the big empty house on Bark Place.

After sleeping in, and enjoying a long soak in her tub, Roxanne roamed from room to room of the large house in her bathrobe and slippers, sipping a cup of tea and musing on time, the past, and the future. Time, she felt, was a known quantity for her, at least so far as the experience of more than two decades had provided. The past, she likewise felt, she had a handle on by dint of her explorations. The future, though, was another matter entirely.

The future, whether she crept into it day by day like the rest of the world, or else jumped ahead by leaps and bounds through temporal bridges, never seemed to arrive. Here she stood, now over a decade into the new millennium, and the future was still nowhere to be seen. Despite the prophets and pundits of the century past, there had come no eschaton, no flash point of history and cosmology colliding in a grand, reality-altering orgasm of change.

Somewhere, Roxanne was convinced, the future must wait, lying beyond the veil of tomorrow. Having seen enough of the past and elsewhere, for the moment at least, Roxanne decided that there were few things better to do with her birthday than to hunt down, for once and all, the future.

As she did before taking any jaunt through space or time, Roxanne girded herself for the task at hand. Climbing the stairs to the second-floor study, she pulled the copy of *Alice's Adventures in Wonderland* fractionally from the bookshelf, heard the satisfying click, and then stepped back as the wall swung open to reveal her private wardrobe.

In the several different eras in which she maintained households within the walls of Number 9 Bark Place, Roxanne did the best she could to remain period specific. It wouldn't do for the day maid in 1890 to stumble across a compact disc player in the dining room, nor for the cleaning staff in 2001 to turn on a Tri-D player that wouldn't be invented for another twenty years; not because it would do anything to alter the flow of time, but because it might tend to raise questions that Roxanne would prefer not to answer, and hinder their performance at their domestic tasks.

Still and all, though, there were some items that Roxanne felt she couldn't live without in any period, hygiene products and the like chief among them. It was only natural, therefore, that she installed a hidden panel in the ground-floor bathroom, accessible only with her palm print. Likewise, she never knew were she might go when leaving an era behind, so Roxanne had decided it best to maintain a standard traveling kit in each of her periods of habitation. To avoid questions and complications, she had built a recessed storage space behind a false wall in the study, and supplied it with the appropriate provisions.

It was at moments such as this, watching the bookshelves swing open to reveal a precisely arranged collection of clothing, boots, shoes, helmets, packs, and other gear, that Roxanne couldn't help but smile. It made her feel a bit like Batgirl in the campy old American television show, steeling herself to go out and fight the forces of evil. Thinking of the old show, though, and others she'd loved in her youth, only tended to remind Roxanne what she had thought the future would hold when she had been a child, and how disappointing the reality had proved to be.

In her childhood in the 1970s, it looked as though the future was just around the corner, the world of tomorrow an asexual, androgyne paradise of white, plastic curves and formfitting bodysuits of synthetic fibers dyed in complementary primary colors. Everyone would have their flying car, or personal jetpack for preference, and would consume knowledge in the form of pills, and three-course meals in gel-packs of liquid goo. Disease would be stamped out, as would ignorance, poverty, bigotry, and war.

Of course, by the 1980s everyone was convinced that the future would be a brutal hell of postapocalyptic biker gangs and mutants, but that was another matter entirely.

Fads and fashions in futurity had changed with as much regularity as the length of women's skirts, but in the end the future never seemed to arrive. It was always just the present, always just today, with things changing more in degree than in kind. Phones became portable, then compact, then wearable, computers following much the same trend.

But in the end, technology was simply a tool to allow people more easily to live the lives they would have led regardless. Nothing changed, in the global sense, but the packaging.

From her unique vantage point, Roxanne had dipped her toes into the water's edge of the future many times, but never much farther than a few centuries down any worldline. For all of her willingness to travel to exotic bifurcating worlds—lines of dinosaur-men, and postapocalyptic waste, and strange desolation—there was something about traveling too far down the future branchings of her own baseline that unsettled her. Perhaps it was seeing too clearly what might become of the world she knew, rather than simply visiting what might have been; or else it was some reluctance to peer too closely into her own future, and that of her friends and family. For all her secret knowledge, the things only she was privy to, there were still areas within which she preferred to maintain a carefully cultivated ignorance.

Now, though, Roxanne resolved to overcome her reluctance to peer too far beyond tomorrow's veil. She would travel into the deep future to see if people, and their world, ever really changed.

The first stop would be a century in the future along her baseline, just to get her bearings. Roxanne would have the Sofia open a temporal bridge to a worldline chosen at random from those branching out into the Myriad. Any one would do.

"*Sofie?*" Roxanne subvocalized.

I am always with you, came the Sofia's response, sounding silently in her thoughts.

Roxanne was never sure, looking back, if she'd named the Sofia herself, borrowing from the Greek goddess of wisdom, or whether the Sofia had simply revealed to her its own name. It amounted to much the same thing, either way. Since she'd first heard the Sofia in her mind, since she'd first learned how to ask the questions only it could answer, its crystalline intelligence had always been present, an echo to her own thoughts, a background to her every waking moment. In her sleep, even, it sounded, whispering to her in her dreams.

We're going to visit the future, Sofie, Roxanne continued, glancing down at the bracelet as she thought. *To see what we can see.*

I am at your side, the Sofia answered. *Instruct me.*

These spatial coordinates, Roxanne thought. *Temporal bridge to one hundred years hence, worldline selected at random from this bifurcating baseline.*

Working, the Sofia responded, and then, *Done.* As they always did, the words came so close together that there was hardly a perceptible gap between them.

With a flash of white light, excess energy bleeding away into the surrounding space as the negative energy qualities of the cosmic string fragment widened and stabilized the chaos of the quantum-foam wormhole, the mirror-ball sphere of the temporal bridge irised open in the middle of Roxanne's private study.

She was wearing as generic a costume as she could manage. Ankle-high leather boots with a low, crenulated sole, slacks of a sturdy cotton weave, long-sleeved white cotton shirt, black leather gloves, and a black leather jacket. On her back was slung a compact leather backpack filled with survival gear and handy gadgets, and on her nose were balanced a pair of wraparound sunglasses with matte-black plastic frames. Her hair, as always, was shorn short, in the style she'd adopted in her early twenties and never seen any reason to change.

Taking one last look around her comfortable Bark Place home, she stepped towards the temporal bridge, reaching up with a gloved finger to touch the surface of the sphere. At the last instant, she smiled, and in a singsong voice murmured, "Happy birthday to me. . . ."

The London of 2112 was not so much changed from that of a century before, with only cosmetic differences. It seemed that the house had changed hands, and had been substantially remodeled. Roxanne opened a spatial bridge to the street outside when she heard voices from downstairs, and the heavy tread of feet on the stairs, not wanting to interrupt the home life of the current inhabitants.

A quick jaunt around the streets beyond the house's door, and a quick perusal of the information on the 'Net showed a world not much altered from any era on the baseline that Roxanne had visited before, and so she opted to move on.

Roxanne found 2212 little different. She wandered the streets of twenty-third-century London, and aside from some intriguing clothes, strange genetic alterations to faces and hands—for the sake of fashion, she assumed—and the maglev cars and buses, was disappointed to see that nothing much had changed.

She next opted for even numbers to keep her notes straight, hopping to 2400 CE directly, appearing in the middle of Oxford Street. She window-shopped for a time, and found a pair of bioorganic shoes with semisentient logic that she would have purchased, if she'd had the appropriate currency, but after reading through the local newsfeeds on the holographic kiosks and visiting the library terminal on the greens at Hyde Park to check on the current state of scientific progress, found that there were still not the earth-shattering and civilization-altering changes she'd hoped for. No interstellar flights, no Star Fleet patrolling the spaceways, no derring-do among the stars.

That was what she was after, Roxanne realized. That was the spice and variety of future she wanted to visit. A world of high science, and rocket ships, and trips to other planets.

She found it, with a little fudging of her instructions to the Sofia, following a branch of worldlines where space sciences were more heavily funded and early experimentations in extrasolar travel more successful. The intelligence of the Sofia, cataloguing each worldline visited in its microscopic but vast crystalline array, extrapolated the probabilities of success and failure and opened the door to the world Roxanne sought.

It was the twenty-eighth century before mankind in this worldline successfully traveled to the stars. If she'd been more specific about her requests earlier, Roxanne was sure, the Sofia might have located a reality branching from her worldline with interstellar travel much nearer her own epoch. This was a good-enough result for the moment, though, so Roxanne set off to explore the London of 2781 CE with gusto, curious to see what changes space travel had wrought on Earthbound civilization.

The answer, as she should have expected, was not very many. Humanity of this far-flung technological age was rather blasé about the whole affair, hardly seeming to recognize the miracle that colonization of other solar systems was. This was the dream of her childhood made actual fact, and yet the men and women Roxanne stopped in the streets of this future London to question about their feelings on the matter hardly seemed to have an opinion one way or the other. The world surely seemed to have changed—Roxanne couldn't doubt that—but the people in it were just the same as they'd always been.

Perhaps, Roxanne decided, traveling to other planets and stars was only a difference of degree, not of kind, to anything man in previous centuries had experienced. Perhaps crossing interstellar space to another planet was not, in the final analysis, so different than rounding the Cape of Good Hope in the eighteenth century, and charting out islands never before dreamt of by European minds. The distances changed, and the technology, but the impact on the popular consciousness was more or less the same. Even now, in this distant future, man still seemed the same animal he'd been back in the caves, though now with better tools, better hairstyles, and somewhat improved hygiene.

The deciding factor, Roxanne concluded, as to whether the future would ever truly change unrecognizably, lay in some discovery or invention that would shatter people's conceptions of reality. A breakthrough that would result in a paradigm shift in thinking of fundamental proportions, one that would truly change the way in which people viewed the world around them.

Time travel, Roxanne decided. If travel in time were to become commonplace, adding a degree of motion undreamt in earlier ages, perhaps that would finally change people for good and all. Roxanne realized she could simply travel back to her own period, and follow a branching line that led to a widespread discovery of the existence of something like the "Eternity Chamber" beneath the ice in Antarctica, but that seemed contrary to the general tenor of her explorations. It was unfortunate that she'd never gotten to the bottom of the mysterious and seemingly impossible "chronium" she'd encountered years and centuries before; if that was genuine, it might spark a revolution in temporal control.

No, Roxanne realized, if her birthday wish was to be granted to the letter, she would need to travel even farther into the future, not back and to some absolute elsewhere. Farther into the future to find a worldline in which the secret to the control of time had been discovered and mastered, and was a matter of public record. Then, surely, she would see some significant change.

It was in the early years of the thirtieth century that Roxanne found what she was looking for. Here, at last, was a world that had discovered the secret of time travel, and would surely prove different from all others before it. There was even a listing in the MemeWeb terminal she visited for something called the Tempus Agency. When the information about the agency was downloaded directly into her memories, advertising services in booking trips to other eras and providing intertemporal commerce support, Roxanne was sure she'd found the future at last.

The woman at the reception desk of the Tempus Agency's London offices smiled at Roxanne with teeth filed to razor points, inviting her to take a seat. The woman's skin had been genetically modified into an intriguing pattern, her coloration altered to produce captivating swirls and Escherlike shapes marching down from her hairline and stretching to the tips of her fingers and toes. Roxanne noted, amused, that the woman likewise had extra fingers grafted onto each hand, but thought that the work could have been done a bit better, the morphology of the new digits not quite meshing with the originals.

The woman greeted her with a string of syllables and grunts that, after some concentration, Roxanne recognized as English after centuries of linguistic drift.

"Pardon me?" Roxanne answered, tilting her head to one side, and pointing to her ear. "I'm a bit hard of hearing," she lied.

"Awh, thas toe bahd, diary. Yus goz soms irius spakspedimen, toe."

As near as Roxanne could manage, the woman had said, "Oh, that's too bad, dearie. You've got some serious speech impediment, too."

Roxanne nodded, painting on a hangdog expression.

"Yes," she said. "It's a curse."

The woman reached over, and with swirls and geometric shapes rippling patted Roxanne's gloved hand, a look of sincere sympathy on her psychedelic features.

"M'nems Miri Assaf, diary," the woman continued, drawing back her hand and lacing her fourteen fingers before her. "Ha kelp yus?"

"My name is Miri Assaf, dearie," Roxanne heard. "How can I help you?"

Roxanne explained that she was interested in the science of time travel: how it worked and to what uses it was put.

The woman whom Roxanne assumed was named Miri Assaf was more than willing to help out, though she seemed understandably confused as to the reasons behind Roxanne's questions. Roxanne was sure that if she were to walk up to the ticket counter at a twentieth-century airport and ask the person behind the counter precisely what an airplane was and how it worked that she would get much the same reaction.

A few decades prior, Miri explained, without resorting to any details that she surely did not know, spacefarers had discovered a strange object positioned in interstellar space between the Earth's sun and Proxima Centauri. The object was immensely long, with an incredible gravitational attraction, and rotating at a phenomenal speed. This object, it was soon discovered, was nothing more or less than a time machine.

Termed the TC1 by early researchers, or Tipler Cylinder One, after the twentieth-century physicist who first conjectured the possibility of such an object, the "time machine" was a cylinder one hundred kilometers in length, ten kilometers in radius, with a mass just slightly more than that of Earth's sun. Through some agency, as yet undetermined, the cylinder had been set rotating at some point in the distant past at a rate of twice every millisecond, approaching luminal speeds in its rotational velocity. Whether the cylinder was naturally occurring, the result of a one-in-a-googol chance collapse of a protostellar object in precisely the right circumstances, or whether it had been manufactured by some unknown alien civilization in the prehistory of the galaxy, no one knew. What was known, however, was that one could use this strange object to travel forwards and backwards in time.

Due to the qualities of the cylinder's mass and relativistic rotational speed, objects approaching TC1 in an orbital pattern entered an area of space-time warpage, wherein their time frame was altered from that of the surrounding space. By orbiting around the cylinder in one direction, one could move into the past, and by orbiting in the other direction, into the future. There were only two limitations to travel: One could only travel back in time to the instant that the cylinder was set into motion, and one could only orbit around the cylinder so long as the fuel and integrity of one's spacecraft held out. Early temporal explorers, drunk with the possibilities of traveling into the far-distant future, had very nearly perished when their fuel reserves diminished to the point that they were nearly unable to leave the cylinder's orbit. Had they gone farther, they would have orbited the TC1 into perpetuity, moving ever farther and farther into tomorrow, never able to return.

Roxanne was intrigued. She'd heard the theories of Frank Tipler, of course, and had even seen some of the correspondence between her father and Tipler when the latter was at Tulane University, but she'd have hardly imagined that such a thing might ever be discovered. The implications to society were staggering. Anyone traveling using such a method, of course, would be locked into a single worldline, just as if they were traveling into the future a day at a time, and would not be able to roam the Myriad as she did; but still and all, the thought that future civilization could chart out the structure of past and future history alike was staggering. Which was to say nothing of the potential benefits in medicine and technology, were breakthroughs from some future epoch to be introduced into the past. This could very well lead to new bifurcating worlds, little Utopias branching off into the Myriad, where sickness, pain, and hunger would be unknown, and where there were no more lingering mysteries about life or the nature of the universe left to solve. Roxanne was dreamy eyed, considering the possibilities.

"So how long of a trip were you planning on taking?" the woman named Miri asked, once Roxanne had been able to decipher her meaning.

"Trip?" Roxanne answered. "A trip to where?"

"Through time, of course," Miri said through her mangled accent. "We have a number of charming packages to Renaissance Italy, and one to the early Mars colony if you're of a more adventurous bent. There is, of course, our trip into the Intergalactic War Era of the Sixth Modern Millennium, but I have to warn you that our indemnity clause absolves us of any personal injury that arises as a result of your travels to any contested epochs."

"I'm sorry," Roxanne answered, smiling a little quizzically, "but I'm afraid that I'm not interested in any kind of travel holiday. I was thinking more of the scientific and cultural applications of the technology."

"Oh, the research market," Miri said, the syllables sliding one into the next. "Well, there was some investment in it at the beginning, but aside from some entertainment and genetic body-modification technology"—she indicated her extra fingers, no doubt completely functionless, with pride—"there really wasn't much money in it. Even at today's prices, an interstellar trip to TC1 isn't cheap, and then you've got to consider the cost of securing and obscuring the craft when you're in some previous epoch. All in all, there just isn't justification enough at present to pursue research, beyond the odd government-sponsored jaunt every year or two, but they typically use outmoded craft and can't travel for very long."

Roxanne goggled, unable to believe what she was fairly certain the woman was saying.

"Do you mean to tell me, then," Roxanne said, "that after discovering something as miraculous as a naturally occurring time machine, just floating out there in space for anyone to use, and with the full panoply of history before you to visit, the best you people can think to do with it is go on holidays?"

Miri shrugged, the patterned shapes and swirls rippling on her bare shoulders.

"I guess," she answered.

"Sod it," Roxanne said, and climbed to her feet. "Sofie," she practically shouted, not even bothering to subvocalize.

I am always with you, came the Sofia's response, sounding perhaps a bit petulant, if such a thing was possible.

"Temporal-spatial bridge to first coordinates," Roxanne barked, glowering at the bewildered Miri. "I'm going home."

The mirrored sphere of the bridge flashed open in the space in front of Roxanne, and she practically jumped into it.

"If that's the future," Roxanne said aloud as the bridge closed, looking around at the comfortable Bayswater furnishings, the rest of her forty-third birthday still stretching out before her, "they can bloody well keep it."

Extract from Roxanne's Memoirs

I find, as I grow older, that I haven't quite the passion for exploration that I once had, and that my tastes turn more and more to reflection and introspection.

Having consumed so much experience, in other words, I find myself now needing to digest.

I've kept journals, and logs, and diaries, continuously and continually through my many years of traveling, and I'm now faced with the challenge of finding some essential meaning in all of it, of extracting some truth or lesson from all that I've seen.

I don't know if any will ever see the products of my labors, and suspect that in fact none will, but with my unique vantage point I feel it would be criminal not to try to distill whatever glimpses of wisdom I might have gained, for the benefit of whomever might come after.

"Labors" is perhaps the appropriate term, for looking at the papers and notebooks in the basement of my Bayswater home, I'm reminded of the story of Hercules, and the Augean stables. I only hope, as I dip my shovel into my own mess, that I don't find that I'm left with nothing but shit.

CHAPTER 12

ACROSS THE UNIVERSE

LONDON, 1956
SUBJECTIVE AGE: 51 YEARS OLD

Roxanne Bonaventure walked through the wide front door of the National Film Theater into a light drizzling rain. She'd had the Sofia backtrack to this variant worldline to catch the London premiere of Orson Welles's *Don Quixote*. Welles himself was in attendance, doing a short introduction to the film and then fielding questions from the audience after the last reel finished. He seemed happier than the variant Welleses whom Roxanne had met on other worldlines, years both subjective and objective ago, who'd all looked as though they'd lived their lives under a constant shadow. This one was both sincere in his thanks in the face of thunderous applause, and eager to embark on his next grand personal vision.

The film, Roxanne felt, was really just passable, if she was honest, and not really all that impressive considering the work other variant Orsons had done. One Welles, in particular, had done a film adaptation of Conrad's *Heart of Darkness* she considered a much more successful work.

Roxanne was strolling down the street, her short gray-peppered blonde hair dampening to the sides of her head in the light rain. She wondered whether she should pick up a bite to eat before heading back to her baseline and era, or whether she should go directly home, when the man stepped out of the side street in front of her, blocking her way.

He was a tall man, well over six feet, dressed in a long topcoat and floppy, shapeless fedora. Around his neck was wrapped an impossibly long scarf, wound over his chin and mouth, leaving only his prominent hook nose visible, the ends of the scarf hanging down almost to his knees. In the dim light of the streetlamp, through the drizzling haze, Roxanne fancied she could see his eyes glowing, like a cat's caught in a glare.

"You are Roxanne Bonaventure," the man said in a strange accent, his voice muffled through the cloth of the scarf. It was a statement, not a question.

"Perhaps," Roxanne answered, crossing her arms over her chest and cocking her head to one side. "It all depends on who is asking, and when."

So far as Roxanne knew, she'd never visited this worldline or the lines from which it branched, coming no closer than twenty or thirty objective years in its past. There'd be no reason for anyone here to know her, or to recognize her. No reason she could think of, at least.

"You will come with me," the man continued, stepping forward and reaching out a bone-white hand to take her elbow.

Roxanne shrugged.

"If you put it like that," Roxanne answered, and dropping back a step swung a side kick in a high arc that connected with the side of the man's head, jarring her to the teeth, and succeeding only in knocking off the man's hat.

The man just looked at her, blank expressionless face over the wrapped scarf, hat lying collecting puddles on the pavement. A mop of curly hair perched on the top of his head canted over to one side, covering up one ear and leaving the other side of the scalp exposed, showing pale, white skin.

"Nice wig," Roxanne said. The man hadn't moved. The kick, the best she could manage at short notice, seemed not to have fazed him. She hopped on one foot, holding her other foot up under her flamingo-style and massaging her now-bruised shin. She wasn't as young as she'd once been, and the fisticuffs tended to take a deeper toll than they had.

"Tell you what," she said, her interest piqued. She bent down, and picked up the man's formless hat from the rain-slicked street. "You seem like a nice guy. Why don't I come with you, you tell me what you're on about, and if I don't like it I give kicking your face in a go again. Deal?"

The man, his face still expressionless, accepted the proffered hat, and nodded slowly.

"Take my hand," he said, righting his wig and perching the hat on top. He held out his bone-white hand again, palm up, like he was inviting her to dance.

"Why not?" Roxanne said. She could always fight him later, or rabbit and run, or else boot him through a spatial bridge into the heart of the sun. What she wanted to know now, though, was how he'd known her name and how to find her, and how he'd managed not to flinch when she delivered a kick that would have knocked the strongest man insensible to the ground.

She took the man's hand in a light grip, and suddenly the world fell away. She had a sick sensation in the pit of her stomach, like riding a roller coaster after eating ten too many hot dogs, and then squeezed shut her eyes when a riot of colors and sounds hit them.

Sounds? she thought, confused.

Yes, she had to admit. Sounds. And tastes. There was some quality to the light she was seeing, a formless mix of every color and hue imaginable, that suggested to her brain every sensation she'd ever experienced, and then some.

Wherever she was going, wherever she was, it was nowhere she'd been before, not in all the worlds of the Myriad.

Roxanne opened her eyes, the nausea slowly passing, and found that she was standing in the middle of a circle of ruins, a purple sky arching overhead. Twin moons, blue and green, hung fat and low on the distant horizon, giving an odd quality to the twilight illumination. The thin air was still and quiet. The ruins, tumbledown arches and pillars, suggested classical motifs, but subtly off, as though the long-ago sculptor had heard descriptions of Greco-Roman architecture, but had never seen it for himself.

Roxanne blinked, looking out on a new world for the first time.

After a long moment of silence, she realized the strange man in the shapeless hat still stood at her side, still held her hand in his cold, pale grip. Roxanne extracted her fingers from his, rubbing the feeling back into her numb joints.

"Nice place," she said, taking a few steps away from the man, giving an appraising glance at the surroundings. "Do you bring all your dates here?"

The man did not reply, but turned towards a raised dais at the forefront of the circle of ruins and pointed.

"Behold," he said in his odd voice.

Roxanne looked, as requested, and was surprised to see the air shimmer slightly. As she watched, five shapes came into view, multicolored spheres that hovered six or seven feet from the surface of the platform, shifting slightly back and forth in the still air, the colors on their surfaces kaleidoscoping.

Bridges? she wondered, thinking of the spherical shape of the Sofia's handiwork.

"WELCOME," boomed a voice from the center sphere, the air buzzing with the volume of the sound. "WELCOME, ROXANNE BONAVENTURE, TO THE END OF TIME."

"Oh, it's my pleasure, I'm sure," Roxanne said, stepping closer to the shapes. "And whom do I have the pleasure of addressing?"

The hovering spheres remained silent for a moment, the colors on their surfaces shifting and changing. Finally, the sphere on the far left began to vibrate, as the center sphere had done, a prelude to enunciation.

"WE ARE THE LORDS TEMPORAL," the far-left sphere buzzed, causing Roxanne's ears to ring. "MASTERS OF TIME AND SPACE."

"Pleased to meet you," Roxanne sang. "And just what, if I might ask, is that supposed to mean? Lords Temporal?"

"ONCE," came the answer from the sphere on the far right, "WE WERE AS YOU, CORPOREAL AND SLAVES TO THE LAWS OF SPACE AND TIME."

"Oh, am I corporeal?" Roxanne said, craning her head over her shoulder and twisting to look towards her rear end. "Is it showing?"

"BUT WE EVOLVED BEYOND OUR LIMITED STATE," the center sphere went on, "TO MASTER THE VERY LAWS WHICH ONCE HAD KEPT US IN SHACKLES."

"Fascinating, really," Roxanne said. She jerked a thumb over her shoulder at the strange man who'd brought her. "And how does your charming friend fit into the picture? He seems fairly corporeal, though I don't know if he'd be much fun at parties."

"HERE," said the sphere second from the left, "AT THE LAST MOMENTS BEFORE THE HEAT DEATH OF THE UNIVERSE, WE ENLIST AGENTS FROM OTHER ERAS TO HELP STEER CIVILIZATION TO THE PATH OF PROGRESS AND GOOD-WILL, AND AWAY FROM THE DARK FORCES OF EVIL AND OPPRESSION."

"How very Baden-Powell of you, if you don't mind me saying," Roxanne answered, crossing her arms casually. "Helping little old civilizations to cross the road, is that it?"

"WE HAVE MONITORED YOUR PROGRESS OVER THE YEARS OF YOUR LIFE," the sphere second from the right buzzed,

"AND HAVE DEEMED YOU A WORTHY ADDITION TO OUR NUMBER."

"YOU ARE INVITED, THEREFORE," the center sphere chimed in, "TO JOIN OUR BODY OF AGENTS, WORKING FOR THE BETTERMENT OF ALL SENTIENT BEINGS."

"TO HELP ALL," the sphere on the far left added, buzzing in, "ATTAIN OUR HIGH STATE."

Roxanne rubbed her chin, gnawing absently at her lower lip, miming concentration.

"You know what? I'm sorry," she said, "but I don't buy it."

The five spheres, and their strange man-thing behind her, remained silent.

"This just doesn't add up, you know?" she went on. "I mean, obviously, you've got some serious science on your side, right? The Sofia is telling me that, yes, I've traveled an inconceivable distance into the future, and a not-inconsiderable distance in space as well. But she can't tell me how you did it. I've had her scanning you five beachballs since you popped in, and your charming gentleman behind me, and what she persists in telling me doesn't make any sense.

"It's as though you aren't really here. The stones of your oh-so-attractive and convincing ruins are here, and I'm here, but you five . . ." She paused, and jerked her thumb again at the man with the long scarf behind her. "Six, forgive me. . . . You six are existing only in some strange approximation of reality."

There was silence for a long moment.

"WE ARE THE LORDS TEMPORAL," the center sphere finally buzzed in response, "AND AS SUCH WILL NOT BE JUDGED."

"That's fine with me," Roxanne answered, waving her hand nonchalantly, "but that hardly changes my findings. You're a puzzle, and no doubt, but not at all what you claim." She paused, and then added, "Besides, if you were half as advanced as you claim, with the control that you insist to possess, you'd know that this malarkey about steering the destinies of civilizations is just that. Malarkey. You'd know that civilizations will steer as they will, and that all you can hope to do is splinter off variants from time to time, and what good that does everyone I can hardly say."

She strode up to the edge of the dais, just beneath the twin shadows of the five spheres.

"But you *do* have the control," she went on, "at least in part, or you wouldn't have been able to drag me from soggy old London to here. Therefore, I can only conclude that you're giving me a bum steer, or trying to sell me something I have no intention of buying."

She reached down to plant both hands on the edge of the dais, and pushed herself up over the rim onto the platform. Straightening, and dusting off her hands palm on palm, she reached up and poked the center sphere with an outstretched finger.

"Well," she said menacingly. "What's it going to be? You going to drop the act and come clean, or am I going to get my feelings hurt here?"

Again, a long moment of silence.

"WE ARE THE LORDS TEMPORAL," the center sphere buzzed, drifting up out of her reach.

"Sure, sure," she answered, interrupting. She hopped down off the platform onto the dusty ground, and walked back a few feet from the man in the shapeless hat. "I've heard it before. Tell you what." She glanced back over her shoulder at the spheres, raising her left wrist in front of her face. "If you guys decide to stop playing, and want to talk, give me a ring."

She smiled at the bracelet on her wrist, and said, "Sofie, home."

A spatial-temporal bridge irised open in front of her. Before stepping through, she turned and pointed to the man in the hat and scarf.

"But please," she said, gracing the spheres with a sardonic half-smile, "if you do call, don't send this charmer to deliver the message. He kind of gets on my nerves."

With that, Roxanne brushed her fingers against the surface of the Sofia's bridge, and was gone.

At the end of time, at the edge of the universe, the Lords Temporal and their agent remained still in silence for a time. Then, one by one, the spheres and man alike winked out of existence, leaving the ruins and the dust alone under the purple skies of the universe's last days.

Extract from Roxanne's Memoirs

I've buried two parents, and too many friends in the various eras in which I've lived. One of the significant drawbacks to maintaining concurrent lives in so many different time periods is the almost continuous sense of loss as so many of my acquaintances leave life's stage, never to return.

I've always found it a great pity that the human life span, for so much of our history, has been so damned short. Now, at the age of fifty-five, I'm just barely in the years of my middle age, as reckoned by my home era on my baseline, but I've reached the age of venerable crone in so many of the past epochs in which I travel. While so many of my old classmates at the Saint Anthony Academy and King's College are now parents of grown children, or even grandparents in so many cases, in past millennia women of my age can count on three, four, even five generations of offspring to surround them as they waste away on their deathbeds.

Still, these things are always a question of averages, and too often the modern mind has difficulty in grasping what it means to say that the average life expectancy in ancient times was no more than eighteen years. This did not mean that a boy was an old man at eighteen years, but rather that so many of his fellows would have died in the cradle, or through the dangerous years of childhood, that by eighteen he would have been one of a select number of survivors.

In the last half of the twentieth century, there was a great deal of talk about concepts like "survivor's guilt," which was said to apply to everyone from those who had lost siblings, to those who weathered terrible natural catastrophes while those around them perished, to those who survived atrocities like the death camps of the Nazis and the pogroms of Post-Soviet Eastern Europe and the genocides of Africa.

What most enlightened twentieth- and twenty-first-century residents fail to realize is that this phenomenon was hardly rare in ancient times. In fact, for most of human history, everyone could be said to suffer from survivor's guilt, having seen the majority of everyone they knew die before their time.

Perhaps this is what drove so many in past epochs to reach beyond their means, and to dare great things. To explore the uncharted reaches of the Earth, like the Polynesian explorers who tamed the Pacific reaches without compass, or map, or defenses. To invent, to discover, to dream great dreams.

I wonder, at times, if this is also why so many in modern eras dare so little, and dream so small. Having seen relatively little of death, they compartmentalize the concept of loss, and fail to realize the true fragility of a human life, and the need for every individual second to count.

CHAPTER 13

HER MAJESTY

From a distance, through the squalor and the milling crowd, Roxanne Bonaventure knew him at a glance. He was as out of place in these surroundings as she was; more so, given the time she'd spent establishing a name and reputation in the era. Neither belonged, but she at least was welcome. She was a traveler, but he was a castaway, or worse, an invader. She wasn't sure yet which.

Roxanne had spent the better part of her sixty years traveling the many worlds of the Myriad, and knew how to avoid disturbances if she wished. Talbot, however, was like a stone dropped into still water, the ripples of his passing spreading out in all directions. Roxanne watched for a moment as he blundered through the crowded streets, narrowly missing a bucket of slops emptied out an upper-story window, elbowing passersby as he gaped at the scenes and structures surrounding him, almost tripping over his own feet every other step.

The pack at his back was heavy, its style incongruous with the native clothes he affected. He'd only just arrived.

"Talbot," Roxanne said in a low voice as he passed by. "Edward Talbot."

He stopped short, startled, and spun on his heel to face her.

Roxanne leaned against a post, arms crossed casually over her chest. She wore a simple black dress and jacket in period style, her gray hair bound up in a bun at the back of her neck. Nothing out of the ordinary for the city at that time, but something in her look seemed to frighten Talbot. He backed away, clutching the shoulder strap of his pack nervously.

"Wh-who are you?" he stammered, edging farther away.

"I'm the Ghost of Christmas Future, Talbot," Roxanne answered. She stepped towards him, reaching out a hand

"You . . .?" Talbot began, eyes darting from side to side. "You come from . . . back there . . . don't you? You've come to take me back."

Roxanne shook her head, her hand still stretched out to him.

"Only if you want to go," she answered.

"The ship," Talbot said, relaxing marginally. "The crash. It wasn't my fault." He paused. In a calm voice, dry and raw like a scab on a recent wound, he added, "The others are all dead."

"I know," Roxanne said softly, stepping forward and taking Talbot gently by the arm. "Let's go somewhere and talk."

A short while later, facing each other across a pitted tavern table, Talbot told her his story, and Roxanne told him hers.

"So with this device," Talbot said, "you can travel through time and space at will?" He reached toward the bracelet on Roxanne's wrist gingerly, as though afraid to touch it, as though it might burn.

"More or less," Roxanne answered, raising the jar of ale to her lips.

"Remarkable," Talbot enthused. "What I couldn't do with something like that." He drew up short, suddenly suspicious. "But I've never heard of the TIA having anything like that."

"I've told you before," Roxanne said, setting the jar down with perhaps more force than was necessary. "I'm not with your Temporal Investigation Agency. From the sounds of it, I doubt I've ever even been near your home Commonwealth."

"So why seek me out?" Talbot asked. "Why now?"

"Because I was asked by a friend to look you up," Roxanne answered. "But that needn't concern you. What I need to know is this: Do you want me to take you home?"

Talbot laced his fingers together, and leaned forward.

"Do you mean to say I have a choice?" he asked. "That you won't try to force me to go with you?"

Roxanne shook her head, smiling. When she'd first seen him, she'd noticed how much younger than his years Talbot looked, no doubt the benefit of medical advances in his future era, but in that moment, wide-eyed, he looked even younger than before. Like a child being told he could spend the rest of his life at a theme park, envisioning endless summers of fun. She couldn't help but feel sorry for him.

"I won't force you to do anything," Roxanne answered. "Stay or go, it will be your choice, and yours alone. But you must understand the risks."

"Oh, I know all about them," Talbot answered, nodding eagerly. "I had to spend months in training before they'd let me come along on the timeflight, and I've been inculcated with all the necessary immunities, so with my knowledge of the period, I wouldn't have any problems at all."

"You're an historian," Roxanne admitted, "so you know all about the past, but the events you studied haven't happened yet. Before it happens, history is still the future. Who knows what might happen?"

Talbot chewed at his lip, listening but unconvinced.

"Your ship is destroyed, and you're all alone," Roxanne went on. "You couldn't even make it to the moon, much less halfway to Proxima Centauri. Without that rotating cylinder, I'm your only way home."

Talbot drummed his fingertips on the rough wooden surface of the table, thinking furiously.

"But to come all this way," he finally said, his tone desperate, "and leave before my studies have even begun. So many great days ahead, significant events, and I'd be turning my back on them all."

"Possibly," Roxanne said, guarded.

"What if . . ." Talbot began, and then broke off. He grew excited, an idea forming. "You say you can go anywhere, and anywhen, with that device of yours, yes?"

Roxanne nodded.

"So it would be no trouble for you then . . ." he said, more to himself than to her. He snapped his fingers. "Yes, that might work. What if you were to leave me here, and just go immediately to some point in the near future? Some years hence, perhaps? That would give me more than enough opportunity to complete my research, while virtually no time would have passed for you, and then you and I could return to the future together."

Roxanne said nothing, but narrowed her eyes fractionally.

"Oh, please," Talbot pleaded. "I know it must be a terrible imposition, but it would mean so very much to me. To get to see the first flowerings of the greatest era in human history with my own eyes, and not from a video monitor in low orbit over the planet. To see it as it happens!"

"How will you live?" Roxanne asked in a quiet voice. "How will you feed and house yourself?"

"Oh," Talbot answered. "I've got serviceable skills, a knowledge of languages and local customs. I could always get a job. And if worse came to worst, I could always fabricate some period currency using the equipment I salvaged from the wreckage." He motioned to the anachronistic pack that lay at his feet.

"They don't treat counterfeiting lightly in these centuries, you know," Roxanne observed, but Talbot dismissed the concern with an imperious wave. "So that's your decision, then?" she asked.

Talbot nodded, but didn't seem to be listening. He was already busy making plans, mapping out strategies and listing high points to visit.

Roxanne picked up her jar of ale, and drained it to the dregs.

"Very well," she said, pushing away from the table and rising to her feet. "I'll wish you luck, and see you in a few years. Shall we say . . . how many? Two? Three?"

Talbot jumped to his feet, shouldering his heavy pack, eager to begin.

"Five," Talbot said, then rushed to add, "no, six. Eight." He paused, doing quick calculations. "Ten," he finally announced, nodding fiercely. "Yes, ten years."

Roxanne whistled low, shaking her head.

"All right," she said reluctantly. "A decade it is. But I should warn you to tread cautiously. You should be careful what rules you break, and whom you offend."

"Oh, I will," Talbot called back over his shoulder, already on his way towards the door. "Just think," he said in his eagerness, as much to himself as to her, "Christopher Marlowe is only nine years old right now."

"So is Shakespeare," Roxanne answered, lifting her wrist and opening a temporal bridge directly before her.

"Who?" Talbot asked, half turning, but by then Roxanne was already gone.

Mortlake, 1583

Two men were in the upper chamber of the house, the candle on the mantel guttering. The younger of the two, corpulent and wearing a black cap close-fitting and pulled down low, was seated on a green chair, the convex black mirror on the short table before him. The older, long beard and flashing eyes, sat at the desk along the far wall, a great folio book open beneath his hand. As they spoke, first one and then the other, the older man recorded every particular, quill flying with incessant scratches over the foolscap.

"Look unto the kind of people about the duke in the manner of their diligence," the younger man said, his voice strange and fluttering.

"What do you mean?" the older man asked, glancing up sharply from his labors. "His own people? Or who?"

"The espies."

"Which?"

"All. There is not one true."

"You mean the Englishmen."

"You are very gross if you do not understand my speech."

"Lord!" the older man implored. "What is thy counsel?"

"I hate to interrupt," came a new voice from the corner, "but I need a moment of your time."

Roxanne strode into the center of the room.

"Oh, dear spirit," the older man said, leaping from his desk and falling to his knees. "Am I to be vouchsafed a visitation of our celestial sponsor Madini? Oh, what great felicity!"

The younger man, at his table, did not move.

"I'm afraid not," Roxanne answered, apologetically. "I'm quite mundane, I must confess." She motioned to the younger man. "I'm here on the queen's business, and need to speak to your assistant."

"See here," the older man answered, bristling and rising up. "I have left standing instructions with the staff and my wife, the lady of the house, that we are not to be disturbed when performing our actions, so I'll ask you to . . ." He paused, looking at the locked and bolted door, and then glanced to the windows, still closed with the heavy drapes tied fast over them.

"Kelly?" the older man said, turning to his companion with mounting confusion. "Can you account for this apparition?"

"I beg your pardon, Dr. Dee," the young man answered, climbing reluctantly to his feet, "but if I might have a moment alone with this . . . lady . . . I believe I can get to the bottom of it."

Roxanne smiled, but kept silent.

The older man looked from one to the other, his eyes narrowed, and slowly made for the door.

"I will be just without, in the hall," he told the young man, his eyes fixed on Roxanne. "But I will allow only a brief span, and then I will have an explanation from you."

Turning on his heel, his long robes swirling around him, the older man unlocked and threw open the door, closing it with a resounding thud as he passed.

"So," Roxanne began, dropping into the chair at the desk, crossing her legs casually, "it's Kelly now, is it? I'd forgotten."

"Has it been ten years?" Talbot said, beginning to pace. He slipped a finger under the edge of his close-fitting cap, scratching the side of his head. He stared off into the middle distance, and bitterly added, "It seems so very much longer."

"I keep pretty close tabs on the time," Roxanne answered.

"So you've come back to me at last," Talbot went on, pacing faster. "And where were you before, when I stood in the Lancashire pillory? Where were you when I was mutilated?"

Roxanne responded with a sympathetic look, leavened with a slight shrug.

"You knew the risks, Talbot," she answered. "I warned you about counterfeiting, didn't I?" She paused, and then added, "I was sorry to hear about the ears, though."

Talbot made a dismissive noise, his hand drifting absently to the cap on his head.

"So you've come to take me back, have you?" he said, crossing his arms and fixing Roxanne with a stare.

"Only if you ask me to," Roxanne answered. "But I have other business, I'm afraid. Bad news you won't want to hear."

Talbot regarded her coolly.

"What do you mean, 'bad news'?" he asked.

Roxanne shook her head.

"Not yet," she answered. "I don't want to spoil the mood. Let's talk of other matters first, you and I." She uncrossed her legs, and leaned forward. "Let me first ask you two questions. In your former life, before your shipwreck here in this era, you were a historian, and a general man of letters. Tell me, Talbot, did your studies extend to the arena of quantum physics?"

Talbot looked at her blankly.

"No," he finally said, flatly, when it became clear Roxanne was waiting for some sort of response.

"In that case, I take it that you are unfamiliar with the axiom which physicists call the Uncertainty Principle?"

Talbot, after a significant pause, shook his head.

"No," he said. "That is, yes, I am unfamiliar with whatever the devil it is you're talking about. But what is this to me?"

"I won't bore you with the details as expressed on a quantum level," Roxanne went on, ignoring his question, "but when stated in a larger scale it translates, roughly, to this: 'The act of observing something affects the state of the thing observed.' Are you with me so far?"

Growing increasingly frustrated and confused, Talbot nodded fiercely.

"Now we reach my second question, Talbot," Roxanne said, stepping nearer his seat, towering over him. "You've insinuated yourself into the life and home of John Dee these past months, after so many years of wandering and observing quietly from the shadows. Why?"

Talbot sat glowering, his hands in white-knuckled fists on the arms of the chair.

"You . . ." he began, then stopped. He blinked, and swallowed hard. "You have no idea how frustrating it is, for someone like me, to be near greatness and not see it. To know that somewhere, behind closed doors, the pivotal events of history are playing out, while I'm stuck filling ampoules with useless powders and potions for hypochondriacs who'll be dead of the plague in a year no matter what."

Talbot pounded his fists on the chair's arms.

"To come so far," he continued, louder. "To suffer so much . . ." He broke off, and ripped the cap off his head. "To suffer!" he repeated. "And to still know nothing!"

Roxanne sighed. She looked at the lumps of scar tissue on either side of his head, the cost of passing base coins.

"So instead?" she prompted.

Talbot, in response, leapt to his feet and wheeled on the black mirror and table.

"So instead," he parroted back, mocking, "I made my own opportunities. My computer, salvaged from the wreckage, easily passed as a supernatural object, dispensing secret wisdom from my historical databases on the period. The curved screen of the liquid crystal display becomes a magic mirror in Dee's eyes, the machine code of the system's processes some angelic script." He paused, and then added, not a little proudly, "It's all in the presentation."

"So you found in Dee something of a willing dupe," Roxanne answered, "someone with a weakness for the arcane that you could use to gain access to the corridors of power."

"I wouldn't say 'dupe,' perhaps," Talbot replied, shrugging, "but yes, something like that."

Roxanne smiled.

"But it hasn't exactly worked, has it?" she asked.

Talbot's shoulders slumped, and he looked away.

"No," he answered bitterly. "Dee keeps me cooped up here all hours, his personal seer, while he ferries back and forth to court, spreading the good word. I've only seen the Queen once, and then only from a far window." He paused, sighing. "Oh, imagine the things I've already missed, the grand decisions she's made."

Roxanne reached out a hand, laying it on Talbot's shoulder.

"It won't happen, Talbot," she said, as gently as she could manage. Talbot looked up at her, confused.

"I wasn't lying when I said I was on the queen's business," Roxanne said. "I told you to be careful whom you offended, but I'm afraid that you didn't listen."

"The queen?" Talbot asked, incredulous. "How could I have offended her?"

"Like I told you before," Roxanne answered, "I was asked by a friend to look you up. Elizabeth doesn't much care for your influence on her advisors."

Talbot narrowed his eyes.

"Now we come to my bad news," Roxanne went on. "As she's been unable to convince Dee to part company with you, she's called him to court less and less over the past months. Now, she's gone so far as to instruct her staff that they are to respond to none of Dee's requests until you are out of the picture. And if Dee can't be at her side when events of great importance occur, you can be sure that you have no chance whatsoever."

When she'd finished, Talbot looked on her silently, scowling. Slowly, his scowl grew into a smirk, and he began to chuckle.

"You think I didn't know?" he asked, his tone sharp. "You think that Dee doesn't rush home and tell me everything he's seen and heard since last we were together? I knew that he wasn't welcome at court any longer, though before now I hadn't known precisely the reason why. But it hardly matters. I've made other plans."

Talbot sank back into his chair, leaving Roxanne to look down at him questioningly.

"There are other princes and prelates of note in this era, after all," Talbot went on. "Elizabeth will not rule forever, and when she dies, someone else must naturally take the throne. I have, you must admit" —he indicated the black curve of his computer's liquid crystal display with a flick of his hand—"some useful information in this regard. The 'angels' have been advising Dee, through my useful mediation of course, that it might be to his benefit to seek service in some foreign court for a time. There are surely other courts more receptive to Dee's talents . . . to say nothing of mine. The angels and I have been focusing our attentions on a certain duke, currently visiting London and soon to return home, who has already developed a keen interest in our celestial conversations." He paused, and then added, "I understand Bohemia is quite nice this time of year."

Roxanne stood over him in silence for a long moment, her look softening.

"I take it you won't be leaving with me," she said simply.

Talbot answered with a curt shake of his head.

"Another decade then?" Roxanne asked. "I'll check on you in another ten years?"

"Certainly," Talbot replied grandly. "Why not? Who knows the grand heights to which I'll have climbed by then?"

Roxanne raised her arm, glancing at the bracelet on her wrist.

"I'll remind you of my two questions, and their answers," Roxanne said, as the reflective sphere of the bridge opened in the room's center. "And I hope you're more careful in the next decade than you've been in the last."

Roxanne reached out her hand to brush against the surface of the bridge, and Talbot was left alone.

Prague, 1593

The man stood on the high parapet, rough stones slicked by the cold rain drizzling down from an unforgiving sky. The intermittent bursts of lightning that divided the darkness flashed on the ribbon of white dangling from the overhanging cornice, dingy sheets tied into a chain and knotted every foot. The chain vanished in darkness as it trailed down the wall. It was uncertain whether it fully reached the ground, or halted somewhere in-between.

The man looked up to the window ledge from which he'd climbed, to the makeshift ladder of bedsheets, to the dim recesses of the ground far below.

"I hope you're not thinking of jumping," came a voice at his back, "when I've traveled so far just to see you."

"I had not decided yet, my lady," the man answered without turning. "I'm still not convinced which of my options will bring me the least pain."

Roxanne approached on sure feet, until she was within arm's reach.

"I take it the past decade has not gone well for you, Talbot," she said.

"Among your many gifts," he answered archly, "you can count understatement as one."

Roxanne reached out, and gently touched his elbow.

"So many things have gone wrong," Talbot continued, clenching his hands in tight, ineffective fists at his sides, his gaze fixed on the abyss before him. "I thought to see such wonderful things. Marlowe and his fellow agents, traveling the countryside incognito as a troupe of players, forging alliances for their queen with the Protestant princes of Europe. Raleigh, extending the Crown's reach into the Western Hemisphere, driving out the Papist Spaniards and French and creating a new nation alongside the Indigenes. Elizabeth, crowned Holy Roman empress and made ruler of three continents. And what have I seen?" Talbot spat on the cold stones at his feet. "Base politics, spite, and the insides of prisons."

"I warned you," Roxanne answered tenderly. "By observing, we change the thing observed. You must tread carefully in these eras, and that which is yet to be is still undecided."

Talbot turned slowly, and Roxanne was unable to say whether the streaks down his cheeks were from teardrops or the falling rain.

"This is no longer the world you knew," Roxanne continued. "You stepped off the path of your worldline long ago. The heroes of your history, here, are little more than footnotes. Christopher Marlowe died only weeks ago, murdered over the matter of a bar tab. Raleigh's colony was a failure, and he is discredited and disgraced, to be executed for treason against the Crown as soon as Elizabeth's successor takes the throne. There will be no grand union of natives and colonists under the banner of Gloriana in the Western Hemisphere. The long era of peace and cooperation that you called home—the line of philosopher-kings, the enlightened nation-state of Pan Europa, the progressive Commonwealth of New Atlantis across the sea—all of them here no more than a dream, if even that."

Talbot seemed to falter, losing his feet, and Roxanne reached out a quick hand to steady him.

"All . . . ." he began. "All of it gone?" His mouth gaped, and he deflated, limp. "My world . . . my history . . . my future? Because of me?"

Roxanne smiled, a little sadly, and shook her head.

"No," she answered. "Not gone. Not really. Just somewhere else, another worldline orthogonal to this."

Roxanne's hand still on his elbow, Talbot slipped down to his knees, folding his hands together in an attitude of prayer.

"Please," he said simply, his voice barely audible over the sound of rainfall on cold stones.

"This is the lesson most people never learn," Roxanne said, bending down to bring her face a handbreadth from his. "The world is what we make it, better or worse. Observing a thing changes it, whether past, present, or future. What one man can do, for good or ill, can scarcely even be measured, and yet it happens every day."

"Please," Talbot repeated, taking Roxanne's shoulders in his hands. "Please, I want to go back. To go home. Can I? Can it be done?"

Roxanne straightened up, and nodded.

"We'll have to go the long way, back again and then forward, but we can manage." She stretched out her arm toward him, and a flash of lightning glinted on the silver of the bracelet at her wrist. "All you have to do is take my hand."

"Yes," Talbot said softly, reaching out and taking her hand in both of his. He stood painfully on worn joints, and repeated louder, "Yes. Take me with you."

Roxanne nodded, and the temporal bridge irised open in the air between them.

"I'm sorry I didn't listen," Talbot said, gripping Roxanne's hand tighter still. "I should have listened."

"Yes, you should have," Roxanne said sadly. "Come on, Talbot. Let's take you home."

Roxanne lifted up their hands, hers and Talbot's together, touched the reflective surface of the bridge, and they were gone.

Extract from Roxanne's Memoirs

In my time, I have known queens, priestesses, and empresses; and I have also known midwives, kitchen maids, and seamstresses. And I have come to learn the subtle differences between ruling from a throne, and ruling from the hearth.

The "modern" woman, since the beginning of the twentieth century, has looked back on the lot of women in historical times in horror. Excepting those rare figures of female authority, the Elizabeths, the Victorias, the Cleopatras, they see the long history of their fellow women as nothing but drudgery, and virtual enslavement to their brother men.

So abhorrent was this notion that women in the midtwentieth century had to invent some glorious past, a Utopian splendor of a world ruled by women alone, matriarchies of goddess worship and male subservience, which was ripped from them by jealous chauvinist males.

Like all lost Utopias, though, this existed only in the imagination of those who dreamt of it.

I have explored the past, or rather the many pasts, of the human race, and while I've found societies with women rulers and female goddesses, I've just as often found civilizations with kings and queens as corulers, worshipping hermaphroditic gods, and cultures ruled by ignorant boy-kings who worshipped certain phases of the moon.

The secret of the history of women in human cultures is not that they lost their power, or had their power somehow stripped from them by jealous men. It is that, from the vantage point of enlightened moderns, we simply cannot recognize the power they always possessed.

No successful society in human history, in all the worlds of the Myriad (and by "successful" I mean those that last any longer than a century), has ever survived without making full use of all its citizenry, letting each member contribute to their fullest.

This is not to say that there were not inequities, nor that slavery and drudgery were not commonplace. But to suppose that the entire gender of womankind was enslaved since the fall of some mythological Neolithic goddess-wor-

ship culture until the coming of the suffragettes is entirely shortsighted, and gives no fair credit or due to countless generations of women who held fair sway over the men in their lives.

That periodically women were unfairly treated, and denied their proper role in society, cannot be disputed, and certainly the early modern history of Western civilization, from the end of the Renaissance forward, is a good example of such a time. But such periods are mere transitions, and over the long haul cannot sustain.

It should be remembered, that viewed in the appropriate context, men never stole power way from women. In the vast majority of instances I have seen, the only power men possessed was simply that which the women allowed them to have.

CHAPTER 14

WHAT GOES ON

I t began with Roxanne in her Bayswater home, simply enough.

She sat in her well-appointed parlor, the mirrored spheres of temporal bridges suspended in midair around her. Through each could be seen a different place, a different time. Her tired feet propped on the low divan, she idly watched events unfold across the Myriad, like other people might watch television, or read the obituaries. It was a way to pass the time.

Over the years Roxanne had developed an interest in others, like herself, who were able to move freely in time. She was still, decades after it first came into her life, always trying to solve the riddle of the Sofia. Now that she was getting older, and her bones not nearly so strong as they'd once been, nor her muscles able to walk nearly so far, most of her explorations were done this way, without ever leaving the safety of her home.

She'd learned how to open temporal bridges that allowed light and sound waves to pass through, but were too small and inaccessible on the far side to be traversable by anything larger than a few molecules across.

In the previous few months of watching, she'd begun to see certain trends developing. Months before she eavesdropped on a small group of agents in one worldline discussing a companion who had gone missing in the thirty-third century. A week later she'd heard temporal intelligence operatives in another worldline discussing anachronistic technological products in late-nineteenth- and early-twentieth-century Europe.

That morning, disparate threads from even more disparate worldlines at last knit themselves together into a single tapestry.

Something very interesting had been going on in a nearby worldline, not far removed from Roxanne's own baseline, in the first decade of twentieth-century London.

This merited a trip out of doors. Roxanne had to see for herself just how things played out.

London, 1910. It was the third week of April, Edward VII was still on the throne, and for what would prove a brief instant the world was at something almost like peace.

Roxanne arrived near the close of the third act, just before all the players were due to take the stage. Tycho Maas, either the villain or tragic figure of the piece, depending on one's perspective, was the first to arrive.

The setting was a generously appointed garden, enclosed by a high wall on three sides and the looming rear of a large house on the fourth. Spring just settling in, the hardiest of the foliage was already blooming, their more reluctant cousins still wrapped in their coats of winter reserve.

Roxanne had found a place near the back wall, on a low stone bench that offered the best view of the house, the garden, and the impending action.

Tycho entered the garden from the wide gallery doors of the house, talking animatedly, hands waving. He wore a white linen suit, a black string tie, and a white Panama hat with a black hatband.

Not unexpectedly, a small sphere the size of a billiard ball floated in midair just behind him, keeping level with Tycho's head. It was constructed of some dull-finished metal, like burnished brass, and chimed a strange little noise whenever Tycho paused in his oration, a mechanical equivalent of a disinterested nod.

Tycho was halfway across the garden when he caught sight of Roxanne, sitting serenely a few dozen yards away on the stone bench, her hands folded primly in her lap. He stopped short, the floating billiard ball halting right behind him.

"You'll excuse me if I seem a mite startled, ma'am," Tycho said, doffing his hat and dipping head and shoulders in the merest hint of a bow. "But if I might be so bold, just how in blue blazes did you get back here?"

Roxanne gave the sort of enigmatic smile that would have given Mona Lisa fits of jealously, and shrugged slightly.

"I just popped in for the show," she said serenely. "Don't mind me."

Tycho shoved his hat back down on his head, and harrumphed. He wheeled around to the floating sphere, intent.

"Halley!" he shouted. "I thought you said the security grids were all in place and activated back—"

He stopped short, his eyes widening, looking from Roxanne to the floating sphere and back again.

"Hell's bells," he shouted, taking off his hat again, wadding it up and smacking it against his thigh. Miraculously, when he regained his composure, the hat did likewise, easing back into its original shape.

Tycho clasped his hands behind his back, and began to pace back and forth.

"Damnation," he spat, stomping across the garden's flagstone. "Twenty years and no one catches so much as a glimpse of you, Halley, and as soon as you give me the all clear that the security baffles are in place, here this withered old plum—" He doffed his hat angrily as he turned back around for another circuit, tipping it in Roxanne's direction. "No offense, ma'am."

Roxanne just smiled, and shook her head.

"Now, as I was saying, here this withered old plum has wormed her way right into the heart of things, and seen the very thing I wanted most hid."

The brass sphere, which had been floating along behind Tycho in his revolutions around the garden, back and forth, chimed again, and then dipped slightly in what could only have been some sort of mechanical bow.

"Your pardon, sir," said the sphere Halley in the voice of an angelic chorus, like a choir of perfect voices in harmony. "But my calculations were not in error."

"Now, dammit, Halley," Tycho said, whirling around and stabbing a finger at the sphere. "You know I don't like you calling me that. 'Tycho,' or 'Maas,' or 'boss,' or anything like that, but none of this 'sir' hoohah. I won't stand for it."

The sphere Halley chimed again, and did a little rotation and dip, a mechanical pirouette.

"As you wish, Sir Boss," Halley sang.

Tycho swore again, and took a swing at the sphere.

Roxanne could tell this was a dance the two had done for long years, and both seemed to know the steps by heart. So caught up in it were the two that they seemed almost to have forgotten Roxanne's presence.

Roxanne cleared her throat.

The sphere Halley stopped its little spins, and Tycho his swings, and both turned their attentions back to Roxanne.

"Now, then," Tycho said, approaching with a slight hint of menace. "Suppose you tell us your business here, ma'am, before I loose my familiar here at you."

Roxanne smiled again, and shook her head.

"While I've no doubt that your drone could do some considerable harm if it desired," Roxanne said, "I do doubt your willingness to allow it. And I'm afraid that we've little time to put the question to the test."

"Oh, do we now?" Tycho said, crossing his arms over his chest. "And why would that be?"

"Because the next players are about to take the stage," Roxanne said.

There came the sounds of a muffled explosion from the far side of the garden, and a hole roughly eight feet across appeared in the wall itself. As the dust and smoke cleared, a fine sprinkling of debris raining to the ground, two figures appeared in the breach.

"Stop, in the name of the Chrono Defense Corps!" shouted the man in the tight-fitting gray bodysuit. Both he and the similarly dressed woman at his side pointed sleek silvery pistols in their direction, eyes narrowed. "You're under arrest for temporal malfeasance."

Tycho Maas handled the intrusion with more grace than Roxanne would have given him credit for. With two strangers training odd-looking firearms at him, he calmly shot his cuffs, straightened his hat, and tucked his thumbs behind his suspenders.

"Now, honestly," he said casually, "was all that hubbub really necessary? Do you know how much that wall cost me?"

The two gray-suited figures didn't move, staring at him stone-faced, their pistols trained.

"Your wit is wasted on this lot, I'm afraid," Roxanne said, crossing one leg over the other. "You'll not find a more humorless bunch than these trumped-up time-cops, though they're more or less harmless."

"All of you, stay where you are," the woman in the gray bodysuit yelled, slowly edging forward. "With your hands where we can see them."

"Point of order," sang the sphere Halley. "While I have suspensor fields capable of dextrous manipulation, my peripherals do not include 'hands' in the literal sense."

"Suspect Maas," shouted the man, coming up beside the woman, "you will instruct your drone to be silent, or we will melt it into slag on the spot."

Tycho turned to the floating sphere, and waved it back with a distracted gesture.

"Halley, do listen to the nice gentleman and keep quiet, won't you?" Tycho said. "We wouldn't want to upset our guests, now would we?"

"Suspect Maas," the woman said, her aim never wavering, "I am Operative Brende Forzane of the Chrono Defense Corps, and this is my partner Anson Lanning. You are under suspicion of six counts of temporal malfeasance, three counts of misappropriation of Corps materiel, and the murder of CDC Operative Clarence Leiber in Hartford, Connecticut, thirty-first December, 3276 CE. Should you surrender without incident—to be transported to the nearest CDC way station for holding, questioning, and trial—your cooperation will be duly noted."

"Just try something, corps-killer," the man called Lanning snarled, his grip tightening on the pistol. "I'm begging you."

"Stand down, Anson," Operative Forzane said. "We'll do this by the book, but he'll still hang for his crimes."

"Now hold on there, missy," Tycho said, holding his hands up in a reassuring gesture. "I don't doubt that I've done all manner of malfeasance and misappropriating and whatnot in my time, but I've never been a killer. Clarence Leiber died that night, I'll grant you, God rest his soul, but I wasn't the cause of it."

"Do you deny possession of Operative Leiber's effects, including restricted weaponry and material-synthesizer technology?" Operative Forzane asked sharply.

"Oh, well, if you mean that shiny doodad of a pistol, and the matter printer . . ." Tycho took a long pause, considering his answer. "Well, then no, I don't suppose I'd deny possession. But I didn't kill him."

"And do you claim not to have extracted from Leiber the location of and operating instructions for the Eternity Chamber, and then made illicit personal use of the Chamber's capabilities?" Operative Lanning barked.

"Well, if you mean that dismal little cave down Antarctica way, with all the shiny doors, then no, I don't suppose I deny that either," Tycho answered. "But I still didn't kill him."

"I don't think they believe you, Tycho," Roxanne said, brushing dust from her knee.

"You," Operative Forzane said. "State your name and your association with Suspect Maas."

"Oh, we've only just met, I'm afraid," Roxanne answered casually. "But I have followed his career with interest for some time now."

Operative Lanning's eyes narrowed, and then a shock of recognition flashed across his face.

"Shit," he said, edging closer to his partner. "Brende, that's *her!*"

"Her who?" Operative Forzane asked, glancing over at Roxanne.

"Don't you remember all the briefings?" Operative Lanning said. "The postings? Temporal Enemy Number One?"

Operative Forzane glanced at her partner, and then back at Roxanne, her manner beginning in casual disbelief, moving quickly through shock, then something approaching terror.

"Her?" Operative Forzane said casually. "*Her?*" she repeated, surprised. "Oh, shit," she went on, blanched, "it *is* her. The Bonaventure."

"Temporal Enemy Number One," Operative Lanning repeated, his voice low.

Tycho turned and looked at Roxanne with new respect.

"Well, I don't know what the hell those two yahoos are talking about," Tycho said, "but you certainly seem to have them in a tizzy."

"It's nice to be remembered, I suppose," Roxanne said casually.

The two CDC operatives had edged toward one another, a defensive huddling instinct, and now stood almost shoulder to shoulder, their pistols pointed now at Roxanne, now at Tycho, and back again, shifting nervously.

"What's your interest in this matter, Criminal Bonaventure?" Operative Forzane said with false bravado.

"Well now, here I am just a measly 'suspect' under suspicion of murder and all," Tycho said, strolling to sit on the bench next to Roxanne, his hands on his knees, "and here you are a full-blown 'criminal.' How'd you manage that?"

"Criminal Bonaventure was tried in absentia for her crimes against the natural temporal order, and found guilty on all counts by the CDC Central Command," Operative Lanning explained, his eyes narrowed on Roxanne, but his voice quavering slightly.

"Standing CDC Directive One instructs all field agents to keep constant vigilance against the Bonaventure," Operative Forzane added.

"You really shouldn't go to all that trouble," Roxanne said sweetly. "Now, I wouldn't want your opinion of me to influence your dealings with Mr. Maas in any way, but I can tell you that he's telling the truth about the death of Clarence Leiber. I looked into it, and Leiber's death was in no way Tycho's fault."

Tycho beamed.

"Thank you kindly, ma'am," he said, tipping his hat. "I do hope you'll forgive my truly unkind comments about your person on our first meeting."

"Don't give it another thought," Roxanne answered with a smile.

"What do you think, Brende?" Operative Lanning said out of the corner of his mouth, eyeing Roxanne and Tycho anxiously.

"We need backup," Operative Forzane whispered back, "but the nearest available personnel are halfway across Europe."

Any further debate was interrupted by the sound of shattering glass.

Everyone—the two gray-suited operatives, the sphere Halley, Tycho, and Roxanne—looked in the direction of the noise.

"Right on time," Roxanne said. "The next set of players enter."

The back gallery doors of Tycho's palatial house had been smashed open from the inside, and two sinister figures now rushed out, aiming ominous-looking rifles.

"Tempus Agency," one of the newcomers said calmly, flashing a gold badge in a leather wallet, his rifle still aimed and ready. "This is a raid. Nobody moves, nobody gets hurt."

A man and a woman, the two new arrivals were dressed in period costume, appropriate for the early-twentieth-century London streets beyond the garden walls. Less appropriate, perhaps, were the strange, sinewy rifles they carried, which seemed the product of another millennium entirely.

"My name is Farid Taffesse, and this is my associate Bethel Razin," the man explained calmly. "If everyone can just keep their heads, I think that we can all be friends and play nice."

Lanning and Forzane had spun around, and aimed their pistols at the two newcomers, who had their own weapons aimed right back at the CDC operatives.

"Who the devil are you?" Operative Lanning snarled, bewildered.

"Taffesse and I are agents of Tempus," the woman called Razin answered, her finger curled tightly around the rifle's firing mechanism. "Agency brass dispatched us from up the time-stream to investigate anachronistic technological developments in this era, and our inquiries led us here."

"Now, I don't know how any of you jokers got through Tipler Cylinder One without alerting any of our monitoring stations," the man called Taffesse went on, "and, frankly, I don't care. There's been a steady stream of international patents filed over the course of the last two decades by the Perihelion, Unlimited Corporation, all of which historical records show weren't due to be invented for decades, even centuries to come. Our inquiries have established that Perihelion is wholly owned by one Tycho Maas, for whom no records exist prior to 1889. Now, which one of you is Maas?"

Everyone, Roxanne included, looked to Tycho.

"Now, this is all a mite perplexing, isn't it?" Tycho said evenly.

Razin kept moving her rifle's aim between Operatives Lanning and Forzane, but Taffesse trained his on Tycho.

"Hold on a minute," Operative Forzane said, stepping between Taffesse and Tycho, her pistol aimed at the Tempus Agent. "Both Suspect Maas and Criminal Bonaventure are in the custody of the Chrono Defense Corps. I insist that you drop your weapons and explain yourselves."

Taffesse smiled and narrowed his eyes.

"Lady, not only do I not know what the hell a Chrono Defense Corps is, at the moment I could care less," Taffesse said. "So far as I'm concerned, you're all implicated in these anachronisms, and you're *all* going to come with us to our jump-ship, to return to the 30C to stand trial."

"Did you say . . . Bonaventure?" Taffesse's associate Razin said in a thickly accented voice.

"What, Razin?" Taffesse asked, glancing over at his associate. "What is it?"

Razin didn't answer a long moment, looking hard at Roxanne.

"The Parachronist," Razin said, her voice hardened.

"You think?" Taffesse said, and took a long look at Roxanne himself. He brightened, smiling broadly. "Well, I'll be damned. Lady," he said to Roxanne, "Tempus brass has a rap sheet on you as long as a mammoth's trunk. Razin and I are going to get ourselves kicked up in rank a few notches for bringing you in, I'll guarantee."

"I don't think so, I'm afraid," Roxanne said, shaking her head in mock sadness. "None of us are going anywhere just yet."

"And why is that?" Operative Lanning asked.

"Because the final players have not yet taken the stage," Roxanne said simply.

There was a strange, humming noise, and the air between the two Tempus agents on the one side and the two CDC operatives on the other began to shimmer, like a mirage.

"Here they come now," Roxanne said, and climbed to her feet.

Both pairs of armed officers backed away from the strange mix of lights and colors bleeding into the empty air. The humming sound grew louder, increasing in pitch.

"Sir," the sphere Halley said, floating to Tycho, wavering up and down unsteadily, "I'm receiving some strange interference with my suspensor arrays."

"Are you, now?" Tycho asked distractedly, looking with amazement at the strange apparition before him.

Suddenly, there was a flash of light, and the shimmering was gone. In its place stood three figures, two men and a woman, who looked like they were dressed in starlight.

"Tycho Maas," said one of the two men in dulcet tones. "Your posterity brings you greetings."

"Now who are *these* guys?" Officer Lanning shouted, rolling his eyes in frustration.

The three newcomers were dressed head to toes in shimmering, formfitting fabric that shifted in coloration with each passing second. As they moved toward Tycho, ignoring the raised weapons of the various agents and operatives, it became clear that they were not standing on the ground, but rather hovering a few inches above it. They were each tall, slender, and graceful, like angels of legend.

"Tycho Maas," the floating man went on, "I am Gareth, and these are my kinsmen/lovers Irma and Rok. Collectively, we represent the

Tychonian Historical Preservation Group, and we greet you with the finest blessings of our world."

"It is our honor, Tycho Maas," the floating woman Irma said, curtsying in midair. She blinked, and Roxanne could see that her eyes were solid silver.

"Our praises to you, Tycho Maas," the floating man Rok said, with a voice that sounded like a choir of angels, like that of the spherical drone Halley.

"Okay, I've had just about enough of this," Taffesse said, pointing his rifle at the foremost of the floating Tychonians. "I want an explanation, and I want it *now*!"

The floating Gareth drifted over to Taffesse, and with long slender fingers reached out and brushed the barrel of his rifle.

"I'm afraid your weapons will no longer function," Gareth said apologetically.

"Nor will yours," Irma said, drifting towards Operatives Lanning and Forzane.

"We could not allow any harm to come to Tycho Maas," Rok sang in his chorus voice. "His existence is too vital."

As Irma drifted nearer the two CDC operatives, Lanning lost his composure entirely.

"Let 'em have it, Brende!" he shouted, and, toggling his pistol to auto-fire, squeezed the trigger.

Nothing happened.

"What the goddamned piss hell is going on here?!" Taffesse shouted, red-faced and approaching incoherence.

"That's quite enough histrionics for one day, I think," Roxanne said, walking forward. "I think if we give Mr. Maas a chance to explain himself, then a great many things will become clear." She turned, and took a very confused Tycho by the arm.

"Erm, that is, what precisely is it that I'm to explain?" Tycho asked Roxanne.

"Why don't you start with your meeting Clarence Leiber, and go from there."

Tycho nodded slowly, and sighed.

"Well, now," Tycho Maas began, addressing the assembled time travelers. "I never had what you might call good fortune. In fact, if not for the generous helpings of bad luck the gods saw fit to drop on me, I wouldn't have had any luck at all. So when I met Clarence Leiber in that Hartford bar, I recognized a kindred spirit.

"Clarence was already well in his cups, and I was catching up close behind, so when he started telling me how he wasn't really from the thirty-third century at all, but had been recruited in the twenty-fourth by some time-police outfit, I thought it was just the drink talking. But then he showed me a matter printer no bigger than one of this era's family Bibles. And it worked—that was the amazing thing. Now, in the thirty-third, we had material-fabrication units that could spit out anything you wanted, from a gold watch to a new pair of shoes to a replacement widget for your hover-car. You just dropped in the raw undifferentiated material at one end, and out came your products from the other. But the smallest fabricator I'd ever seen was at least twenty feet square, and weighed a ton. This thing of Clarence's could do the same job, printing out bits of your product one at a time, that would adhere if you touched them together as strong as if they'd been made out of one piece of tempered steel. And it was portable, and would run forever without servicing.

"He showed me his weapon, an emp-gun, he called it. A short-range EMP generator, it was capable of shorting out any electrical system, even the electrochemical process of the human brain. This thing could stop a clock, and stun a human without any permanent damage.

"Then he pulled this little brass ball out of his pocket, and the damned thing started floating around. It was a drone, with a weakly superintelligent AI that he called Halley, after the comet. Halley had a full array of suspensor fields, and was a surprisingly good conversationalist.

"Well, I said to Clarence, how did he expect me to believe he was from the twenty-fourth if he had all this gear that we hadn't dreamt of in the thirty-third. And then Clarence told me all about this room, buried under the ice in the Antarctic, full of doors into time. About how he'd traveled up and down the time-stream for millennia in either direction, and how it was all the same. Great gadgets, great food, even a great job with these time-cops, but at the end of the day, no matter what city or century he was in, Clarence always went home alone.

"Well, God rest his soul, I could tell he was a loser right away. But he seemed a decent-enough loser, so I went on helping him drink his sorrow away.

"Last call is at five in the morning in thirty-third-century Hartford, so when the bar closed up there wasn't much of anywhere for me and Clarence to go. I myself wandered off a ways, if you'll excuse the indelicacy, to relieve myself against the building, while Clarence ran out into the motorway to hail a cab. Ran out into the motorway, and smack into the path of an oncoming hoverfreighter. Well, that was it for poor Clarence. So as the freighter driver was calling up the authorities, I rushed to Clarence's side.

"He was a goner, we both knew, but he had a few breaths left in him yet.

"'Tycho,' he said to me, 'Tycho, you're the only thing like a friend I've got in this era.'

"Which, when I thought about it, was a sad statement indeed, as we'd just met hours before, but drinks tend to bring out the camaraderie in the forlorn, so I let his statement stand.

"'Tycho, my friend,' Clarence said, 'you've got to take my emp-gun, and my printer, and Halley. The authorities can't find this tech, or it might do irreparable harm to the time-stream. Just hide it away where no one can find it, and everything will be fine.'

"And then he died.

"Well, I wasn't about to let my good friend Clarence down. I took his gun, his little printer, and Halley, and got out of there quick.

"I'd like to tell you that I did what Clarence asked, and hid his effects away, so no one could find them. But I can't. I'd spent my whole life at the bottom rungs of the ladder, never able to get ahead, never able to make a buck. And now here this angel Clarence had dropped deliverance in my lap. I could sell his gadgets off as my own inventions, and make a bundle.

"But then it hit me. Why sell the matter printer once, when I could go somewhere else and sell the fabricated products instead? Then I'd just be printing money. Or why couldn't I just print *money*? Now, as I've said, in the thirty-third we had matter fabricators, and while a pint-sized version might make some headlines and get me a couple of fat payouts, it wouldn't be an endless gravy train. But if I were to travel back to some earlier period in history, before anyone had even heard of matter fabrication, then I could literally print money, or gold, or diamonds, or whatever I might want. I could live like a king, and no one would ever be the wiser.

"So I rented a personal flier with the last of my bank account, packed up some provisions, period costumes, and Clarence's effects, and flew down to the Antarctic. I found that buried room Clarence had talked about, but couldn't figure which door went where. I decided to gamble, hopped through one of the doors, and stepped through into the year 1889.

"Of course, I didn't know it was 1889, not just yet. First I had to get back to civilization. Halley turned out to be an even greater asset than I'd thought, as his suspensor fields were enough to carry both him and me across the Antarctic ice, across the freezing Atlantic reaches, up into South America. We finally made it to Brazil.

"Now, I'm Connecticut born and bred, but I knew that I couldn't pass for a native. I just didn't know enough about current events, and my accent was too far removed after a dozen centuries of linguistic drift. But I didn't much care for the idea of learning a whole new language, either. So I decided on London, which as near as I could make out, was the commercial capital of the era. I printed up some local Brazilian currency, bought passage on a ship, and wound up here in London."

"But that's not the end of it, is it, Tycho?" Roxanne said.

Tycho shook his head, his eyes on hers.

The operatives and agents were looking on, their eyes narrowed and suspicious, while the Tychonian angels watched beatifically.

"First you had to establish some sort of identity in the era," Roxanne said, "but not knowing enough about Hartford or Connecticut or even America of this period, you couldn't create a convincing history for yourself. So you borrowed someone else's. The only Hartford resident you could remember from this period. A celebrated author who'd written and said enough that you could quote him for years without ever repeating a phrase. You borrowed his signature dress, his manner of speech, and his deportment, and then Tycho Maas, thirty-third-century loser, became Tycho Maas, nineteenth-century Connecticut Yankee and bon vivant."

"Well, yes, ma'am," Tycho said, hanging his head, "I suppose that's true."

"And after printing up enough money to buy a house, and a staff, and enough luxuries to last a lifetime, you decided it wasn't enough," Roxanne went on.

Tycho nodded slowly.

"You went into business, setting up your own company, Perihelion, Unlimited," Roxanne said, "using the matter printer to fabricate prototypes of inventions that wouldn't otherwise be introduced for decades or centuries. By the turn of the century, Perihelion was one of the largest and most powerful corporations in the world."

Tycho nodded again.

"But still your products weren't selling enough for your tastes, with all of England, America, and half of Europe already buying," Roxanne said. "You realized that those who weren't buying your products typically couldn't afford to buy anything. In order to expand your market, you had to expand your customer base. So you helped finance Parliament members who voted for legislation that was good for business. Children's Acts, to get children out of factories and lined up for your new cinema theaters, pennies in hand. Shorter working days for miners, so they'd be free at night to drink in your pubs. Secondary education to increase literacy, so that more customers could read your advertisements, and recognize your brand names."

Tycho sighed guiltily.

"But it didn't stop there," Roxanne went on, a sly grin on her face. "You wanted to expand your markets overseas, into Europe and Asia and beyond. So you foot the bill for any government official willing to look for alternatives to warfare and armed conflict. You bought politicians in Europe, America, Germany, France, Russia. You had influence over czars, presidents, kings, and popes. All for the sake of your own profit, your own selfish ends."

Tycho hung his head even lower, and wiped at his eyes.

"Yes, yes," he said, anguished. "It's all true. I betrayed a dying man's trust, and exploited the poor primitive people of this era, all for my own ill-gotten gain."

Roxanne couldn't help herself, and started to laugh.

The CDC operatives and the Tempus agents were at their wits' end. Having heard the full recitation of Tycho's crimes, many of which they'd only suspected, they now wanted blood.

"He's polluted the time-stream," Operative Lanning said, stabbing a finger at Tycho.

"God only knows what damage he's done," Farid Taffesse snarled, aghast.

"It will take years to try to undo the damage," Operative Forzane said. "For all we know these Tempus idiots are from a rogue time-stream that Maas's actions spawned into being."

"You lot are from the rogue time-stream," Bethel Razin sneered, "and we'll prune it off at the source."

"Can I offer anyone a refreshment?" asked the spherical Halley, still unsettled after the Tychonians' dramatic appearance.

The Tychonians stood by serenely.

"Oh, you people miss the forest for the leaves, not even noticing the trees," Roxanne said, laughing. "You're all from alternate world-lines, branching off from this period in history, but you miss the essential point. Separate intent from results for a moment, if your minds are capable, and try to realize what's happened here. Tycho Maas, for purely selfish reasons, has been a greater force for positive social change in this era than any single figure in history."

The agents and the operatives looked at her, angry and confused.

"Without intending to do so," Roxanne went on, "Tycho has improved the general welfare of the average citizen in over half of the civilized countries on the globe. Literacy rates have soared, infant mortality and crime are down, and international tensions are at the lowest point in centuries. The First World War, which was to have begun just a few short years from now, will be delayed a full decade due to his efforts. And when that war is done, there will be no Second World War to follow, if Tycho is left in this era, as he will spearhead efforts to rebuild all of Europe, and modernize Asia, to increase his company's consumer base."

Officer Forzane stiffened.

"But this time-stream is an aberration that threatens all of future history," she snapped.

"Oh, grow up," Roxanne said. "Tycho's done nothing but create one more worldline, which does nothing to threaten your own. It's only because you've both arrived at this common point in your shared histories"—she pointed at the CDC operatives and the Tempus agents —"that you could even travel here. Whether Tycho goes or stays, your histories will continue unaffected."

Roxanne turned, and waved her hand at the Tychonian Historical Preservation Group.

"If Tycho goes, however," Roxanne went on, "*their* worldline will not come into existence. The Tychonian era, which begins in the late twentieth century in this worldline and continues for millennia, is one of the few, true Utopias I have ever encountered in all the worlds of the Myriad. The social reforms and technological innovations introduced by Tycho, out of context and centuries before their proper time in history, engendered faster and farther-reaching improvements in human civilization than in any other period, before or since."

"Their civilization is a Type Omega culture on the Barrow scale," Roxanne explained, "able to harness the fabric of space-time itself, able to travel instantaneously to any point in space or time. Their citizenry is a mix of organic humans"—she pointed to Gareth—"enhanced humans"—she pointed to Irma with the silver eyes—"artificially intelligent software and hardware"—she pointed to the angelic-voiced Rok—"and every possible combination in-between. The Tychonian civilization flourishes as a direct result of the decades Tycho Maas spent in the late nineteenth and early twentieth centuries."

She turned to Tycho, who stood openmouthed, with the sphere Halley hovering right beside him.

"Tycho Maas, these are your children," Roxanne said, her arm spread to the Tychonian angels. "Well, I suspect Rok is more the child of Halley, but he is still the result of your efforts in a general sense."

Tycho opened and closed his mouth, unable to speak.

"I . . . I don't know what to say," Tycho answered.

"I wouldn't either, in your position." Roxanne laughed. "Though you are ultimately a small, selfish, and self-involved little man, however charming, you have inadvertently given rise to the marvel of the ages. The highest peak of human development, a high watermark for the species, and the closest to perfection the Earth will ever know."

The agents and operatives were still aghast and bewildered. They tightened their grips on their weapons, as though willing them to work again.

"It is all as she says," Gareth said.

"Ours is a near-perfect world," Irma added.

"And always improving," Rok sang.

Taffesse snapped.

"If you think I'm going to entrust the welfare of all future generations to a thief, on the word of the greatest threat the time-stream has ever known," he shouted, "you've got another think coming."

"Oh, enough," Roxanne said.

Two temporal bridges opened up, one on either side of the garden. They hung in midair, mirrored windows into other worlds.

"Halley, if you would be so kind?" Roxanne said. "Those two into that hole, and those two into the other?" Roxanne pointed at the CDC operatives and one bridge, and the Tempus agents and the other.

"With pleasure, mistress," Halley sang, and scooped the agents and operatives up in his suspensor fields, and shoved them towards the bridges.

Screaming their defiance all the way, as soon as they came into contact with the bridges, they disappeared from sight, followed soon after by the bridges themselves.

"Where have you sent them?" Tycho asked, wide-eyed, trying to take it all in.

"Oh, I've just sent them to their homes," Roxanne said with a sigh. "Once upon a time I might have done something a bit more dramatic, but I'm an old woman now, and I suppose I always want the best for people, even if they don't deserve it."

Tycho looked at the three beatific Tychonians, and then back to Roxanne.

"What's to become of me?" Tycho said, addressing Roxanne and the Tychonians both.

"It makes no difference to me," Roxanne answered, smiling. "Do whatever suits you."

Gareth raised a slender finger.

"If I might suggest," he said in his honeyed tones, "my kinsmen/lovers and I, in our capacity as the Tychonian Historical Preservation Group, had hoped that you might visit our world with us, if briefly."

"We want to show you the wonders you have brought us," Irma added.

"And the wonders still to come," Rok sang.

Tycho, whose eyes had begun to mist, looked back to Roxanne.

"Is it allowed?" he asked in a small voice. "Can I see it for myself?"

"It is entirely up to you," Roxanne answered with a smile. "But I would recommend returning here eventually, as you have more work yet to do."

Tycho broke into a broad grin, and bustling forward caught Roxanne in a hug.

Roxanne smiled awkwardly, uncomfortable with the contact, but understanding Tycho's reasons.

"Thank you, my good lady," Tycho said, now crying openly. "I'd never thought anything like this possible."

Roxanne gently broke from his embrace, and smiled warmly.

"No one of any substance ever does," she said. She opened a temporal bridge to take her home, leaving Tycho Maas, his angelic children, and the floating sphere Halley alone in the garden.

Extract from Roxanne's Memoirs

I feel that I am rapidly approaching the end of my long life, and now, just days short of my ninetieth birthday, I pause to reflect.

I have seen things, and visited places, and met individuals, that no one else in all the worlds of the Myriad ever has.

I have seen the beginnings of life on Earth, and the countless ways in which it might end.

I have unlocked the secrets of existence, and solved the riddles of the ages.

I have walked with poets, and kings, and messiahs, and killers, and saints, and known each as an individual, and not merely a collection of quotations.

I have seen worlds ruled by sentient dinosaurs, and worlds peopled by talking mice, and worlds dominated by winged humanoids who blot out the sky in their millions.

I have witnessed the birth and death of great dynasties, and seen the cherished moments of history's anonymous multitudes.

I have explored the limits between fact and fiction, and tested the boundaries between fantasy and reality.

And yet, at the end of it all, I have no one with whom to share it. No one but the Sofia, who is always at my side, singing to me in my sleep. But where she came from, I have never learned.

CHAPTER 15

THE END

LONDINIUM, 220
SUBJECTIVE AGE: 100 YEARS OLD

"I'm so very tired, Sofie," Roxanne Bonaventure thought, bringing the yarrow flowers she'd picked close to her nose. She could smell so little, these past years, and missed it. "I just want to stop."

Roxanne, bent with age, her hundredth subjective birthday only a few days away, shuffled slowly through the flower-dappled meadow south of the Roman fortifications, on the site where her Bayswater house would be erected some sixteen centuries hence. Lonely and alone, with only the Sofia for company, she'd traveled back along her worldline to this more tranquil spot to warm her weary bones, the London winter of the late twenty-first century proving too much for her fragile constitution.

I am always with you, came the Sofia's answer in her mind. *Instruct me.*

Roxanne smiled, her wrinkled and spotted skin shifting over the visible bones of her skull, her eyes twinkling but damp. All this time, all these years, only the Sofia had always been at her side, always there in her mind.

Her hearing had begun to fade long before her sense of smell, so it was some time before Roxanne heard the approaching sounds of heavy footfalls, and the shouting of coarse voices. When she did, finally, the men were almost upon her, stopping just a few dozen yards away.

"Good morning," Roxanne said casually, her hand holding the yarrow blooms clutched close to her chest. She turned, and saw a half dozen armed and armored Roman soldiers, ragged and rough-looking. Some brandished swords, some daggers, and a pair of them carried drawn bows, arrows already notched.

"I told you I'd seen her appear, Septimus," one of the men told another, in rough-hewn Latin. Roxanne smiled, incongruously, pleased to find that she hadn't lost her ear for the language.

"She's a Briton witch," said another, tightening his grip on the sword in his hand. "Come to ensorcell us."

Roxanne shook her head, chuckling a dry, rasping laugh.

"Not Briton, exactly," she said, in the best Latin she could manage, "and hardly a witch." She winked at the men, smiling wider.

"She's fixing her evil eye on you, Septimus," the first man shouted, looking away, horrified. "You must stop her."

The man in the lead—Septimus, she presumed—the obvious leader of the men, shielded his eye with the back of a callused hand.

"Archers!" he shouted. "Fire!"

"Wait—" was all that Roxanne managed to say, and in English at that, before the Roman arrow pierced her side.

Reflexively, Roxanne instructed the Sofia to open a bridge back to her home at Bark Place, in the late twenty-first century, and fell into and through the temporal bridge before another of the Romans could act.

Lying on the hardwood floor of her bedroom, blood pooling on the antique rug below her, Roxanne managed to pull the arrow from her side before losing consciousness.

Why? she thought weakly, before blackness overcame her. *Why, Sofie?*

You instruct me, the Sofia answered, perhaps with a trace of tenderness. *You said you wanted to stop.*

Since the age of seventeen, when she'd first learned of the Sofia's true nature, Roxanne had felt more or less invulnerable, though she'd been under the protection of its crystalline intelligence unknowingly since just after her eleventh birthday.

In addition to opening doors to different points along a worldline, bridges in space and time, and cataloguing and storing information about every instant in space and time it encountered, the Sofia also steered through the countless worlds of the Myriad, at every instant, without any conscious thought from Roxanne. At every point, every instant of the constantly moving Now, from the near-countless worlds branching off from the current moment, the Sofia selected one in which the host Roxanne came to no harm.

If an attacker were to try to shoot Roxanne, the Sofia would simply steer instant by instant, segments of time too short to be measured, to a worldline in which the gun backfired, or the shot went wide of the mark, or something else came in the path of the bullet—any probable outcome that would leave Roxanne unscathed.

The only way, in fact, that Roxanne could ever be injured, she'd learned at an early age, was if she were to inform the Sofia to let it happen. And why, she'd thought with the wisdom of a seventeen-year-old, would she ever want that?

Roxanne drifted in and out of consciousness, over the course of what must have been a few minutes but felt to her like additional centuries wearing down on her. The gored Roman arrow lay on the floor a few inches from her pale, bony fingers, the blood seeping from her side staining the surrounding floor in an ever-widening pool.

If she could stay awake long enough, Roxanne knew, she could instruct the Sofia to open a bridge to the hospital. Or she could drag herself across the bloodstained floor to the phone and call for help. But she didn't.

The Sofia, Roxanne realized, had read her intentions correctly, though she'd never have been able to admit them to herself. She was old, she was tired, and she just wanted to stop. Whether this way, or any other, Roxanne found she didn't really care.

There were two things she had to do before stopping altogether, though—two places to visit, two people to see. She'd worked it out, years before, the mysteries and the secrets of her life slowly coming together in their puzzle shapes with age, but Roxanne had been sure there would always be time. She'd lived her life as the mistress of time, invulnerable and untouchable, and just knew that there would always be another day ahead, another year to explore, before she'd have to make that final trip. But she had been wrong. There were no more days ahead. This was the last.

Pushing herself up on shaky arms into a sitting position, pressing her hands to her side to stanch the flow of blood, Roxanne whispered to the Sofia to open a temporal-spatial bridge to northern California, some eighty-nine years before. The mirrored sphere appeared just before her, and with red-stained fingers she reached out to touch the surface.

The girl was so much younger than she remembered, and so much smaller. Delicate, tender hands reaching out to brush the chalk-white hair from Roxanne's wearied face. This couldn't possibly be the one, Roxanne knew. The Sofia had brought her to the wrong place, and the wrong time.

The girl asked what she could do to help. There was only one thing, but Roxanne couldn't bring herself to say it yet. She had to be sure.

"What is your name, child?" Roxanne asked, straining to make herself heard, blocking out the pain radiating from her side to the tips of her fingers and toes.

"Rox-roxanne," the girl answered nervously, her voice breaking. "Roxanne Bonaventure."

Roxanne smiled, and reached up a bony hand covered in skin the thickness of brittle paper to brush the girl's cheek.

"Roxanne," Roxanne repeated, unable to nod. She tried for a smile, but her muscles weren't quite equal to the task. "I have a question for you."

The Sofia had informed her, years ago, when first she'd learned to hear the voice of its crystalline intelligence, that when first placed on her arm it was bound to the very substance of Roxanne's being. It had become a part of her, inextricably woven into the fiber of her body and life. It could be removed, the Sofia insisted, but once.

The Sofia snapped closed on the wrist of the younger Roxanne, closing the loop of its existence. The young girl looked from the bracelet to the older Roxanne and back, her face a riot of fear, excitement, and amazement.

The young girl opened her mouth as though to speak, but the older Roxanne wouldn't have it.

"The Sofia will have the answers you need, when you know the questions to ask," she explained to her younger self. "It will be years yet to come, but it will all make sense in time."

"But . . ." the girl sputtered. "I don't . . ."

"Shh," Roxanne shushed, and reached out to touch the face of the Sofia's crystalline intelligence. "There's no time now." The ancient

Roxanne paused for a moment, and couldn't help but laugh—a sick, rattling sound that shook her body from the lungs out.

Through their last, lingering contact, the elder Roxanne and the voice of the Sofia spoke one last time. There was a final door Roxanne needed opened, a final mystery to solve. She had just enough strength, she hoped, to see it through to the very end.

Sofie, she said in her thoughts. The jewel on the bracelet, shrunk perfectly to fit the wrist of the young girl, was warm to her touch. *I need to go to the end.*

I was always with you, from the beginning, came the voice of the Sofia in her mind. *Instruct me.*

There was a strange sensation that ran like electricity over Roxanne's wrinkled skin, something she hadn't felt since her father had died, decades before. It felt like good-bye.

"All right," the ancient Roxanne said, her voice cracking. "It's time."

In response, the Sofia snared a wormhole from the quantum foam a few inches to Roxanne's side.

Good-bye, came the voice of the Sofia, whispering in her thoughts before she broke physical contact.

Roxanne smiled, a tired old-woman smile, and fell into the bridge, leaving the Sofia and the young Roxanne bound together in the woods, alone.

Roxanne opened her eyes, her lifeblood spilling onto the dusty ground even faster than before, and looked up at twin moons set on a purple sky.

Just before blackness overtook her again, she managed to eke out a few words.

"Come on, then," she said. "I haven't come all this way for nothing. . . ."

∞

Roxanne's eyes fluttered open, weak, and she saw the man in the shapeless hat and improbable scarf standing over her.

"It's about time," she meant to say, but the words came out only as a dry croak.

The man, his eyes expressionless over the fabric of the scarf, knelt down, reaching a hand out to her crimson-stained side.

As the fingers of the man's hand came within inches of her flesh, they seemed to twist at an impossible angle, and disappear from view. Roxanne felt something cold, like pinpricks, and a strange shifting sensation in her side. While the man knelt close, his arm ending in a bare wrist a hair's breadth from her abdomen, Roxanne felt the skin and viscera of her belly knit and heal.

"Well," Roxanne tried to say but couldn't, "I wasn't expecting that."

The pain of it too much for her, she slipped from consciousness again, eyes closing on the purple skies above.

When her eyes opened again, she was stronger, more alert, feeling more alive than she had in years. The fabric of her ruined shirt still stuck to her flesh with a thick glue of clotted blood, but the skin beneath was smooth and unmarred. Roxanne found that she had the strength to sit up.

The man stood over her now, expressionless and strange, waiting for her to speak.

"I didn't come here for a handout," Roxanne said, sensing an inadvertent pun in her words, "but I thank you all the same."

The man was silent and still.

"I want to see your bosses," Roxanne said, propping herself up on suddenly strong arms and fixing the man with a stare. "Whistle them down from hyperspace, will you?"

The man looked at her, the hint of some surprise in his expressionless eyes. He didn't speak, but reached up a bone-white hand to his head, removing the hat and wig and tossing them to the dust at his feet. His scalp was smooth and unmarred. Next he unraveled the long scarf, letting it flutter to the ground, and shrugged out of the topcoat, shirt, and pants.

He stood before her, naked and disclosed, and Roxanne at last understood.

His face, below the hooked nose, was featureless and unmarked, smooth alabaster skin covering an expanse of flesh that stretched down to his chest. He had no mouth, and no chin. His body, Roxanne could see now that it was exposed to view, was not that of a man, but of a rough approximation of a man. A manlike shape that could pass, disguised, for the real thing, but would not hold up under close scrutiny. There were no rib bones visible at his sides, no obvious joints at shoulder, elbows, or knees, the space between his legs smooth and uninterrupted.

As Roxanne watched, the man-thing seemed to retreat and approach at the same time, moving in ways that hurt her eyes and made her head swim. An arm shape dwindled from view, disappearing entirely, a strange globular shape floating detached from the body mass taking its place only an instant later. The man-thing melted and shifted, a kaleidoscope of flesh and bone, quartz-glass and steel, flowing up together into a perfect sphere, hovering a few feet from the ground over Roxanne's head.

"There you are," Roxanne said, smiling.

"WELCOME BACK," the sphere buzzed, dipping down almost within her reach.

"I should have guessed your agent was one of you," Roxanne said, shaking her head and chiding herself. "That was the one thing I hadn't considered."

"WHY HAVE YOU COME, SEPARATED FROM YOUR RING?" the sphere asked, suggesting sympathy.

"I'm at the end of my days, and I thought I'd finally come here to the end of time to learn the truth," Roxanne answered, reaching out a gnarled hand to brush against the surface of the floating shape. It was warm to the touch, and tingling.

"THE TRUTH," the shape buzzed. "WHAT IS THE TRUTH?"

"You can't be from around here," Roxanne answered. "I figured that out years after our last little visit. I thought and thought about it, and the way your man dragged me across space and time was flatly impossible. As near as I've been able to work out, you simply plucked me out of space-time altogether, moved me through hyperspace, and reinserted me at another point on the hypersurface of the universe. The Sofia may be able to bend the laws of physics, but what you did broke them outright. Either everything I and scientists on countless worlds of the Myriad believed to be true about the universe was wrong, or else you were something else entirely."

The sphere hovered, silent.

"You're not from around here, are you?" Roxanne asked again. "You're from some higher-dimensional space."

The sphere buzzed, suggesting something approaching laughter.

"I knew you would be the one to come," the sphere said, and began to shift and flow, as the man-thing had before.

The shape kept changing, slowly at first, and then with increasing speed, through a dizzying series of forms, colors, and textures. At one moment a single blob of flesh, the next it would be a constellation of bone and skin hanging in midair, the next a pair of quartz rods. Roxanne couldn't follow the progression, and with eyes watering had to look away.

"There has always and only ever been me, a Traveler," came a chorus of voices from the heart of the maelstrom of shapes. "Standing outside the curved circle of your world, I have looked in, visiting beginning and end, looking for the one who would join me as the Companion."

Roxanne shielded her eyes.

THE END | 271

"I don't understand," she said, though she had begun to suspect.

"I was like you, once—that was not a lie. A traveler through space and time in my own universe, another sphere far across hyperspace. When my own universe approached its death in heat and compression, I found a way to escape, rising above the four-dimensional limitations of space and time to grow into a being of five dimensions, able to survive in and navigate the larger world beyond."

"So you could enter the 4-D hypersphere of *my* world at any point, past and future," Roxanne said, "seeing the universe as a whole, time and past alike, from outside."

"Yes. But I found that I was lonely, in the reaches of the higher dimensions, able only to observe and record all I saw. Better, I thought, to find some companion, some other who would join me for all time. So I seeded your world with the keys to the mysteries of time and space, in the hopes that someone might discover the secrets of the higher dimensions and join me in a larger world."

"Keys?" Roxanne said, climbing to her feet unsteadily and walking into the center of the swirling mass of shapes. "I don't understand. I thought you'd just brought me here as some kind of joke, all those years ago."

"No. I left magic lying around the corners of your world. A room of doors through time hidden under your Earth's eternal ice. A spinning tunnel through time perched just beyond the gravity well of your sun. I even rained pieces of myself onto your Earth from time to time, sections of my larger self extended into your space, and would drag men along the surface of the universe's hypersphere to past and future."

"The chronium," Roxanne said, remembering, realizing finally why the crystalline shapes in the orbiting mass had seemed familiar. "The Eternity Chamber, the TC1, all of it you?" She bristled, thin hands bunching into angry fists at her side. "Some kind of elaborate joke on humanity," she snarled. "Is that it?"

"Not a joke, but a test. And an invitation. To find the way here, and uncover the secrets of the higher world. To come with me, to be my Companion and never leave my side."

Roxanne stalked away across the dusty circle of ruins, but stopped, a thought pushing its way into her mind.

"The Sofia," she said, whirling on the mass of shapes, pointing an accusing finger. "Was that another of your bloody little keys?"

"No," came the answer from the chorus of voices. "The creation of your remarkable device is a mystery even to me. I can divine its workings, and the nature of its manufacture, but I had no hand in the origins of your device."

Roxanne sighed, trying to take it all in. What surprised her most was how unfazed she was by it all, how much it came as no surprise. Had she suspected it all along, and never admitted it to herself? She felt that she should despise this strange, monstrous creature of the higher dimensions, but found that she couldn't. Instead, she felt only pity, and understanding.

"You felt alone," Roxanne said, her tone softening. "Unique in all the world."

"Yes," the mass of shapes answered.

"And did this, all of this, to find a companion." She was stating fact now, not asking a question.

"Yes," the mass of shapes replied.

"But I don't understand," Roxanne said. "Even if you could coax and lead someone like me into divining your true nature, how would that help you at all? You would still be only a momentary intrusion into the lower dimensions of a 4-D universe, alone in your larger world, right?"

"I could lift them up," the mass answered, shifting faster now, "free of the shackles of space and time, and make of them a being like myself."

"You could do that?" Roxanne asked, disbelieving.

"I have that power."

THE END | 273

Roxanne turned away, her mind racing, ancient hands clenching and unclenching at her sides. To go on existing, but always with a companion at her side. To see the mysteries of space and time from a whole new perspective, with whole new dimensions of space to explore.

To never be alone again.

Roxanne swallowed hard, and made her decision.

"I'll do it," she said, stepping forward into the midst of the constellation of mass that shifted into a final configuration and became a collection of five perfect spheres hovering around her. "I'll join you."

The process was painful, but shorter than Roxanne would have expected. Her body retained its basic form, but extended out in all directions into the fifth dimension. Her mind wavered, on the brink of insanity, but at the final instant the segmented intrusions of the Traveler looked on her and spoke with gentle tones.

"It is accomplished," he said, his voice a chorus of angels, and lifted her up out of the flow of time and space.

Roxanne, her mind adjusting to the dazzling sensations of the higher dimensions, was unsure which was the more startling: the appearance of the manifold hypersphere of her former home stretching below her, or the wonder of the Traveler seen in all his glory.

Seen whole, in all his dimensions, he was no longer the unsettling collection of shapes and globs, but was a smooth, well-formed creature with head, arms, and legs not terribly different than Roxanne's own. She regarded her own extended form, compared it with his, and marveled.

"Welcome," he said, smiling at her across the expanse of the higher dimensions. "Welcome home, my Companion."

He took her hand in his, and led her to explore the wonders of her new world.

From the reaches of the fifth dimension, the hyper-Roxanne was able to look down on the universe's curve of space and time as a whole, seeing past and future in one unending tapestry. The branches of the Myriad, which she'd followed the long days of her life, were just other threads worked into the skein, all of them visible here from above.

When she'd grown used to viewing the world in this way, and could perceive the shiftings and turnings of the world from above, the Traveler led her to a quiet corner of the universe's manifold sphere, and showed her the thread of her own life.

Other lives—other existences, of particles, people, and planets—spread out over the fabric of the hypersphere in an ever-increasing complexity. Only Roxanne's thread, singular, followed a single track. It looped back on itself, a silver thread joining beginning and end, a silver ring in the tapestry.

"It's so lonely," Roxanne said, looking at her own life. "So alone in all this splendor."

"It has the Sofia for company," the Traveler answered, placing a hand on her shoulder.

Roxanne nodded, but was unconvinced.

Time passed, immeasurable in the expanse of higher space, and Roxanne and her companion, the Traveler and his Companion together, found a kind of peace in one another's arms. No longer alone, no longer unique, each had found a perfect mate, who would never leave their side.

In time, their substances mixed, the crystalline substance of the Traveler's inner form mingling with a seed of Roxanne's own long wisdom. Though it was only partially aware, incapable of independent action, Roxanne could not help but look upon this offspring as their

THE END | 275

child, and the Traveler did not dispute it. They named this offspring after a goddess worshipped by those long dead in the world at their feet.

Not wanting their offspring to live its existence of semisentience alone, they found a place for it in the world below, a place where it would never be alone, would never want for a companion.

The Traveler constructed a home of impregnable silver for it, and Roxanne netted a fragment of cosmic string to adorn it. This done, they dipped into the flow of time, anchoring an aspect of its higher-dimensional self as an intrusion into the simpler spaces. Moving from the more complex reaches of its parents' world into the more confined space of its new home, the offspring appeared at all points along its new existence simultaneously, from beginning to end, an unbroken ring through the Myriad. From the moment the young girl first touched its smooth surface in the forest, to the instant the dying woman removed it from her arm, and then the moment of the young girl again, an eternal and endless cycle. Forever wed to its new companion, forever at home.

In the final instant, before leaving their offspring behind forever, Roxanne leaned in close, from behind the veil of the higher dimensions, and whispered to the child she had made.

"I am always with you," she said, and it was done.

Author's Notes

Stories should explain themselves. I've always felt that any story that required a foreword or afterword or appendix or glossary to be fully understood was, in some very crucial sense, unsuccessful.

I'm also someone who feels deeply cheated when a DVD doesn't include a full boat of extras, or when a trade paperback collection of a comic series doesn't include sketch pages or script excerpts.

This is a contradiction, I'll admit, but I'm large enough to contain a contradiction or two.

With that in mind, and in the fervent hope that the preceding stands on its own without a supporting scaffolding of explanations and apologia, I offer the following notes:

ON THE ORIGINS OF
HERE, THERE & EVERYWHERE

This novel had a strange and circuitous genesis.

It began life when I was part of a Texas-based writers' collective called Clockwork Storybook. Every Labor Day of the group's brief and tumultuous existence, we took part in a combination writing exercise/ publicity stunt that we called the Annual Clockwork Novel Weekend, in which we would write a complete (if short) novel over the course of seventy-two hours, posting chapters online as we went. Our small (but dedicated) group of readers could follow along as the stories progressed, interacting with us and with each other on our message boards, trying to guess where the stories were going next, catching typos, that sort of thing. We'd stolen the idea from Harlan Ellison, who did this stunt long before us, sitting in a store window and composing stories on a manual typewriter, man-uscript pages taped up one at a time to the glass. Writing as per-formance art. Writing as a dare.

(It only makes sense that a certain kind of writer would be drawn to this sort of thing. Many of us, down deep, are frustrated rock stars, or actors, or comedians, hungry for applause that we'll never hear. Turning writing into a spectator sport is just one way of filling this void.)

The result of my labors over the 2001 Labor Day weekend was the nucleus of this book, a novella of thirty thousand words that carried the name *Out of Joint*. It covered Roxanne Bonaventure's life in broad strokes, and shared with this final version the first chapter, the last chapter, and bits of the middle.

When our writers' collective decided to start our own print-on-demand imprint, I thought it only natural that we should publish Rox-anne's story. At its original length, though, the novella was far too short to stand on its own, so I wrote an additional twenty-five thousand words, bringing the grand total to fifty-five thousand. This expanded edition (which added the chapters about Roxanne Grant, and Nigel, and Atalanta Carter) was released under the title *Any Time at All* in 2002, to positive reviews in *Asimov's Science Fiction*, the *New York Review of Science Fiction*, and *Infinity Plus*, and extremely tepid sales.

After the release of *Any Time at All*, I expanded Roxanne's story yet again, adding another twenty-five thousand words (including the chapters about Tycho Maas, and Julien, and the death of Roxanne's dad), and started looking for a proper publishing house that would be willing to print it. The revolution that POD technology had promised to writers and the small press had, I felt, failed to materialize, and I decided it was time to try more traditional routes. However, the expanded novel was rejected by several outfits as being "not commercial," one even remarking that the book was "too smart."

Enter Lou Anders, to the rescue.

Lou and I met at a convention a few years ago. He first was a drinking companion (as most acquaintances at conventions are), then a frequent e-mail correspondent, and before long a valued friend. In his capacity as editor, though, he's something closer to a patron.

What began life as *Out of Joint*, and went through an awkward adolescence as *Any Time at All*, has now matured into *Here, There & Everywhere*. Like any parent, I can only hope for the best, and hope that my offspring will write home if it finds work.

ON THE BONAVENTURE FAMILY

During my tenure with Clockwork Storybook, I published four novels, three of which centered around members of a large extended family, the Bonaventure-Carmody clan (one such was Roxanne's many-times-removed great-uncle, Hieronymus Bonaventure, first lieutenant of the HMS *Fortitude*, in *Set the Seas on Fire*; another was research magician and world-saver Jon Bonaventure Carmody, in *Cybermancy Incorporated*).

Encoded in *Here, There & Everywhere* are references to these and others among Roxanne's relatives.

The notion of an extended family of adventurers and explorers is one I initially encountered in the works of Philip José Farmer. Chancing upon a battered copy of his *Doc Savage: His Apocalyptic Life* at an early age, in the words of Paul, scales fell from my eyes. The notion that fictional characters might inhabit the same world, might in fact hang from the branches of one enormous family tree, was one that stuck with me through the years, and which colored my later work. The generations of the Taylor family in my novel *Voices of Thunder* certainly make this influence plain.

Wrapping up *Voices*, it occurred to me that the Taylor clan touched on something central to my obsessions, but was inadequate to serve as a framework for all of the types of stories I intended to tell. I found hints of potential solutions in the work of three other writers: the von Bek-Beck-Begg stories of Michael Moorcock, in particular those in the collection *Fabulous Harbors*; Alan Moore's pastiche/homage/commentary *Supreme*, replicating genre forms while analyzing and revitalizing them; and the generations-spanning Diogenes Club stories of Kim Newman, both those with and those without vampires. Stealing shamelessly from these fine men, adapting bits and pieces of their approaches to my ends, I approached something like the Taylors from a completely different angle, and the Bonaventure-Carmody family was the result.

The generations of the Bonaventure-Carmody family play a central role in my work and, like an entire roll of bad pennies, will appear in some capacity in all of my novels for the foreseeable future. Roxanne is featured in a forthcoming series of books for young readers called *Young Explorers*, will make a brief appearance in *The Celestial Empire: Fire Star*, and will have an uncredited cameo in my young adult novel, *AEGIS*. Whether she is hiding in the background of my *Paragaea: A Planetary Romance* I leave to the reader to decide.

ON SANDFORD BLANK

Sandford Blank, consulting detective, shares something in common with a great many predecessors, with some influences less obvious than others. The most obvious, in fact, was likely the farthest from my thoughts when creating him, while the most unlikely influence was the one on which I drew most heavily.

Blank was inspired largely by the research of Jess Nevins, author of *Heroes & Monsters*, *A Blazing World*, and the forthcoming *Encyclopedia of Fantastic Victoriana*. His writings on Sexton Blake, and Victoriana in general, were of inestimable use in the Blank chapter, and for this and his many other good deeds, Mr. Nevins has my continuing thanks.

Sandford Blank, for his part, will return in the pages of *End of the Century*, in which he is forced to cooperate with his arch nemesis Monsieur Void, the Ivory Mandarin, to solve a string of brutal murders on the eve of Queen Victoria's Diamond Jubilee.

ON SOURCES

As a writer there is the danger, in citing sources, of giving the appearance of one who wishes too hard to impress. As though to bolster up sagging confidence in whatever text may have preceded it, an afterword filled with scholarly citations makes a writer look like he's trying to seem smart. *Look at my syllabus*, the writer says, stepping out from behind the curtain. *See how much I've read! I can't be all bad, right?*

Keeping the preceding firmly in mind, I find myself unable to resist giving credit to the handful of books that allowed me to write this one. Thanks are due, in no particular order, to Kip Thorne for *Black Holes and Time Warps* (W. W. Norton & Co.), David Deutsch for *The Fabric of Reality* (Allen Lane, Penguin Books), Michio Kaku for *Hyperspace* (Anchor Books), Rudy Rucker for *The Fourth Dimension* (Houghton-Mifflin), and Clifford A. Pickover for *Surfing through Hyperspace* (Oxford University Press). Many thanks are also due to Norman and Jeanne MacKenzie for their *H. G. Wells: A Biography* (Simon & Schuster), and to the makers of *The Beatles Anthology* documentary series.

Chris Roberson
Austin, TX

AUTHOR'S BIO

CHRIS **ROBERSON** crafts stories of all shapes and sizes. His critically acclaimed short fiction has appeared in the anthologies LIVE WITHOUT A NET (Roc, 2003) and THE MANY FACES OF VAN HELSING (Ace, 2004), with appearances in the pages of ASIMOV'S SCIENCE FICTION, BLACK OCTOBER, FANTASTIC METROPOLIS, REVOLUTIONSF, TWILIGHT TALES, OPI8, ALIEN SKIN, ELECTRIC VELOCIPEDE, and LONE STAR STORIES.

In 2003, Roberson and his business partner and spouse Allison Baker launched the independent press MONKEYBRAIN BOOKS, an imprint specializing in nonfiction genre studies. Releases include the extraordinary talents of Michael Moorcock, Alan Moore, China Miéville, Jeff VanderMeer, Paul Di Filippo, Jess Nevins, Matthew Rossi, Rick Klaw, and more. The upstart company has already garnered strong commercial and critical success, including a nomination for the prestigious International Horror Guild Award.

On February 19, 2004, the couple became the proud parents of a daughter, Georgia Rose Roberson. The family resides in Austin, Texas.